Texas Yankee: Homecoming

Jerry P. Orange

DEDICATION

Texas Yankee: Homecoming is dedicated to my wife Tracye Lynn Orange. Tracye has been with me through thick and thin and makes my life better by being in it. She brings out the best that is in me. I am blessed to have such a great wife.

CONTENTS

ACKNOWLEDGMENTS

I want to acknowledge my father, Dr. Larry F. Orange (Pop), for his encouragement on this project. Pop raised me on Jesus, John Wayne, and Louise L'Amour. I also want to acknowledge my mother Janet Orange for her lifelong support and encouragement through times when even I didn't want to be around me. Shaken and stirred by life, seasoned with the love of a great family, I'm the end product of that recipe.

Chapter One; Heading Home

April 1, 1866 somewhere in west Tennessee, Joshua Granger was sitting near a small campfire re-reading a three-month old letter from his distant cousin Sarah Lynn Smith in Texas.

> My dearest Joshua,
>
> I hope and pray that this letter finds you well and happy. You and my brothers have been in my prayers daily these long years of the war. We are so fortunate that both John and Jesse made it home safely. I long to hear from you my darling. These four years of war with no news of you have been pure torture on my poor heart. Please write to let me know that you are alive and well.
>
> I turned twenty-one in June. I'm well old enough to marry now. When mother asked why I didn't accept the attempts of some local gentlemen to court me proper, I told her it wouldn't be right to toy with their affections since I was intent on marrying you. That made her so mad she had a fainting spell and she took to her bed early that night.
>
> Papa talked to her and told her it was the Christian thing to do to forgive you for fighting for the Yankees. He said since my heart has been set on this for all these years it is only right to give you a chance to prove yourself worthy of my hand in marriage.
>
> I think he's afraid that I'll run off to find you if you don't come for me. It's already a bit of a scandal that I'm waiting to marry a Yankee. So my darling, I close with this humble and earnest request that you make haste to save me from utter disgrace for I've sworn to join a convent if I cannot have you for my husband.
>
> With all my love,
> Sarah Lynn Smith

Joshua smiled as he refolded the letter and put it back in his coat pocket, "She always did have a flair for the dramatic."

He thought back over the last ten years to when he first met Sarah. His father had taken him and his older brother to Texas to sell some breeding stock Kentucky Saddle Horses to his father's favorite cousin in Georgetown, Texas. They had visited for two weeks before hitting the trail back home to Shelbyville, Kentucky.

Joshua pulled a flask from his saddlebags and took a sip of the good Kentucky Bourbon to ward off the chill of the early spring night as his mind drifted back in time. Sarah had been ten years old with auburn hair and a few freckles when he met her on that first trip to

Texas. He had been a carefree boy of twelve whose only interest had been horses; at least until he'd met her. The two of them had played together for those two weeks because their older brothers would go off together and wouldn't let them come along. On the day Joshua and his father and brother left to go back to Kentucky, Sarah had kissed him on the cheek when no one was looking. She had whispered to him, "When I grow up enough I'm going to marry you." After all these years the letter still surprised him. He took another sip and put the flask back in his saddlebags.

One of Joshua's horses snorted bringing his mind back to the present. His eyes searched the darkness to see why his battle proven stud horse was standing at attention ready to fight. Joshua pulled one of his .44 Remington pistols and pointed it in the direction the horses were looking.

"Step into the light slow and easy with your hands in the air," he said softly.

A young black man stepped into the firelight. He was just short of six feet tall, his shirt-tail was out, he was bareheaded, and barefoot. He had his hands shoulder high holding the reins of a skinny bareback mule that stood around fourteen hands. The man looked to be in his mid-twenties, well muscled and confident. There was no fear in his eyes.

"Good evenin' Suh," he said. "I smelled yo coffee and bacon and wondered if you might have enough to share."

"I might," returned Joshua. "Are you alone?" Joshua watched the man's eyes; they never wavered from his own.

"Yes Suh, jest me and my mule."

"What are you doing way out here at night?"

"Same as you Suh, I'm goin' to Texas."

"How do you know I'm going to Texas?" Joshua asked a bit surprised.

"I heard you talkin' at the store when you passed through town today. So's I followed you Suh, hoping you might let me travel with you."

"Why would I do that?" asked Joshua. His pistol still pointed at the young man who was starting to show signs of nervousness, like this wasn't going the way he expected.

8

"Cause you gonna need some help when those men from town try to kill you and take yo hosses and money tomorrow."

"Is that a fact?"

"Yes Suh, nobody pays no mind to a po' Negro cleaning up the barroom. I heard them talking 'bout it."

"How many?"

"Four. Can I put my hands down now?"

"Sure. Help yourself to some coffee and bacon; there's a biscuit left, you can have that too. What's your name?"

"Thank you, Suh." The young man lowered his hands and squatted by the fire. "My name is Nathan. I don't have a last name yet. I won't take another man's name just to have one, 'specially my old massa's. So I figger I'll make my own name. I want it to mean something. What's yo name Suh?" asked Nathan as he picked a piece of bacon from the skillet warming by the fire and put it on the biscuit.

"My name's Granger. If you plan to stay the night, put your mule on the picket line with my horses. So four men want to kill me for my horses?"

"Yes Suh, Mr. Granger. They say if they'd had hosses like yo's when they was ridin' with Gen'ral Mogan, they'd a never been caught in Ohio."

Joshua chuckled, "I was riding horses like these. In fact I was riding that stud and was right up front when we caught General John Hunt Morgan. So I guess they are going to try to ambush me."

"Yes Suh, but they don't want to jest shoot you and take yo hosses. They says they wants to hang ya for bein a Yankee." Nathan stuffed another piece of bacon on the biscuit and then took a bite. "They say they gonna get you when you cross the river at the ferry tomorrow."

"Is there another place to cross?"

"Not another good crossing place for a day's ride in either direction."

Joshua pondered the situation. Nathan nodded toward the coffee pot indicating he'd like a cup of coffee. Joshua nodded to Nathan that was fine then stood and holstered his .44. He was wearing two of them butt forward in military style flap holsters.

He figured he had at least two advantages; one, he'd been warned so he'd be ready, and two; they wanted to hang him so they'd want to take him alive. He wouldn't be that particular.

9

"So how does a barefoot negro riding bareback on a skinny mule plan to help me fight off four Rebs that want to hang me?" asked Joshua.

Nathan stood and lifted his shirt slowly to reveal the .44 Army Colt tucked into his pants. "I got this and the skinny mule is gun broke. My old massa used to bird hunt off him."

"Why would you help me?"

"Mr. Granger, I needs to go to Texas and find my brother. My old massa sold him off to a family goin' to Texas before the war. My mama's dying request was for me to find him. I give her my word that I would. So Mr. Granger, I's going to Texas and I need some help getting there. I ain't never been more than a few days ride from here in any direction. All's I know how to do is raise tobacco, break hosses and mules to harness, and milk cows. I might be wrong but you carry yo'self like you's been places and seen things and can prob'ly teach me what I needs to know. So I'll help you fight those four men tomorrow if yous'll take me to Texas with you."

"What if I say no?"

"Well then I'll get back on this skinny mule and make my way south and west as best I can. I reckon if I ride that direction long enough I'll get to Texas." Nathan stepped up beside the mule with the reins in his hand. "Thank you for the coffee and bacon. Should I put my mule on the picket line or ride on?"

"Put him on the picket line," said Joshua. "There's some corn in that pack yonder. Give him some. He looks like he can use it."

"Yes Suh," Nathan said with a grin.

Chapter Two; Outlaws

The next morning after a breakfast of more bacon, biscuits, and coffee, the two men rode down the road together toward the river. Joshua rode his Kentucky Saddlehorse stud leading a couple of fine young mares with packs on their backs. Nathan rode his skinny mule.

"Mr. Granger, those is some fine hosses. Why you taking them to Texas?" asked Nathan.

"I plan to breed them. There's lots of horses in Texas, wild mustangs aplenty. But, most of them are small. It's hard to find one fifteen hands tall. I plan to gather me some of those mustangs and

10

cross them with these Saddlehorses. I'll cull the herd by size first and sell anything under fourteen hands. I'll keep the mares for breeding. I'll geld the rest and break them to ride or drive, maybe both. I want to get a contract for selling horses to the army. But first I have to get to Texas. You ever used this ferry before?"

"Yes Suh, once."

"What can you tell me about it?" asked Joshua.

"There's an old man that runs the ferry. He's friendly enough. He has a pretty black girl who stays with him. That's about all. I think he'll feed you for a price."

"You're sure that is where they plan to make their move?"

"Yes, Suh."

"Well, the river is just up the road around that curve. Pull your pistol and when I start shooting, you start shooting," Joshua pulled one of his pistols and untied the lead on the mares, knowing they wouldn't stray far.

As they rode around the curve they heard a woman cry out. Joshua spurred the stud and galloped ahead with the mares and mule right behind him. When they cleared the curve, they saw three mounted men watching a fourth man on foot chasing a Negro woman. All four men were armed with long guns and pistols. One of the mounted men was holding an older skinny white man at gunpoint. Everyone stopped and looked as Joshua and Nathan came galloping around the curve. No explanation was needed for what was going on.

Joshua fired at the outlaw holding the old man at gunpoint and dropped him from the saddle. The outlaws' startled horses jumped at the gunshot. Joshua missed his second shot grazing the hip of one of the horses, causing it to go into a bucking fit. He heard Nathan fire from his left. He was surprised to see the man on foot go down just as the man was bringing his rifle up to fire. Joshua's stud slammed into an outlaw's horse knocking horse and rider to the ground. Joshua fired down into the outlaw's body as his stud jumped the downed horse. By this time the old man had picked up the rifle dropped by the dead outlaw and shot the last outlaw out of the saddle while he was trying to get his bucking horse under control. It was over in less than a minute.

Joshua cued the stud to stop and looked around. Nathan was off the mule and comforting the crying Negro girl. The four outlaws were dead or dying. Joshua looked at the old man and said, "You alright mister? I hope you don't mind us buttin' in."

"I'm fine son. You came along just in time. You must be the one they were waiting for; three nice saddle horses, riding a Texas saddle, wearing a Union Army coat and carrying two guns. Yeah, I reckon you're the one."

"Sounds like me don't it?" Joshua said with a grin. "I'm gonna gather the horses. If you don't mind, me and my companion will be staying for lunch before we cross the river."

"Young man you can stay as long as you want."

Joshua gathered his and the outlaws' horses. He tied seven horses and a mule to the porch rail and looked around. The Negro girl stopped crying and after some comforting words from the old man, went inside the house to fix lunch. Nathan carried firewood into the house for her while the old man studied the outlaws. He gathered their guns, belts, and long guns and put them on the porch.

"These fellows ain't from around here," he said. "I know most folks in these parts and I don't recognize the men or the horses either."

One of the outlaws groaned. Joshua pulled a pistol as he and the old man walked up to him. The outlaw opened his eyes. The downed horse had rolled over top of the outlaw while scrambling to get back on its feet. The outlaw looked at Joshua. "I can't feel my legs," he said.

"Mister," said Joshua looking at the unnatural angle of the man's hips, "your back is broke and you're gut shot. You're dying. Where're you from? You got kin you want notified?" asked Joshua with no compassion as he holstered his .44. The man wasn't a threat anymore.

"I'm from Alabama. We all are. We were heading to Montana. I don't reckon I'd want anybody back home to know I got myself killed trying to rape a nigger girl while I was waiting to hang a Yankee and steal his horses."

"Well mister you go on and die so we can bury you and be on our way. We're going inside and have lunch. If you got any manners left at all you'll die before we come back to check on you," said Joshua coldly.

The outlaw coughed up blood and wheezed, "You go to Hell Billy Yank."

"After you Johnny Reb," said Joshua as he turned and walked into the house.

After a lunch of beef, beans, and cornbread, Joshua and the old man sipped coffee while Nathan helped the girl with the dishes.

"Sir that was a good meal, your girl sets a fine table. You know, in all the excitement, we didn't get a chance to introduce ourselves. I'm Joshua Granger and my companion is Nathan."

"My name's Griffin son, the girl is Suzy. She stays with me and helps me run the place."

"Mister Griffin, what do think we should do with those fellas' horses and belongings?"

"Well Joshua, they was planning to abuse my Suzy, kill me, hang you for entertainment, steal your horses and burn my place out of meanness. They ain't from around here and no folks to send anything to. Hell, we don't even know their names. I say we bury them and divide their things amongst us."

"Sounds reasonable to me, how many shovels you got? I'd like to get those graves dug and over with."

"I got two."

"Let's get it done. I got a feeling Nathan ain't had much experience with this kind of thing so if you don't mind helping me we can take care of this pretty quick." Mr. Griffin nodded in agreement.

"Nathan, take the horses around back and put them in the pen by the barn after you unsaddle them."

"Yes Suh, Mr. Granger," said Nathan.

Joshua and Mr. Griffin buried the outlaws and walked back to the pen where Nathan and Suzy were watching the horses. They hung a hat and coat on the fence post and dropped a pair of boots on the ground.

"Suzy," said Mr. Griffin, "go inside and get my extra pair of socks for Nathan. I think these boots will fit him." Suzy nodded and went to the house. "Nathan, try on this coat and hat," he said.

13

The coat was a little big but the hat fit. Suzy came running out of the house with the socks in her hand. She smiled as she handed them to Nathan.

"Thank you," said Nathan. "I don't know 'bout wearin' a dead man's clothes."

"You'll get over it as it gets colder tonight," Joshua replied.

"Reckon I might at that," said Nathan as he pulled on the boots. They fit too.

"Let's go around front to the porch and get you a long gun. It'll come in handy in Texas. Let's see what we have to choose from," he said.

Joshua sat down on the porch steps and picked up the long gun nearest to him. It was a double barrel shotgun. The finish was worn and the ramrod was homemade. It looked to be a 20 gauge. "It's seen some hard use but still looks like it works. Mr. Griffin, do you mind if we take it?" he asked.

"Joshua, you help yourself to whatever you want. Suzy and I do alright and have about everything we need. What you don't want I'll most likely sell the next time I go to town," Mr. Griffin said.

Joshua picked up the next one. It was a Sharps carbine, a short, breech loading single shot weapon that used a .52 caliber paper cartridge and a musket cap. The third one was an Enfield .58 caliber muzzle loading rifled musket.

The last one was a seven shot Spencer carbine. It fired a .52 caliber rimfire metal cartridge and was very sturdy.

"Nathan, I think we've found your long gun," said Joshua.

"Mr. Granger ain't that the same kind you's carrying?" asked Nathan.

"Yep," said Joshua. His unit hadn't been issued the Spencer but he bought it from a cousin who fought with Confederate General Forrest and had taken it from a captured Yankee. His cousin hadn't stuck around for the official Confederate surrender and rode home on a captured Yankee horse with a full set of Yankee Cavalry equipment. He'd been hard up for money to buy seed to plant his crops, so Joshua bought the Spencer from him.

"Try this on," he said and handed Nathan a belt with a holstered .44 Army Colt, cartridge box, and a sheath knife on it. "The way you handled that Colt today, I figure you should stick with it. This pistol is

14

the same as the one you have so you should be able to do just fine with it."

By the time they finished, Nathan was completely outfitted with a horse and saddle, a change of clothes, a belt and holster for his Colt, blankets, ammunition, and a $20 gold piece. He felt like a rich man and stood straighter than before without even realizing it.

"I want to keep another saddle for the mule for when I finds my brother," Nathan said. "But I don't know which one would be best."

"Well, unless you plan on chasing cows I'd recommend keeping the army saddle," Joshua said. "It's light. It'll most likely still fit the mule if he fattens up, and it's made so that you can strap lots of stuff to it. You could use it like a pack saddle until you find your brother."

"Reckon that's what I'll do then," said Nathan.

Joshua took a thoroughbred looking mare and the guns. Nathan picked out a 15.1 hand sorrel gelding about 8 years old according to his teeth. Mr. Griffin was happy with the two horses and saddles for himself and Suzy and an Army Colt .44. He already had a shotgun in the house for hunting and that was enough guns for a peace loving man.

"Joshua, it's getting late in the day. Why don't y'all stay for supper? You can sleep in the house where it's warm and I'll take you across the river after breakfast in the morning," offered Mr. Griffin.

"That's mighty hospitable of you Mr. Griffin. I do believe we'll take you up on your offer," Joshua replied.

The next morning they had a breakfast of ham and eggs with biscuits and gravy. Mr. Griffin ferried them across the river and they resumed their trip to Texas.

"Mr. Granger," asked Nathan after a while, "Why's we ridin' west when I heard Texas is southwest?"

"That's a fair question. Nice to know you're paying attention. We're going to Memphis. At Memphis we'll cross the Mississippi river into Arkansas and head for Little Rock. From there we'll head south and west into Texas."

"I'm curious why we ain't goin' southwest across the country. It seems to me that would be the fastest way."

"It would be if there weren't any farms with fields of crops and cattle and towns in the way, but most of the area we will be passing through is settled to some extent. I prefer to stick to the road and not upset the locals by trespassing. Some folks are right touchy about that. If we stay on the road we don't have to worry about it. The road also takes us to the river crossings and towns along the way. In the towns we can eat someone else's cooking once in a while, sleep under a roof, get supplies and our horses shod. It makes for a more comfortable trip. Between riding to Texas twice before, herding cattle on a drive north, riding for the Pony Express and then the Union Cavalry during the war I've had plenty of uncomfortable in my life. I can handle uncomfortable without complaint when I have to but that don't mean I like it."

"Mr. Granger you said you rode fo the Pony Express. I've heard of it but don't rightly know what it is."

"Was," said Joshua. "It ain't around no more. The Pony Express was mail delivery from St. Joe, Missouri to California across the plains and the Rocky Mountains. We carried the mail on horseback riding as fast as we could go. We'd switch horses ever ten miles or so for about thirty miles and then we'd pass the mail on to the next rider. The mail never stopped. We had riders going east and west switching horses at the stations along the way. Nothing stopped us. We rode through heat, blizzards, lightning, and Indians and only lost one shipment of mail.

"But the telegraph came along and they strung lines all the way to California. It was faster to send a message by telegraph than to send a letter so the Pony Express went out of business."

"Did you ever fight the Indians, Mr. Granger?" asked Nathan.

"Mostly I had fast horses and would try to out run them. Most of the time, I was able to. I did have to fight a couple of times though. There was the time they attacked the station while I was waiting to make my next run. I fought off four while I was riding once too. They were waiting for me at a narrow spot in the mountains. I saw them coming. I spurred my horse and pulled my pistol. I ducked low and dodged arrows but one of them got me in the leg. I'm glad they hit my leg instead of my horse or I wouldn't be here to tell the tale. I kept riding and spurred that horse so hard I drew blood. When they closed in on me I shot two of them and their horses as fast as I could. The Indians were right up on me when I shot them. I could almost touch'em with the pistol barrel. By then my horse was pulling away from them and I guess they gave up."

16

"Why'd you shoot the hosses?"

"The horses were bigger targets," Joshua laughed. "I knew for certain that they couldn't catch me on foot and I only had five shots so I made them all count. I got plumb lucky with the first horse and hit it in the head. It just crumpled and rolled over top the Indian riding it when it went down. That caused the last one to swing his horse to the right, which gave me a broadside shot at his horse so I shot it twice in the body. It ain't that I wanted to kill the horses but hitting a man on a running horse from a running horse with a pistol and shooting behind me, well it wasn't a likely proposition. I figured I might be able to hit something as big as a horse and a shot horse wouldn't be able to catch me."

"What did you do about the arrow in yo' leg?"

"I rode like hell for the station. It took about half an hour to get there. I passed the mail on to the next rider and dismounted. The old mountain man who kept up the station was there to see the mail hand off. He'd done some 'have to or else' kind of doctorin' of arrow and bullet wounds in the past.

"He took me inside and handed me a bottle of whiskey. Then he sat me in a chair and cut open my pants. After he looked at it he said he would have to take it out and it would hurt like hell. 'Don't be afraid to holler' he said. He took the bottle and took a swig for himself then handed it back to me. He stood up, put his foot on my knee and told me to just look the other way and relax. I was taking another swig of whiskey when he grabbed that arrow and pulled. God damn that hurt! I choked, spit whiskey across the room and hollered but then it was over. I was doing fine until he took the whiskey and poured it on the wound. That's when I passed out. I was laid up for a couple of days and not able to ride."

"Mr. Granger, you ever been to Memphis before?" asked Nathan.

"Nope."

"You reckon it's a big city?"

"So I hear," said Joshua. "The reason we're going there is I figure we can cross the Mississippi there and stock up on some things we'll need. I figure Memphis is probably pretty well stocked with anything we might want. I'm not sure what we'll find the further west we go and I'm sure whatever we do find further west will be more expensive. I was thinking I'd get some good cloth, needles, thread,

17

things that a woman might want since I'm getting married when I get to Texas. I know that during the war the blockade shut off a lot of supplies to Texas and times are hard there from what I hear."

Chapter Three; Sarah Lynn

Georgetown, Texas, April 4, 1866

Outside the post office, Sarah Lynn Smith clutched an unopened letter in trembling hands. The letter was dated February 27, 1866 and was addressed to her in a strong masculine script. It was from Joshua.

Wanting to burst from curiosity she maintained her composure and walked quickly down the dirt street to Parker's General Store. Her brother Jesse was there bartering cattle and homespun wool cloth for supplies for the family ranch. The fall of Confederate paper money had left even old Texas families who had large ranches with little or no money.

As she stepped through the door of the store Mrs. Parker and Jesse turned to see who came in.

"Well, hello Sarah, it's so good to see you," said Mrs. Parker.

"Thank you Mrs. Parker it's a pleasure to see you too. Is Jessica available? I thought I might drop in for a visit if that would be alright."

"I'm sure she'd be glad to see you. You know you are always welcome in our home," Mrs. Parker said.

"Jesse, would you mind picking me up at the Parker's house when you finish here?" asked Sarah.

"I'd be glad to. It will give me a chance to pay my respects to Jessica. That is if it's alright with you Mrs. Parker."

"Well, I suppose it wouldn't hurt anything," Mrs. Parker said pleasantly.

"Thank you and it was good to see you Mrs. Parker," Sarah said as she hurried out the door and down the street.

"Jessica is my best friend; we've known each other our whole lives," Sarah thought to herself as she hurried down the dirt street. "She'll understand if I cry because Joshua says he isn't coming and she'll laugh with me if he is. She won't think any less of me either way. That's what best friends are for."

18

Stepping on to the porch Sarah knocked on the door. Jessica opened the door and hugged Sarah, inviting her in.

"What a pleasant surprise," she said. "Please, come in! It's so good to see you! What brings you to town?"

"Jesse was coming to town to get some supplies. I came along to drive the wagon so he could drive the cattle we brought to trade. I was hoping there might be a letter from Joshua at the post office," said Sarah and she held up the letter for Jessica to see.

"Oh Honey, you come right on in here. What did he say?"

"I…I don't know yet. I was afraid to read it on the street for fear I might make a scene. I wanted some place safe and private to read it." she said.

"Sarah Lynn Smith, you go right in there and have a seat in the parlor. You can make all the scene you want too. I'm the only one here and I'm going to make us some lemonade in the kitchen while you read your letter."

"Thank you, Jessica, I knew you would understand." Alone in the parlor, Sarah sat on the sofa and opened the letter:

> My dearest Sarah,
>
> After all these years your letter came as a pleasant surprise. To think that you still want me for your husband after these years apart warms my heart. I have loved you from the start and there has never been another woman for me.
>
> Don't join a convent! I'm coming and I'm coming to stay. I must get some affairs in order for I do not plan to return to Kentucky except to visit. I hope to see you in the spring.
>
> I know your mother wants you to marry well. Rest assured that while I am not rich, I am not poor either. My brother has worked the farm my father left me and has saved half of that money for me over the years. I was able to save 75 dollars a month of the 100 a month wages from riding for the Pony Express. My army wages were meager and didn't go far, but I am selling my farm to my brother since I do not plan to return. Altogether it comes to a respectable stake with which to begin a new life in Texas with you. You will not marry a pauper.
>
> My heart has been as midnight since we last said good-bye and shall be until the sunlight of your lovely eyes brightens it like the dawn over our beloved Texas. God willing, I will see you the spring.
>
> With all my undying love,
> Joshua Yerby Granger

Sarah read the letter again and then again. Jessica walked into the parlor with a tray of cookies, a pitcher of lemonade, and three glasses. Setting it all on the coffee table, she said, "I take it from the grin on your face that he's coming."

Sarah jumped to her feet and grabbed Jessica's hands.

"Yes! Yes! Yes!" she squealed, jumping up and down and swinging them both in a circle. "I'm so happy I think I could fly!" she said.

"Well I'm happy for you then! What did he say? Read it to me!"

They sat on the sofa and Sarah read the letter aloud as Jessica poured the lemonade. "Well? What do you think?" asked Sarah. She set the letter on the table and accepted a glass of lemonade from Jessica.

"I think it sounds wonderful so long as your brothers don't kill him for fighting for the Yankees. Why, why, why did he do that? He was one of us. What was he thinking?"

Sarah shook her head, "my brothers won't kill him because they know I love him. They may not have much to do with him but Papa has approved Joshua's coming back so they won't kill him. The last letter I got from him before the war broke out and stopped all the mail, said that he had been to California and believed the Union should be preserved. Together we are a great nation and divided we would become just so many powerless provinces. He truly believed that was worth fighting for. I cried so hard when I read that letter. I thought for sure I'd never see him again. He closed the letter by giving me the horses he left here when he went north with the cattle drive. He told me that if I still wanted to marry him when the war was over to send a letter to his brother's house in Kentucky. So I did and now he's coming.

"I haven't seen him since Christmas six years ago. You and I were still in school in New Orleans and he defended my honor."

"I remember that. He was a mess when the headmaster pulled him off those two boys," said Jessica. "Did he ever tell you what they said?"

"No he didn't," Sarah replied. Then she continued, "two years later when we finished school, the war was raging and I came home without him," Sarah paused. "Why did you bring three glasses?"

"Honey child, you weren't the only one at that school getting letters from Texas. Your brother Jesse is also quite the romantic, in case you didn't know. Now that he's home I'm expecting him to ask Papa for my hand any day. That glass is for him. I'm sure he'll be thirsty after loading the wagon."

As if on cue there was a knock at the door.

"There he is now," she said. Jessica smiled as she poured a glass of lemonade, pinched her cheeks to give them some color and answered the door with lemonade in hand.

Riding home in the wagon that afternoon, Jesse asked Sarah, "What's bothering you? You're being awfully quiet."

Staring off at the horizon with a faraway look in her eyes, Sarah said, "I'm planning my wedding Jesse. I want it to be perfect."

"You know Mother isn't going to be happy about this. Sarah, I just don't understand what you see in him. You've turned down marriage proposals that lots of women just dream about. Right here in Austin and Georgetown, you turned down two Texas gentlemen of good families with wealth and position to wait for this damned Yankee with nothing but a couple of horses and some big ideas...Ow!" Jesse rubbed his cheek where Sarah had suddenly slapped him. "What did you do that for?"

"I'll not have you curse my intended!" she said with fire in her eyes. "You know my Joshua is as brave, strong, and honest as Texas is hot in July! He may not be as handsome as Joseph Carson the banker's son, but you remember back in '57 when the Comanche raided our ranch. We were holed up in the house. Mary Louise loaded one gun while you shot another and I did the same for Joshua.

"When me and Joshua ran out of bullets that one Comanche tried to come through the window. Joshua smashed him in the face with the rifle butt and knocked him back out the window. That's when Papa showed up with Uncle Fernando and his vaqueros and ran them off."

Jesse rolled his eyes as he stared off at the horizon. Yeah, he remembered the fight and he knew the story that was coming next. He still hadn't decided whether Joshua was really brave or just plain stupid but he had to admit the boy was tougher than a pine knot.

"One of those Comanche had jumped on Diablo to ride off on him and I started crying," Sarah got choked up again just thinking about losing her favorite horse.

Jesse never did understand what Sarah saw in that runty little palomino gelding. The horse only stood fourteen hands even and was ornery as hell. But he was her favorite to this day. She thought he was just dandy.

"That good for nothing heathen made the mistake of riding past the porch," Sarah continued. "Joshua jumped off the porch and knocked him off my horse." Sarah punched her fist into her hand and raised her voice as she remembered the fight. "They hit the ground rolling around grunting and fighting and Joshua tried to kill him with his Bowie knife. I was afraid that heathen would kill Joshua after he broke Joshua's ribs with that tomahawk. But one of the Comanche's buddies scooped him up and they rode double out of there."

Jesse silently mouthed the next couple of sentences like reciting scripture in Sunday school. He'd heard the story so many times he knew it by heart.

"Joshua was a bloody mess when he led Diablo back to the porch. He was sweaty and dirty from fighting the Comanche. His face was streaked with pain and powder smoke. He was bleeding from his ribs. He must have cut the Comanche because his knife had blood dripping from it. When he said, 'Sarah honey you can stop crying. I didn't let them take Diablo.' I knew that he was the man for me; one that would knife fight a Comanche just to save my horse. Maybe it wasn't too smart but he did it for me and that's what counts!" The wagon team flinched as she slapped the wagon seat for emphasis.

"But Sarah…" Jesse began, but she cut him off like he hadn't said a word.

"As for my marriage propositions," she continued, "you know good and well that Mayor Jones is a widower with six children. He was more interested in my dowry and someone to look after those children than he was interested in me. Besides, he's twenty years older than me! It would be like marrying Papa.

"Now Joseph Carson, I had to stop and think about it when he asked me to marry him. He's smart, handsome, and a snappy dresser. He's got a future ahead of him too. So when he proposed, I told him I'd have to think about it. It took me two weeks to make up my mind.

What with the war going on, I didn't know if I'd ever see my Joshua again. Then one day it occurred to me that young Mr. Carson's mouth was full of war talk and his hands were empty. If he really meant what he said about loving Texas and supporting The Cause, he'd of had a musket in his hands proving his love and support with his deeds instead of being here trying to sweet talk me into marrying him. He's got his good points but he's more talk than substance. Joshua didn't talk about taking my horse away from that Comanche; he just did it then told me it was done."

"But Sarah," said Jesse, "he fought for the Yankees in the war. He fought against Texas. After we accepted him into our home, he fought against us. How can you accept that?" he asked.

"He believed that keeping the Union together was the best thing for all of us and that it was worth fighting for," she said. "Sam Houston agreed with him by the way."

"But old Sam didn't fight!"

"Only because he was too old! Joshua didn't have that excuse!"

Jesse shook his head and looked back to the road. He knew the futility of arguing with a Texas redhead. This wasn't the first time he'd tried it. The conversation would only go downhill from here, so he clucked to the horses and popped them on the rump with the reins.

"We better get on home before it gets dark," he said as the horses broke into a trot.

They arrived at the ranch just before sundown. Sarah jumped from the wagon and ran into the house.

"Mother! Mother! He's coming!" she yelled. "Joshua's coming home and he'll be here in the spring! Isn't it wonderful? Papa, we have to discuss my dowry!"

"Whoa, girl, slow down!" Her father, Frank Smith stepped into the parlor. His beautiful wife, Juanita, was frowning and panic flashed in her dark eyes. She opened her mouth to say something but Frank stopped her with a look. They had been together for almost thirty years and he knew what was on her mind as if she'd said it out loud. This wasn't the time for it.

"Slow down darlin' and start at the beginning. Who's coming home?" he asked softly and smiled. Sarah Lynn had always been his Daddy's girl and he didn't want to spoil this for her.

This had been ten years coming. Joshua Granger came from good stock. His father, Thurston Granger had been Frank's first cousin and best friend growing up in Kentucky. They were the same age and being hungry for adventure, they had hired on with the American Fur Company at age fifteen and had spent the next five years trapping beaver and fighting Indians in the Rocky Mountains. That last winter in the mountains they had stayed in the high country too late and got snowed in. They had almost starved to death. They'd eaten their dog and then their horses and were boiling beaver pelts to eat before the spring thaw came and they could get down the mountain.

They figured that was enough adventure to suit them just fine. They decided that since they each had a small fortune saved, it was time to do something else. They parted ways in St. Joe, Missouri. Thurston was an only son and went home to Kentucky to run the family farm and raise high-grade saddle horses.

Having come so close to freezing to death, Frank decided he'd take his small fortune and expand it in the warmer climate of Texas. Being the third son of five, he figured there wouldn't be much inheritance for him to go back to anyway. He and Thurston had kept in touch over the years as much as mail and distance would allow. Now his best friend's son was coming to Texas to marry his only daughter. He couldn't think of a better man for her. He thought about this as he watched Sarah continue breathlessly.

"Papa, Mother, Joshua is coming home to marry me. I have his letter right here."
Sarah read the letter to them.

"Mother, I'll need your help making my dress and we'll need to go to San Antonio to talk to the Padre. Papa, my dowry, I love that section on the San Gabriel west of here. Can I have it for my dowry? Please Papa," she asked fluttering eyelashes and giving him her sweetest smile. She knew that look had always gotten her the answer she wanted.

Juanita looked at Frank and he saw her distaste for this marriage flash like lightning in her eyes. Frank took his cue.

"Darlin', you know your mother and I will do the best we can for you. You just need to catch your breath and calm down a little. We'll have plenty of time to work out the details. Now war can change a man honey, and you and Joshua haven't seen each other in several

24

years. You're going to have to get reacquainted. You will have a courtship of at least one full year or I will not consent to this marriage.

"Also, he is a grown man and must prove to me that he can and will provide for you. He cannot live here. You are still and always will be my little girl and I love you. I have high standards for the man who wants to take my little girl away.

"Now don't look at me like that…" he said as Sarah stared at him with heartbreak in her eyes. She was on the verge of tears and her lip trembled. "I'm not saying you can't marry him. I'm telling you that you have been raised a lady and deserve a proper respectable courtship and you will have one. You've waited this long for each other; one more year won't kill you." With that he wrapped his arms around her and gave her a big hug. He kissed the top of her head. "I'm happy for you Sarah Lynn." Over her shoulder he glanced at Juanita, a smile had replaced the frown on her face. A nod and slight curtsy silently said, "You handled that well. This may work out after all."

From the kitchen doorway, Mary Louise, their Negro housekeeper and cook said, "Mr. Smith, supper is ready. Would you call the boys? Miss Sarah, I'm so happy for you. I just had me a feelin' we was gonna have something to celebrate when you got home so I cooked up those doves your Papa got this morning, just the way you like'em and made a pecan pie just for you."

Later that evening as everyone was getting ready for bed; Sarah heard a soft knock at her bedroom door. Putting her robe over her nightgown she asked, "Who is it?"

"It's Mary Louise, Miss Sarah. Can I come in?"

"Of course Mary Louise, come in."

Closing the door behind her, Mary Louise said, "Sit down at the vanity child, and let me brush your hair for you."

Mary Louise had been ten years old when Sarah Lynn was born. She had changed her diapers, given her baths, fed her and generally cared for her ever since. She knew Sarah Lynn was upset over her mother and brothers' reactions to Joshua coming to marry her. She also knew that brushing her hair would help soothe her.

With Sarah Lynn sitting in her chair facing the vanity mirror, Mary Louise began to brush Sarah's long dark red hair. "My little baby doll is all growed up and ready to get married," she said softly. "I remember the day you was born like it was yesterday," she continued. The long slow brush strokes were soothing as Sarah relaxed in the chair with her eyes closed. "I was scared to death. I'd never seen a baby born before. My Mama, God rest her soul, made me stay and help her with your Mama." Mary Louise chuckled, "Your Mama hollered and I turned to run. My Mama grabbed me and pulled me back. She said, 'Girl, go get me a clean cotton towel. We gonna have us a baby in a minute.' I ran and got that towel and heard the awfullest yelling and crying and going on. I was sure your Mama was dying. Then things got quiet and I heard you crying. I poked my head through the door and your Mama weren't dead. She was smiling and oohing and awing over you and making baby talk. Then my Mama took you back from your Mama and cleaned you up. She waved me into the room and wrapped you up in that towel. You was all red faced and wrinkled and you had all that dark red hair. Your Mama took you to feed and while you was feeding, your Mama told us that your red hair was because her family was from a place called the Canary Islands and they have lighter hair and skin than most other Spanish folk.

"Now here you is all growed up and ready to marry. The man you want is coming for you. Why you got that sad look on your face child? You should be happy."

"I am happy, Mary Louise. It just seems like I'm the only one. They're all angry that he fought for the Yankees. It puts a shadow over my happiness. Then too, I'm a little scared. It's been six years since we've seen each other. What if he doesn't think I'm beautiful anymore? What if he changes his mind? OW!"

"Sorry," said Mary Louise, "I must have hit a tangle too hard. You need to quit all that worrying nonsense. You's a beautiful woman. Joshua saw that when you was a young'un. He's seen how beautiful your Mama is too. The boy may be reckless, but he ain't dumb. He knows the filly grows up like the mare and the horse colt grows up like the stud horse. He picked you out when you was little like he'd pick out a filly for breeding. He ain't gonna be disappointed.

"Look at you with your smooth skin, your bright green eyes, and all this pretty long red hair. You got a fine womanly figure too. You might want to stick to one piece of pie for dessert now that you're growed or that'll get away from you. You're strong and healthy with good hips. You ain't gonna have no trouble birthing babies."

"I'm worried about my wedding night too. I've never been with a man before. What if I do something wrong?" asked Sarah.

"You'll do fine darlin'. It'll all come natural enough. Don't you let them old prudes that complain about their husbands worry you none neither. They make it sound like a chore and a bother to be a wife in bed and I suppose at times it can be. But let me tell you child, the Good Lord knew what he was doing and it can be real good if you let it."

"Mary Louise you've never been married. How do you know all this?"

"I've been in love child, and God forgive me, we couldn't get married but we didn't let that stop the rest of it."

"Why Mary Louise!" said Sarah with feigned shock. Then she asked mischievously, "So who is this mysterious man in your life? I know everyone you know."

"Don't you worry your pretty head about it child. That's between him and me and the Good Lord," said Mary Louise.

"Why how silly can I be? It must be...OW!"

"You got the dangedest tangles in your hair tonight. Hush and think about how happy you are that your man is coming for you. No telling how many of them tangles I'll hit if you keep distracting me like that."

Smiling quietly, Sarah Lynn sat back and closed her eyes while Mary Louise finished brushing her hair. "There now," said Mary Louise softly a few minutes later. "All done. You need to go on to bed now. Your Papa's gonna want you to help him with that colt he brung in yesterday. He knows you're the best horse handler in the family."

"Thank you, Mary Louise. I'm all relaxed now. You've always been good to me. I don't know what I'd do without you."

"You're welcome Miss Sarah," said Mary Louise as she left closing the door behind her.

27

Chapter Four; The Wagon

On April the fifth, they rode into Memphis. Nathan thought it would probably be a good idea to put his pistol in his boot and cover it with his pants. They put his Spencer on one of the packhorses. Nathan put the McClellan saddle on the mule and rode it into town letting Joshua put his gelding in the string of horses being lead.

"I jest got a bad feeling about ridin' into town on a nice hoss carrying guns," Nathan said. "It might upset some of the white folk to see a Negro carrying guns and riding a better hoss than they is. I think I'd rather just try to blend in and avoid trouble."

It was a little after two in the afternoon when they rode into town. They made their way through the busy streets toward the river and found a livery for the horses. Just across the street from the livery was a hotel, so Joshua went in to get them some rooms.

"I'd like two rooms for me and my companion," Joshua told the desk clerk.

"I'm sorry sir but we don't rent rooms to niggers," the clerk said.

"I'm paying with gold coin and I want two rooms," Joshua repeated sternly.

"I'll be glad to rent you two rooms sir but your nigger ain't staying in this hotel," the clerk replied.

"It's alright Mr. Granger," Nathan said softly, "I should stay at the stable and tend the hosses anyway." With that he turned and headed for the door. Joshua followed.

"What was that all about?" asked Joshua when they were outside.

"It's about not causing a fuss and stirring folks up. We's only gonna be here a couple of days at most you said. I'll go over to the livery and sleep in the hay loft. I'll manage jest fine."

Joshua went back to the hotel and checked into his room. "Where can I get a hot bath?" he asked the clerk.

"For fifty cents we'll have a tub and fresh hot water brought right to your room." the clerk said.

"Alright, I'll have the bath," Joshua said. In a few minutes a couple of black men had carried a tin bathtub to his room and filled it with hot water. After his bath and a change of clothes Joshua decided to get some early supper and find a card game. He learned to play poker on the cattle trail and developed his skill at cards during the

28

war; it was a favorite way to pass the time in camp. He enjoyed a good game, especially when he was winning.

It was about dark by the time Joshua found a diner. This place had ham and eggs, fried potatoes, biscuits, and red-eye gravy for supper with a piece of dried apple pie for dessert. He washed it down with fresh milk, and a cup of strong black coffee.

Walking out into the night with a full belly and a good mood, he decided to have a smoke. Since he left his pipe at the hotel, he stopped in a store to buy a cigar. While lighting his cigar, he heard a piano playing and followed the music through the crisp night air to a saloon. Sure enough there was a card game going on inside.

Before going inside, Joshua walked across the street to admire a six-horse hitch of Norman draft horses. They were hitched to a Studebaker freight wagon in front of a warehouse. It was a real nice setup. The horses looked like they could each pull anything you wanted to hook them to. The team was four geldings and two mares. The wagon itself was four feet wide and twelve feet long with a bowed canvas top.

Joshua walked back across the street and went in the saloon. He walked up to the bar and ordered a shot of whiskey. The piano player was playing a lively tune while some sporting girls stomped around the floor with a couple of inebriated customers who thought they were dancing. Some riverboat men were playing cards with a teamster, the house dealer, and a couple of businessmen. Listening without appearing to, Joshua discovered that the stakes were high and the teamster had been winning.

Joshua walked over to the table in between hands. "Gentlemen, do you mind if I join in a few hands?"

"Pull up a chair," Smitty, the house dealer, grunted from around his cigar.

An hour later Smitty was dealing to Joshua and McKnight the teamster. The other players had found this round too rich for their blood and folded. Joshua held three kings, an ace, and a six of spades. McKnight raised the pot to six hundred dollars. Joshua called and they drew their second round of cards. McKnight took three so the best he could have had was a pair. Joshua discarded the six and the ace taking two cards. The bid was up to McKnight.

Joshua just drew a fourth king. McKnight smiled. He looked confident and bid fifty dollars. Joshua bid high to test his confidence.

"I'll see your fifty and raise you another hundred and fifty."

McKnight was frustrated. A frown had replaced the smile on his face. He considered his cards a moment and drew long on his cigar as smoke curled around the table. He tilted his head back and blew the smoke at the ceiling; he picked up his whiskey glass, took a long gulp and made his decision. "Granger, I don't have two hundred dollars but my wagon and team out there are worth six hundred dollars horses, harness, wagon and all. If you'll accept that instead of cash I'll see your one fifty and raise you another four hundred."

Joshua pushed four hundred dollars more into the center of the table. "I'll see your four hundred and call."

Smiling like the cat that ate the canary McKnight laid his cards down with a flourish. "Full house, 3 queens, and 2 aces," he reached for the pot.

"Hold on," said Joshua and he laid down his cards. "Four kings."

McKnight stared in shock. "It can't be."

"It can be and it is," Smitty said sliding his hand inside his coat.

"But...but," McKnight stammered his face growing red. The other players started sliding back from the table. "It took me two years to put that wagon and team together."

"You should have thought about that before you made the bet," one of the other players said tersely. "It was a fair play and you lost. Don't go doing something foolish. Write the man a bill of sale and be done with it."

For a tense moment everything was quiet. The piano player, dancers, and all the patrons were watching to see what happened next. McKnight made his decision and stood up quickly to find Smitty's shoulder holstered pistol in his face.

"Easy Smitty," said McKnight throwing up his hands. "I'm just going to the bar to get pencil and paper. Granger, you played a good hand. Since I'm broke why don't you buy me a drink at the bar while I write out the bill of sale?"

Everyone in the room relaxed. "Be glad to," said Joshua.

After the bill of sale was completed a dejected McKnight looked to Joshua, "Let me introduce you to your team. They're good horses, take care of them."

Thirty minutes later the transaction was complete. Joshua had inspected his new rig with the former owner. Joshua walked back into the bar and went up to Smitty's table where the game was still in progress. He smiled at Smitty, "Deal me in gents I'm still feeling lucky."

By midnight Joshua called it quits after losing a couple of big hands in a row. A hundred dollars, a wagon and team ahead, he climbed up on his new wagon and drove it back to the livery stable. He pulled up in front of the stable singing loudly and feeling no pain.

"Nathan? Nathan? Where are you Nathan?" he yelled into the livery barn.

A figure stepped from the shadows of the full moon night and Nathan said, "I's right here Mr. Granger."

Joshua jumped up with a start and fell off the wagon. "Oh that hurt." Joshua groaned as he sat up. "You spooked me Nathan. I expected you to be asleep."

"I was asleep," Nathan said, helping Joshua off the ground, "til some damned fool Yankee woke me up singing about John Brown's body moldering in the grave at the top of his lungs. I figgered I'd come out and see who was gonna shoot you so's I could point them out to the sheriff in the morning."

Joshua dusted himself off, "You're a good man Nathan. Thanks for looking out for me." He staggered over to the horses, "How do you like my new rig? Ain't these some fine looking horses?"

"Yes suh, Mr. Granger, they's as fine a team as I ever seen. You do have an eye for good hosses."

"Thank you Nathan…Nathan, you're the only friend I've got. You should call me Joshua."

"Yes suh, Mr. Joshua."

"Nathan?"

"Yes suh, Mr. Joshua?"

"I never drove a six-horse hitch before."

"Me and the hosses could tell suh."

"Nathan?"

"Yes suh?"

"Will you take care of my new horses for me? I really need to go to bed before I pass out in the street."

"Yes suh, I'll take care o' them for you. You go on to bed."

"Thank you Nathan."

With that Joshua staggered to the hotel and stumbled into his room. Sitting down on the bed he leaned back and was asleep before his head hit the pillow.

Late the next day, a queasy Joshua made his way to the stable. He found Nathan, and they went around back of the stable. They took a seat on the top rail of the fence to admire the new team and wagon.

"So I really did win a wagon and team last night. I thought I might have dreamed it," Joshua said. He reached into his pocket and pulled out his money. He started to laugh but his head throbbed. "Oooh..." he said. "I guess I didn't dream that either." With that he told Nathan how he came by the wagon.

"Nathan it's a nice set up but what am I going to do with it? I think I was just impressed by the sheer size of those Norman horses and got caught up in the moment."

"I thought maybe you was gonna carry yo' supplies to Texas in it," said Nathan.

"That is a good idea. You ever drove a six-up?" asked Joshua.

"Yes suh, I've drove one enough to know how. You want me to drive it to Texas for you?"

"Would you?" asked Joshua.

"Might as well, I's going that way," They both chuckled.

"We'll buy supplies and load it up tomorrow," said Joshua. "I guess if you're going to work for me, I ought to pay you. The Army pays thirteen dollars a month and found. I guess I could match that. How does that sound to you?"

"Mr. Joshua, I ain't never been paid regular, much less that much. Thirteen dollars a month sounds real good to me but I ain't lost so why you wants to find me?"

Reaching in his pocket Joshua pulled out thirteen dollars and handed it to Nathan with a smile. "Thirteen dollars a month and found means thirteen dollars a month, a place to stay, and your meals. There's a full month's pay for April in advance. I'll pay you another thirteen dollars at the end of May. Go buy whatever you think you need for yourself. I'm gonna go sleep off this hangover. Check the horses and wagon and make sure they are ready for travel. Make a list of what you think we'll need that we don't already have and we'll get it tomorrow."

"Yes suh!" said Nathan and he jumped off the fence.

"I'll see you in the morning," said Joshua as he headed for the hotel.

"Yes suh, Mr. Joshua. I'll be ready."

The next morning, Joshua met Nathan at the barn. "Got your list ready?"

"Mr. Joshua, I was so excited yesterday that I forgot to tell you I can't read nor write. I got my list in my head."

"Oh," Joshua said. "I guess we need to get something you can learn to read, write, and do arithmetic with. It'll do you good to know how."

"I'd surely like to learn."

"I ain't claiming to be no school teacher, but I reckon I can show you enough to get by with. I had a little schooling when I was a boy. My Mama made me read the Good Book to her at night so she would know I knew how to read and be a good Christian. My Daddy made me do my sums helping him on the farm raising horses, and tobacco and counting money with him. What do we need and I'll put it on my list."

"Well," said Nathan, "we need some grease for the wagon wheels. We need harness leather, a leather awl, and some heavy thread in case we has to repair any harness. We's gonna need corn for the hosses. We got one water barrel but another one won't hurt and I doubt we can load this wagon so heavy these Normans can't pull it. Can't never have too much water. That should cover it."

"Good, let's hitch up the wagon and go load it up. I'm getting anxious to get to Texas," Joshua said.

By the end of the day, their shopping was complete. In addition to what Nathan wanted, Joshua also purchased four hundred rounds for their Spencers, two hundred rounds of .44 for their pistols, and percussion caps for the pistols, rifles, and shotgun they acquired from the fight with the outlaws and one hundred rounds for each of the rifles. They also had twenty-five pounds of #6 shot, ten pounds of .00 buckshot, a small keg of gunpowder, and card stock for the shotgun. Joshua figured the guns weren't much use with no ammunition and it

33

was better to have more than you need than to run out. Besides one hundred was a nice round number.

Joshua bought a new black suit, white shirt, and black tie to get married in. He also bought some things for Sarah Lynn: a gold wedding band, bolts of muslin, silk, and wool; thimbles, needles, and thread to match the fabric, a silver hair brush and hand mirror set, a lace kerchief, and a small bottle of perfume.

He bought horse supplies, a plow, gardening tools, and seed. He also bought a new coat to replace the Union army one he'd been wearing, as well as food for the rest of the trip, cooking utensils, and a wall tent. Finally he picked up a New England Primer with paper and pencils for teaching Nathan to read, write, and do arithmetic.

The next morning they crossed the Mississippi with Nathan driving the loaded wagon and Joshua leading four pack horses and the mule. If they took their time and rested the horses every seventh day, they could keep the horses in good shape. Grazing them at night and for two hours at the noon break, in addition to feeding them corn would keep them fit. Joshua felt well supplied for the rest of the trip and thought he would be able to start off well when he and Sarah got married.

When they got off the ferry and on the road toward Little Rock Nathan asked, "Mr. Joshua, is you a rich man?"

"No," Joshua said smiling to himself at the question.

"I 'spose it ain't rightly none of my business. It jest seems like a good idee to know if you's working for a rich man or a poor man. I ain't never seen as much money as you spent yesterday. I'm sorry for being nosey; I'll go back to minding my own business."

"It's alright Nathan. I believe I can trust you so I'll tell you. I'm not rich but I'm not poor either. I sold my farm to my brother before I left Kentucky. That's why I have a little money to buy things with. Well, that and a good night at the poker table.

"Maybe someday I'll have some money to buy a few things myself," Nathan thought as they rode on in silence enjoying the warmth of the sun.

Chapter Five; Orphans and Prostitutes

April 21, 1866

Two weeks later Joshua and Nathan rode into Little Rock. They found a livery stable for the horses since they planned to stay two nights. Joshua found a hotel and Nathan stayed at the livery in the wagon yard. It was late so they went to a diner and had some supper. Gold coin trumped skin color and Nathan was allowed to eat in the diner with Joshua. While they were eating, they noticed a dirty little boy wearing ragged clothes come in and take a seat by himself at a corner table. The boy looked around the room expressionless. Without making eye contact with anyone he sat quietly in the corner. When the waitress saw him, she went in the kitchen and brought out a bowl of stew, a glass of milk, and a small plate of cornbread. She set it down in front of the boy. Glancing at her without acknowledgement he began to eat.

As she filled their coffee cups Joshua asked, "What's with the kid?"

"His name is Luke. He's an orphan," she replied. "His mother was my friend. I feed him when he comes in."

"He doesn't seem very appreciative. He didn't even say thank you," Joshua said.

"He doesn't talk much, never has, most of the time he doesn't talk at all. He's thankful enough. You don't see it because you don't know him."

"Won't anybody take him in?" Joshua asked.

"Some have tried but he won't stay. Last fall some folks tried to send him away to an asylum. These men came and put him in a cage wagon and took him away. He put up quite a fight for a kid before they got him in the wagon. It was heartbreaking. As they were driving off, he was banging his head against the bars of the wagon and crying and screaming. Two weeks later he showed up again and nobody has tried to bother him since. He spends most of his time sitting by his mother's grave or hanging around the blacksmith shops. He knows I'll feed him so he comes here when he's hungry."

"That's sad. What happened to his folks?" Nathan asked. "Don't he have no kin that can take care of him?"

"We don't know of any. His mother showed up here in '56 pregnant with no husband. When her parents found out she was pregnant, they gave her fifty dollars and turned her out. They said she was a disgrace to the family. She was on her way to California to find Luke's father but got news that he was killed in an Indian attack before he got there. He had promised to send for her when he struck a good claim. She had Luke here and lived in a shack on the edge of town. She worked here and got by the best she could. When she died last spring, little Luke just kind of ran wild. People call him retarded because he doesn't talk but he ain't stupid. He's just different. I got to get back to work," she said and headed back to the kitchen.

When Luke finished his stew and cornbread, he got up and walked quietly to the door. At the door he stopped and looked around for the waitress. When she looked his way he held her gaze briefly, looked away and walked out the door.

The next morning, Joshua met Nathan at the stable. They took most of the morning to check all the shoes on the horses. Eleven horses and a mule made forty-eight feet to pick up, clean out, and inspect. They both had a basic knowledge of shoeing horses and could trim hooves and replace thrown shoes if necessary.

While they were inspecting the horses, little Luke came up close to watch them work. After they finished horse number six, they took a break, with only the saddle stock left to do. Joshua set down the last foot of one of the Norman geldings and looked up. "What the hell?" Little Luke was bent over holding the off hind foot of Joshua's stud and examining the shoe. The stud looked back at Luke, ears perked up with curiosity but no signs of aggression.

"What?" Nathan looked up and Joshua pointed to the stud. "I thought you said that stud wouldn't let jest anybody pick up his feet," Nathan said.

"I did say that," Joshua replied. "I guess the kid ain't just anybody."

Luke stopped when he heard them talking and set the stud's foot down. "Shoes good," he said without looking at them and walked away.

Joshua and Nathan walked over to the stud. The stud laid his ears back at Nathan. "Just stand back. He'll stand still for me," said

Joshua. Then he checked all four feet and found that sure enough the shoes were in good shape.

Joshua and Nathan finished with the saddle stock and went to lunch at the same diner where they ate the day before. On their way there, they saw Luke checking shoes on horses tied to the hitch rails along the street. He wasn't hurting anyone or the horses so the townspeople were leaving him alone.

They finished their lunch, stepped out on the porch of the diner and looked for Luke. They saw him down the street, still checking shoes on horses in front of a saloon. A large man stepped out of the saloon and saw Luke bent over checking the shoes on his horse. "What the hell are you doing to my horse, kid?" the man yelled. Before Luke could react, the man kicked him in the ribs and knocked him flat. The man kicked him again cursing him, and drew back to kick him a third time when Joshua tackled him, slamming him into the hitch rail and knocking the wind out of him. Joshua slammed his knee into the man's groin and stomped the arch of his foot as hard as he could. He felt the satisfying crunch of the bastard's foot breaking. Joshua took a step back and the man sagged against the rail but started to straighten up. Before he could fully recover, Joshua hit him in the jaw with a right hook and then a left. He followed up with an upper cut to the man's gut just under his breastbone. The man blew all the air out of his lungs and fought for breath. Joshua grabbed him by the shirtfront and was pounding his face when a shot was fired.

Joshua stopped and looked around to see the local sheriff standing on the sidewalk with a smoking Colt pointed leisurely in his direction.

"That's enough, son," he said. "Let him go." Joshua let go of the big man and he fell in the street. The sheriff holstered his pistol.

"How's the boy, Christina?" he asked the waitress from the diner. She was holding the crying boy in her arms as Nathan felt of his ribs.

"I think the bastard broke his ribs and may have given him a concussion," Christina said. "I'm taking him down to the doctor." She picked up the crying boy and walked off speaking softly to Luke as he cried, with his head on her shoulder. Nathan followed right behind her.

"A couple of you get Rupert here down to the doctor too," the sheriff said to the crowd gathered around. "Now as for you," he said

37

to Joshua, "I saw what happened so I'm not going to arrest you for whipping Rupert, but I have to keep the peace and I want you leaving town at first light tomorrow."

"Yes sir. Anything else?" asked Joshua.

"No, I think that will do it," the sheriff replied.

"Then I'm going to check on the boy."

The sheriff nodded and Joshua walked off toward the doctor's office. A few minutes later, Joshua found Luke sitting drowsily in a chair at the doctor's office.

"I gave him something to put him to sleep," the doctor told him. "I want to clean him up so I can check for any other injuries and that's the only way I could think to get him to hold still. He's going to have a headache and his ribs will hurt for a while, but kids are tough and he'll recover just fine.

"Rupert on the other hand is in worse shape. Not that he deserves any better, mind you. But he won't be able to ride, walk, or eat very well for quite some time. You smashed his groin. I don't think the damage is permanent, but he's going to be swollen and sore there for several days. You broke his foot, so he will need a cane or crutch to walk for a while and he's missing his top front teeth. He'll have to rearrange his eating habits, I expect. By the time the swelling around his eyes goes down to where he can see again, I reckon he'll think twice before he kicks another child."

"So the boy is going to be OK?" asked Joshua.

"He'll be fine in time," the doctor said.

"I'm glad to hear it. Nathan, we need to finish up checking the harness and buying some more corn so we can leave at first light tomorrow. The sheriff is running us out of town. We have to leave in the morning."

"What about the boy?" Nathan asked.

"You heard the doctor, he'll be fine."

"I don't like it," Nathan replied.

"Neither do I but I don't see many options. Come on. We'll check on Luke again after supper," Joshua said.

"I'll take good care of him. You gentlemen go do what you have to do," the doctor told them. "Christina, you have a supper crowd to get ready for. Luke will be fine."

38

As they were leaving they heard Luke mumbling in his sleep. The only thing they understand was Mommy.

In his dream little Luke wasn't in pain and he was happy. His mother had come to visit.

"Hi, Mommy! I sure do miss you. When are you coming back home?" asked Luke in his dream.

"I can't come home my darling. I miss you very much and I love you so much it hurts not to be with you. I can only come and visit like this sometimes. But one day you will get to come live where I live and we will be together again," his mother told him.

"I want to come live with you now Mommy. I don't like it here. People do mean things to me. I'll just come live with you now."

"Oh sweetheart, I really wish you could but it's not time yet. One day you will understand but for now you must trust me and do what I tell you. Alright sweetheart?"

"Yes Mommy."

"You know who Mister Joshua is darling?" she asked.

"Yes Ma'am."

"Do you like Mister Joshua?"

"Yes Ma'am, he stopped the mean man from kicking me."

"I know, honey. He is a good man and I want you to go with him when he leaves in the morning."

"Mister Joshua is leaving?"

"Yes dear. The sheriff is making him leave because he hurt the man who kicked you. I want you to go with him."

"Will you be coming with us Mommy? I don't want to go if you aren't coming with us."

"I'll come visit you like I have since I had to go away. I'll always be with you when you need me."

"OK, Mommy. As long as you come with us I'll go. I don't like it here anyway. Where are we going Mommy?"

"We're going to Texas dear. Now you get some sleep and be a good boy for the doctor and Mister Joshua when you wake up."

"Yes Ma'am.

"I have to go now sweetheart. I love you. Sleep well."

"Bye Mommy," said Luke.

The doctor looked across the room when he heard Luke say goodbye to his mother. Unaware of Luke's visitor he wondered to himself how such a tortured soul could sleep with such a look of peace on his face.

Down the street, Joshua stopped in at the sheriff's office. Sitting at his desk the sheriff looked to be well into his forties with a slight potbelly but the calloused hands and weather worn face indicated that the "easy life" of a town sheriff had not always been his occupation.

"Sheriff," Joshua said as he closed the door, "we're headed down to Texas, just above Austin and we were hoping to meet up with a wagon train headed that way. There's a lot of rough country between here and there and having some company would be a good thing. Since you're running us out of town can you introduce us to a wagon train? We're well armed and provisioned. I've fought Indians and I fought in the war. My hired man, Nathan has been in one engagement with bandits while he's been with me and he did fine. We'd be an asset to any train we joined."

"The next train of immigrants ain't set to leave for a week. Most of them are using oxen to pull their wagons. Oxen are cheaper and easier to take care of than horses or mules but they're slower too. It'll take'em a long time to reach Austin. Let me think on this a while son," the sheriff said.

"Fair enough, what about the boy?" Joshua asked.

"What about him?"

"What's going to happen to him?"

"Oh, I reckon Doc will nurse him back to health and he'll go back to running wild."

"That's too bad," said Joshua.

"Yeah, life is tough sometimes. Check back with me this evening about seven. I may be able to make that introduction for you."

Back at the stable Nathan was rearranging the load in the wagon.

"What the sheriff say?" he asked Joshua.

"He said check with him this evening and he might be able to introduce us to a wagon train." Joshua answered.

"What about the boy?" Nathan continued.

"You heard the Doc. He'll be fine."

"What I mean is what's gonna become of him?"

"Only God knows and He ain't telling. The sheriff says he'll probably go back to running wild."

"I don't like it.

"Neither do I but I don't know what to do about it," Joshua said as he walked off.

Later that evening about six o'clock Joshua went to the diner alone. He welcomed the quiet of being the only patron for the moment and took a seat at a table in the back of the room facing the door. Christina came out and took his order then went back into the kitchen. It had been a long day. Tired and frustrated he leaned his head back against the wall and closed his eyes.

"May I join you Mister Granger?" said a soft feminine voice.

Opening his eyes he saw a pretty, modestly dressed, woman in her late twenties. The calloused hands and lines around her eyes told of a hard life but the light in her eyes and smile spoke of peace.

"Please do," he said as he stood politely. "How do you know my name?" he asked when they were both seated.

Blushing slightly and glancing self-consciously at her folded hands she said, "I think everyone in town knows who you are after this afternoon."

"Great," he replied sarcastically. "What can I do for you ma'am?" he sighed.

"I want to talk to you about Luke. He's a good boy. He isn't like most children but he's smart and loving if given a chance and he really likes horses. I know he doesn't talk much but he can when he needs to. He just needs someone to love him and look after him." Silent tears ran down her cheeks. "I'm sorry. I told myself I wasn't going to cry," she said as she dabbed the tears from her eyes and face with a monogrammed handkerchief. "It's just that life has been so hard for him since I…since his mother died. I came to ask you to take him with you when you leave. He likes you and he'll be good for you. I promise."

Closing his eyes again and rubbing his temples to soothe the oncoming headache he asked, "And just who are you to be making that promise for him?"

41

"Here's your supper. Who are you talking to?" asked Christina as she set his plate down.

Joshua opened his eyes and stared at the empty chair across from him. "Where'd she go?" he asked.

"Where'd who go? You're the only one in here," Christina replied.

Joshua reached across the table and picked up the monogrammed handkerchief from the table. "I was talking to a woman. She left this. It's still damp from where she dried tears from her eyes," he said as he held up the kerchief for Christina to see.

"OH MY GOD!!" Christina cried. "That, that's Anna's handkerchief!" she stammered and backed away from the table.

"Who the hell is Anna?" Joshua asked in confused frustration.

"Anna Miller. She's Luke's mother. That handkerchief was her favorite possession. She said Luke's father gave it to her the night before he left for the California gold fields. He said it was to remind her of him until he could send for her. Neither one of them knew she was pregnant at the time. She never told us his name. We buried her with that handkerchief." Visibly shaken, Christina went back to the kitchen.

Joshua put the kerchief in his vest pocket and said aloud, "I'll give it to Luke when he's old enough to understand." A cool breeze brushed his forehead. It wasn't until he finished his supper that he realized the windows in the diner were closed.

At seven o'clock, Joshua headed for the sheriff's office. When he walked in he saw a well-dressed couple in the office with the sheriff. The woman appeared to be in her late twenties or possibly early thirties. She was blonde with blue eyes, well put together with a medium build, wearing a dark blue dress. She had a pretty face and the dress was of the latest fashion as was her hairstyle. The man was wearing a simple but tailored black suit. He had a handlebar mustache and his watch chain was gold. He appeared to be in his mid-thirties with dark eyes. His hands and face indicated that he hadn't spent a lot of time outdoors in recent years. "I'm here sheriff," said Joshua. "Anybody else heading south?" he asked as he shut the door behind him.

"Joshua let me introduce you to Miss Luella Johnson and Mr. Slim Edwards. They are headed to Dallas and are interested in hiring you to be their guide," the sheriff responded.

"Mr. Granger," the woman presented her hand and gave him a firm handshake. "I'm Luella Johnson, lately of Cincinnati. Mr. Edwards and I are going to Dallas to join my brother in a business venture there. We're in need of a guide who is familiar with the ways of the frontier and we're hoping you may be that man. We are willing to pay for your services."

"Why don't you just take the stage?" asked Joshua.

"The cost is prohibitive sir," replied Slim with an obvious British accent. "We have several associates traveling with us. That, and the accompanying baggage, renders the stage an option that is not suitable."

"We hired a man in Cincinnati but it seems he had a drinking problem and was unreliable. Therefore we terminated his employment," Miss Johnson continued.

"The wagon train is the safest way to travel. Why don't you join them?" asked Joshua getting an uneasy feeling.

"Due to the nature of our business, the good people of the wagon train voted to keep us out," Miss Johnson replied a bit defensively.

"Just exactly what is the nature of your business?" Joshua asked with raised eyebrows.

Miss Johnson cleared her pretty throat, "My brother runs a saloon and sporting house in Dallas. Mr. Edwards is a piano player and card dealer. Our six associates are young ladies who will work in the sporting house."

Joshua turned slowly to the sheriff. "You're kidding me. I ask you to introduce us to a wagon train and you set me up with a half dozen whores and a piano playing card sharp? Damn, sheriff. How can I ever thank you?"

"Mr. Granger," interjected Miss Johnson firmly. "Whether you take the job or not, I will not tolerate such disrespect for my girls and Mr. Edwards. They all make an honest living providing welcome services to their clients."

"Yes Ma'am, I bet they do," he said sarcastically. Then embarrassed with himself he continued, "But you're right Ma'am. My Mama would be ashamed of me. I apologize. I just can't imagine

43

how you expect one man or even two to get you to Dallas in one piece when your cargo is pretty, young women. There are two types of country between here and Dallas. There is rough and there is rugged. The rough has Indians and the rugged has outlaws."

"We are aware of the dangers Mr. Granger. We are prepared to face them," Mr. Edwards chimed in. "I am no stranger to battle. I served some years in Her Majesty's infantry in India. If it comes to a fight you will not find me wanting."

"What about the rest of you?" Joshua asked Miss Johnson. "Are you prepared to kill in self-defense? Are you prepared to cook over a buffalo chip fire? Can any of you drive a team? How many wagons do you have?" he continued in frustration.

"Mr. Granger," Miss Johnson began. "I can understand your reluctance. I'm sure you are quite capable of handling yourself but the idea of escorting eight tender feet, I think you westerners call us is surely intimidating. As for killing in self-defense I am sure that I, and most if not all, of my girls are capable. As for the cooking over a buffalo chip fire, I'm afraid I'm not familiar with that type of wood. Mr. Edwards, myself, and a couple of my girls have driven the wagons from Cincinnati and the rest are learning. We have two wagons pulled by four horses each. My girls are very resourceful and open to learning whatever is necessary to make a new life in the west. The good sheriff here assures us that you are capable of seeing us to Dallas and teaching us what we need to know in the process."

"And just how the hell would you know that after one fifteen minute conversation sheriff?" asked Joshua hotly.

"Calm down, son," said the sheriff calmly. "It's my job to know who's in my town. You came in from the east riding a Kentucky Saddlehorse stud and leading two fine young brood mares. You're riding a Texas saddle, wearing California spurs, your belt knife is in a sheath with a Crow Indian bead pattern, and your gunbelt has a Kentucky State Militia issue belt buckle. So you're probably from Kentucky, you've been to Texas before, and California by way of the Rocky Mountains.

"You carry a rope on your saddle. The only people who do that are people who know how to use one. So I can safely assume that you came up from Texas on a cattle drive at one time or another.

"Then there are the guns; two .44 Remingtons in military flap holsters carried butt forward and a Spencer carbine. They were Union cavalry issue. They were for sale in lieu of wages for soldiers mustering out of service since the army had more guns than money after the war. That, your belt buckle, and the fact that you're not broke tell me you fought for the Union in the cavalry. If you'd fought for the Confederacy you'd be poorly armed, broke, and wearing parts of your old uniform.

"You're not afraid of going to Texas alone and you seem to know how to get there but you're smart enough to want some company. You're prepared for trouble but not looking for it or you'd be wearing those guns low in open top holsters. You can handle yourself pretty well. The way you had old Rupert whipped before he even knew there was a fight tells me it wasn't the first scrap you've ever been in. The way you favor your left side and right leg once in a while are probably from old wounds. You didn't get that scar on your face from shaving either. I've been around son and so have you."

"Mr. Granger," Miss Johnson asked, "is the sheriff accurate in his assessment of your past?"

"Yes, Ma'am," answered Joshua sheepishly.

"Then Mr. Granger I am convinced that you are our man and I'm prepared to offer you one hundred dollars cash to take us to Dallas."

"That's a lot of money for a three week trip," said Joshua. "A trail boss gets a $100 a month for moving a herd of cattle to market."

"Mr. Granger, I assure you that the welfare of my girls is much more important to me than any herd of cattle is to a rancher. My offer reflects that. Is the nature of our business the reason you hesitate?"

"No ma'am, I just can't promise you that we'll all get there in one piece. We could get hit by Comanche and all of us lose our hair. I wouldn't want to be responsible for that."

"Mr. Granger you are willing to take that risk as are we or we wouldn't be here. My business requires that like the sheriff, I too have to be able to tell who I'm dealing with. I saw the way you defended the little boy today. I am certain that a man who would do that would not let any harm come to us if it were in his power to prevent it. So unless you have other objections I will see you in the morning. We will wait for you at the south end of town."

45

"There is one more thing," said Joshua. "If the little boy will come with us I intend to bring him. If that's a problem you'll need to find another man for the job."

"It's not a problem. I'm sure the girls will spoil him rotten by the time we reach Dallas. I'll see you in the morning Mr. Granger."

Everyone said goodnight. Miss Luella Johnson and Mr. Slim Edwards left. Joshua turned to the sheriff. "You got a problem with me taking the boy?"

"If he wants to go he's free to go, but I'll not have you forcing him. Let's go see how he's doing."

At the Doc's office they found Luke clean, dressed in new clothes eating supper. When they walked in Luke stopped eating and looked up. Seeing Joshua he got up and gave him a hug, sat back down and continued eating. Nathan and the Doc were there.

"I bought him some new clothes," said Nathan. "Doc say he gonna be fine."

"Can he travel Doc?" asked Joshua.

"He'll be sore but other than that it won't hurt him," the doctor replied.

"Good," said Luke to everyone's surprise. "Mommy says for me to go with Mr. Joshua and Mr. Nathan. We're going to Texas," and he went back to eating.

Joshua smiled at the other three men as they stared at each other in amazement. Joshua pulled the handkerchief from his pocket. Showing it to them he said, "The lady who gave me this, asked me to take him with us."

Chapter Six; The Dowry

April 21, 1866

West of Georgetown, Texas, Sarah was riding along the San Gabriel River with her father. They were looking over the section, six hundred forty acres, that she asked for as her dowry and the half section plus twenty acres next to it that her mother insisted he put with it for a total of one thousand acres. It wasn't quite one tenth of his ranch. Frank Smith was impressed with his daughter's choice and the reasons she gave for her selection. The grass and water was good but it was also the outer section of his ranch and the land to the west was very open and only sparsely settled, with plenty of room to expand. It was good country for cattle and horses. In fact there were wild cattle and horses already on it. Some of them carried his brand and some were still unbranded.

He glanced at his daughter riding beside him and listened to her lay out her new home in her mind; house here, corrals there, garden yonder, he smiled to himself with pride. She was definitely a lady of the Texas frontier. She was beautiful, strong willed, and smart like her mother. The years of school in New Orleans put a refined finish on her strong frontier character. Today she rode astride in a divided skirt of her own making even though she knew it annoyed her mother. "Ladies should ride sidesaddle or in a buggy," Juanita told her repeatedly. "Mother you know I can't rope a calf or colt riding sidesaddle." He heard the old familiar argument in his head.

When Sarah's brothers were off to war she filled in for them helping her father on the ranch in their place until he sent the women to live in town because of the increased Indian raids. She learned to ride, rope, hunt, shoot, and brand cattle like a man. Instead of wearing pants while doing man's work she made herself some divided skirts to maintain her modesty. Yet Sarah was quite an accomplished horsewoman and rode very well in a sidesaddle, when it suited her.

She'd also put together a nice herd of her own horses using the stud and mare Joshua gave her when he joined the Union. She used them as foundation stock and crossed them with the best local stock she could find. Her herd rivaled his own in quality if not quantity. He'd been selectively breeding and improving his herd for over ten years. He sighed to himself wondering why she insisted on riding that ornery little palomino when she had some of the finest horses in Texas to choose from.

The family went broke like everyone else when Confederate currency became worthless and they lost some cattle and horses to the Comanche. But they still had their land. They still had some cattle and horses and they would recover. Right now cash was scarce.

"Papa do you think Joshua will be pleased?" asked Sarah. "Have I done well?"

"Yes Darlin, you've done fine. You've already got fifty head of the finest horses in Texas. We'll go ahead and start building you a cabin to go with the land after we finish the spring round up. It will

47

be modest; probably a two room with a loft, but it will be strong and warm. You're mother and I started out that way. I expect you'll be able to build a bigger nicer house in a few years. So you don't want to put the cabin where you think you'll want the big house. I suggest we dig a well between the cabin and where you'll want to put the big house. That way it won't be too far from either one. The river water will be fine for bathing, cleaning, and watering your stock but I think you should use a well for your drinking and cooking water. It will be cleaner and taste better.

"There should be enough big lumber along the river to get the cabin built. The rest is small stuff but it will make good corral poles and fire wood."

"Papa, I'm going to tell Joshua he should homestead the land northwest of this section on the other side of the river. That way we'll have deeded land on both sides and control of both banks. I checked at the land office and it's open to homesteading. Last month the Constitutional Convention in Austin passed an ordinance that anyone can homestead 320 acres, a ½ section, and if they stay on it for three years it will be theirs and all they have to pay for is the survey."

"How do you know all that?" asked Frank a bit surprised.

"I read it in an Austin newspaper. I found it in Georgetown last week when I went to town to help Jessica sew on her wedding dress. She's going to make Jesse a wonderful wife. I'm so happy for them.

"But with the war over and the soldiers coming back to protect us from the Comanche, more homesteaders will be coming. The open range won't last forever and access to water will be the key to successful ranching."

"Sarah, that's pretty sound thinking. If you want Joshua to homestead, we should wait and build the cabin on the homestead. You think about it and we'll make a decision after Joshua gets here."

"Papa, you haven't said a word about Joshua fighting for the Yankees," Sarah said uneasily.

"Honey, just between you and me, I thought secession was a bad idea. I voted against it. But when the rest of Texas voted for secession I had to decide to support Texas or leave. I chose to support Texas. Joshua did what he thought was best just like the rest of us did. The war is over and he wants to come home. I can't fault him for doing what he thought was right. He is still his father's son and

48

welcome in our home. You have a right to know what I think of your intended and now you do. I still care for him as my best friend's son and I respect him as a man. The war is over and so is this conversation. You will not bring it up again.

"Now let's go look at that piece you want him to homestead." With that Frank touched spurs to his horse's flanks and continued west at a lope. Beaming from ear to ear, Sarah loosened the reins and Diablo took off to catch her father's horse.

Chapter Seven; Escort to Dallas

April 22, 1866 in Little Rock, Arkansas:

Shortly after daylight Joshua, Nathan, and Luke said goodbye to Christina after finishing breakfast in the diner. They mounted up and headed south out of town to meet the ladies. The ladies and Mr. Edwards were waiting for them just outside of town in two wagons. Mr. Edwards was driving one and Miss Johnson was driving the other. The girls were riding in the wagons with the baggage. Without a word or slowing down, Joshua waved them in behind the Studebaker. He considered stopping to talk but decided against it. The sheriff wanted them all out of town sooner than later so he kept going. They kept a good pace all morning. Around eleven o'clock they crossed a creek and Joshua called a halt for lunch.

Joshua led the wagons about two hundred yards off the trail and had everyone dismount. Before anyone could wander off, he called them all together. "Gather round folks. We need to get acquainted and lay down some rules for this trip. Y'all line up so I can see who we have here."

The girls looked at him like he'd lost his mind.

"Well, go on!" said Miss Johnson. "You heard the man. Do what he says. He's in charge here."

The girls lined up beside the wagons. Miss Johnson and Mr. Edwards fell in at each end of the line.

"OK," said Joshua. "I'm Joshua Granger. Miss Johnson has hired me to get you to Dallas. In order for me to do that in the most efficient manner possible I need to know who and what I have to work with.

"Nathan is driving my wagon and taking care of our horses. The boy is Luke and he is going to Texas with us. I'm glad to see that y'all are modestly and practically dressed. Advertising your line of work before we get to Dallas will only bring trouble. We'll have enough to keep us busy without asking for more.

"When we are in camp, everyone will have assigned chores. Do not get out of sight of camp and no one goes anywhere alone. When you answer the call of nature take a friend with you. One person will stay where you can see the camp and the person doing their business.

"I see the looks on your faces and I don't care if you don't like what I'm telling you. You need to understand where you are. To the east we have Arkansas. You've just left the most civilized place in the state. To the west we have the Indian Territories. We will be traveling southwest into Texas and then south to Dallas. The closer we get to Texas the more chance we have of running into outlaws and maybe even some Indians. When we reach Fulton, Arkansas we will be one hard days ride from the Indian Territory to the west, Louisiana to the south, and Texas to the southwest.

"That means outlaws can kidnap pretty young women in the morning and have them across the state line of their choice shortly after dark. At that point any law that might be chasing them has to stop. You can then be carried across the Indian Territory and sold to the Comanche or Kiowa, who will keep you as a slave or carry you on down to Mexico and sell you to some Mexican bandit who likes fair skinned women. Either way you can expect to be beaten, raped, and tortured for their amusement until they get tired of you. Then they will kill you in the most entertaining way they can think of. This ain't Cincinnati.

"I need to know some things about each of you so we will go down the line one at a time. I want to know your name. Can you drive a team? Can you cook over a fire? Do you know how to load and shoot a gun and if so, did you bring one with you? If you brought a gun, I want to see it after we finish here. I think that is the longest speech I've ever made. Mr. Slim, we'll start with you and work our way down the line to Miss Johnson."

"My name is Jonathan Edwards. My friends call me Slim; it is the name I prefer. I can drive a team, and while not a gourmet, I can cook edible food over a fire. I served a term in Her Majesty's service as an

50

infantryman and am quite familiar with certain firearms. I have my fowling piece and my Cogswell pepperbox revolving pistol with me."

"My name is Matilda Brashears. I've never cooked over a fire or driven a team or shot a gun, but I'm willing to learn. I did bring a derringer with me but I'm embarrassed to say I don't even know how to load it." Matilda was a smiling rather plain and medium built brunette of about eighteen years.

"My name is Rachael. I don't know about any of this stuff and I don't have a gun. I just want to get to Dallas and start making some money." Rachael was a woman in her mid-twenties, attractive with dark hair and a hardness to her that made Joshua think it had been a while since she had smiled without getting paid for it.

Next in line was a smiling big blonde haired woman. She was young, maybe twenty, about six feet tall and built stout. "Guten Tag, My name is Helga Verner. Slim is teach me to drive wagon. I like cook but never over fire I have. I never shoot the gun. But smart girl, I am learn quickly." She was obviously fresh off the boat from Germany.

"My name is Teresa Laboe. I can drive a team; shoot a rifle, pistol, or shotgun. I can kill it, clean it, and cook it over a fire. I brought my Colt pocket pistol with me and I know how to use it." Teresa was about five foot four inches tall and thin with brown hair and freckles.

"My name is Ruth Jones. I don't know much about guns or horses but I can cook. I don't have a gun but I'm willing to learn whatever you want to teach me." Ruth was a mulatto girl with nice features and medium build.

"Bonjour, mi amour, I am Esmeralda Lafayette. My friends call me Frenchy. I don't know any of this frontier stuff but if you can take care of me to Dallas, cowboy, I can take care of you. I don't have a gun but I can keep yours clean," said the pleasantly plump and pretty woman in her late twenties with a wink and smile that made Joshua blush so hard his ears burned.

"That's enough Frenchy," said Miss Johnson smiling as the rest of the girls suppressed their giggles. "I guess it's my turn. I'm Luella Johnson. I can drive a team and shoot my Henry rifle and Remington pocket pistol but I am not a cook."

"OK, here's what we are gonna do," said Joshua. "We are going to set up camp here for the night. We will have lunch and after lunch we will assign camp chores. Then those of you who have guns will show me what you can do with them. After that I will look to your provisions, horses, harness and wagons to make sure they are fit for travel. We will get an early start in the morning. We will travel six days and rest on Sunday. We should reach Dallas in about three weeks."

That afternoon was spent just as Joshua said it would be. Miss Johnson pulled out her new Henry rifle. Joshua saw a few of them during the war. The fourteen rounds it held earned the Henry the title of "that damned Yankee rifle that you load on Sunday and shoot all week," from the Confederates. Luella wasn't kidding when she said she knew how to use it. When Joshua complimented her on her choice of firearms she told him, "I really can't take the credit. A gentleman friend in Cincinnati took me to a store with a large selection of guns. I told the storekeeper I wanted the best rifle available for this trip. He sold me the Henry and several boxes of ammunition. My gentleman friend taught me to use it. The pistol was a gift from another gentleman friend in New York some years ago."

Luella's Remington pocket pistol was a small .31 caliber revolver and she shot it well also. In the same extravagant style indicated by the use of a Henry Rifle the Remington was nickel-plated and elaborately engraved.

Slim shot a few sticks thrown in the air with his fowling piece, which was a twelve-gauge single barrel shotgun. Satisfied, Joshua asked to see his pepperbox. The Cogswell Pepperbox was an English made .36 caliber revolver that had revolving barrels instead of a revolving cylinder. The shape of the gun lent itself to discreet carry in a trouser pocket. Slim could hit what he was after with it out to about twenty feet. That was good enough for a card table kind of gun like a pepperbox.

Teresa Laboe pulled out her Colt Pocket Model. It was a .31 caliber five shot revolver very common among people who wanted to carry a gun discreetly without being weighted down. Small and easy to use, it was a respectable gun, one of Sam Colt's best sellers. True to her word, Teresa was proficient with it.

Joshua gave Matilda instruction on using her .41 caliber single shot muzzle loading derringer and worked with her until she was able to load it herself and hit a man size target at twenty feet. Once Matilda was comfortable using her derringer Joshua told them all to keep their guns loaded and their pistols on them at all times.

Even though he had enough guns to arm the rest of the women, Joshua decided against it at this point. Guns in untrained hands would be as dangerous as running into outlaws or Indians and an accident would be even more likely. Without the time to train them in the proper handling and use of the guns it would be a bad idea.

The major chores of cooking, gathering fuel for the fire, and horse care were divided up two girls to each task. Nathan would oversee the horse care and showed Matilda, Helga, and Luke how to unharness, curry, water, grain, and hobble the horses before turning them out to graze. Slim would be in charge of the cooking with Teresa and Ruth to assist him. Luella, Rachael, and Frenchy would gather the fuel for the fire and make sure the water barrels were full. Joshua explained how dry wood gave off less smoke and was therefore more desirable than wet wood because smoke would give away their location to Indians or outlaws. It was all Joshua could do not to laugh when he explained "what kind of wood" a buffalo chip was and saw the resulting looks of disgust from the three women.

Feeling somewhat better about the whole situation, Joshua took Luella and Slim and went over their horses, harness, wagons, and supplies. The eight horses were of average size; about fifteen hands each, give or take an inch or two per horse. While they were not outstanding they were good quality stock and should have no trouble making the trip. Joshua was pleased to note that they were geldings ranging in age from six to ten years old. Geldings would be more even-tempered and easier to handle due to the lack of sexual distractions. These horses were old enough to be past the behavioral problems of young stock and young enough to not need the special attention of older horses.

The harness was new and in good repair. The wagons were made by Old Hickory Wagons out of Louisville, Kentucky. Joshua was familiar with them and they made a good wagon. These wagons were not as large and heavy as his Studebaker but would be good for this trip and many more. They were three and a half feet wide and eight feet long. They had large wheels in back and smaller wheels in front giving them a shorter turn radius.

Luella showed Joshua their food supply. It consisted of an adequate amount of rice, beans, flour, coffee, salt pork, some spices and seasonings as well as several cans of condensed milk. Joshua saw condensed milk a few times during the war but never thought about buying some for his own use. When he commented on it, Luella told him it made nice gravy to go on biscuits for special occasions. Joshua had always been fond of biscuits and gravy. They also had pots, pans, and cooking utensils.

"Miss Johnson, I am impressed with your outfit," Joshua told her when they finished. "I wasn't expecting you to be so well prepared."

"Thank you, Mr. Granger. I have approached this trip as I approached any of the other business ventures I've gone into. I find out everything I can about it, hire the best people I can find, and give them the best equipment I can. The only mistake I made this time was the first man I hired to get us to Dallas."

"What happened?"

"When I hired him he was sober and came with good references. As you can tell by our outfit he was doing a fine job. But when we reached Little Rock, he ran into an old friend and they went into a saloon for drink. He couldn't stop at one and was drunk for a week before I gave up and fired him. We were camped on the edge of town and he came into camp still drunk demanding his job back. When I refused he became violent and pulled a knife on me. Slim was in town and unable to assist me at the time. It was terrible. When he threatened to 'open me up from crotch to eyeballs,' I pulled my pistol from the pocket of my dress and shot him dead. I didn't want to kill him but I was afraid for my life. I did what I had to do.

"I tell you this Mr. Granger, not to intimidate you; I don't think I could if I wanted too. I tell you this so that you will understand that while I am not a frontierswoman, I am neither frail nor helpless and you may rest assured that I can rise to the occasion whatever it may be."

Joshua chuckled. "What's so funny?" Luella asked defensively.

"The sheriff ran you out of town too, didn't he?" Joshua replied with a smile.

"Yes, he did," she replied with a smile of her own.

That evening at supper Joshua told them all; "There is one more thing we need to cover and that is night watch. We will have three shifts, three hours long. Slim and Matilda will have the first shift from eight to eleven. Miss Johnson and I will take the second shift from eleven to two. Nathan and Teresa will have the two to five shift.

"Our day will start at 5 a.m. We will have breakfast, water and grain the horses, hitch up and roll out. We will travel until around 11:00 when we will stop for a two hour break and noon meal. Around 1:00 we will roll out and continue until around 6:00 when we will stop for the night. This will probably vary some depending on water and other things but we should be able to do about twenty miles a day. That should put us in Dallas in about three weeks."

Later that night, sitting on the wagon seat of the Studebaker, listening to the horses as they grazed and dozed, Luella turned to Joshua and asked, "Well, when are you going to ask me how I came to be a whore?"

A bit shocked by the question Joshua replied, "It hadn't occurred to me to ask."

"Really? Why not? It seems to be a favorite question of men I meet," Luella said with a tinge of resentment in her voice.

"Hell, I don't know," said Joshua defensively, "Maybe because it ain't none of my business?"

After a long silence Joshua asked, "Is there something bothering you, Miss Johnson? You act like you got a burr under your saddle."

"I would like some conversation Mr. Granger. This quiet and solitude that you seem to be enjoying sets my nerves on edge. I'm sorry if I offended you. It's just that particular question seems to be of interest to most men and your answer took me by surprise."

"I don't reckon a little conversation would hurt anything. Just keep your voice low. Sounds travel further at night and we don't want to attract unwelcome guests."

"What kind of guests?"

"Outlaws and Indians."

"Are there really hostile Indians around here or are you just trying to scare us girls into good behavior?" asked Luella in a mock whisper.

"The Indians between here and Dallas are not openly hostile and some of the Cherokee are as civilized as you and I. But there are those that would slip in and kill you with a knife while you sleep. Others would just steal our horses. Then there are white men who would do that to. There's also the possibility of a raiding party coming down from the Indian Territory. There are outlaws who ride in groups of five to ten who just take what they want from whoever they can by force. They are a bigger threat around here than the Indians. The further west we go the more chance we have of running into hostile Indians. I really don't expect to see hostiles as far east as Dallas but the Indian Territory isn't very far north so it is possible. I'd rather be overly cautious than be mistaken and lose my hair."

"What will we do if we run into them Mr. Granger?"

"We'll make the best stand we can and try to fight them off. If there's a bunch of them and they see how many women and horses we have they'll be determined. I think the next town we come to we should get all of you some men's clothes and I better teach the rest of the girls how to shoot. If we look like eleven well-armed men from a distance they are less likely to attack. But if they see all these horses and seven women they won't be able to resist. They'll hit us for all they are worth. They like horses, cattle, women, guns, and scalps. Not always in that order."

"Are all the things the sheriff said about you true Mr. Granger?"

"Yes Ma'am."

"How old are you?"

"I'm twenty-three Ma'am,"

"So young and yet you've done so much."

"I don't feel young."

"So let me see if I've got this straight; you're from Kentucky and you're going to Texas. But you've been to Texas before. You've been on a cattle drive and you've been to California and back. You were in the Union Cavalry during the war but you still want to go back to Texas."

"Yes Ma'am."

"So what takes you back to Texas?"

"A girl."

"She must be really something for you to go back to Texas after fighting for the Union."

"She is. I'm gonna marry her."

"Tell me about her."

"Can't really."

"Why not?"

"Haven't seen her in almost six years. I expect she's changed some."

"You're going to Texas to marry a woman you haven't seen in six years. What makes you think she'll marry you?"

"Her letter said so."

"Mr. Granger if it's not being too nosey, I'd love to hear how you two met."

"Well, I guess it won't hurt nothing to tell you. When I was twelve years old, my father took me and my brother to Texas with him to sell some Kentucky Saddlehorse breeding stock to her father, Frank Smith. That's when we met. We stayed two weeks with them before we went back home. She was the prettiest little ten year old girl I had ever seen. Our older brothers would run off together and wouldn't let us come with them, so we played together. When we left she kissed me on the cheek while nobody was looking and whispered she was going to marry me when we grew up. It sounded like a good idea to me. So being kids we told our parents that we were going to get married when we grew up. They seemed to think it was a good idea too and they let us write letters to each other. It was almost like an arranged marriage except, we arranged it."

"That was eleven years ago," Luella commented. "So you must have gone back to Texas at some point."

"Yes Ma'am. By the time I was fourteen my father and mother had passed away. I was living with my brother and his new wife on our farm in Kentucky. I ran off in the middle of the night with a shotgun, a four year old stud horse and a fourteen year old mare. I run off because I heard my brother and his wife arguing about sending me away to school. I was underage and since our Ma and Pa were passed he was my legal guardian. I didn't want to go away to school so I lit out for Texas."

"Your brother just let you go?" asked Luella.

"No Ma'am. The next day he damned near killed his best horse catching up to me. I seen him coming and took off. My stud was doing fine but my mare was in foal. I didn't want to hurt the foal so I slowed down and he caught up to me.

"When he did, we talked about it. That morning when they found the note I left, his wife started crying and told him she was going to have a baby and she was scared she couldn't take care of a baby, him, and me too. She said she was sorry and if I'd come back she wouldn't go back to her mother's like she'd threatened the night before.

"I told him I really wanted to go to Texas and start my own horse ranch. When he realized I was serious, he gave me his Colt Dragoon pistol and the $37 he had on him. He told me to be careful, write often, and that I was always welcome to come home. I went on to Texas but things didn't work out like I planned."

"What happened?" asked Luella.

"When I got to Texas and told her father that I'd come to marry Sarah Lynn, he explained that she was too young and that I'd have to wait until she was at least seventeen. I told him I supposed I could wait five years but I'd need a job and asked him if he needed a good hand.

"For the next two years I worked for him and he treated me almost like a son. Then one night at supper he announced that Sarah had been accepted at a finishing school in New Orleans and she would be going away to school.

"After about a year I got restless and hired on with a cattle drive going north. When we finished the drive I went to St. Joseph and hired on as a Pony Express rider. The pay was a hundred dollars a month and I figured if I couldn't see Sarah, I could make some money so we wouldn't be broke when we got married. I got out to California riding for the Express. I was riding for the Pony Express when the War broke out. When the Express shut down I went back to Kentucky and joined the Union Cavalry."

"So you just rode off and left the love of your life and didn't hear from her for six years but she still wants to marry you now? That doesn't make sense," said Luella.

"No, that's not how it went. Sarah and I continued to write letters the whole time right up until the war broke out and the mail stopped. In my last letter I told her I planned to fight for the North if it came to war and that I wanted her to have the horses I left in Texas. I told her if she still wanted to marry me when the war was over to send a letter to my brother's house.

"After the War, it was just natural to go back to Kentucky again. My Daddy had left me a little farm when he passed away so I went back to it. When the letter came from Sarah Lynn asking me to come back to Texas so we could get married like we'd planned before the war, I sent her a letter telling her I was coming. My brother Paul said I was welcome to stay and I had the little farm to work. He suggested that I marry Sarah Lynn and bring her to Kentucky."

"That sounds like a reasonable plan to me," Luella commented.

"I told him I might come back to visit but that I was going to Texas to stay. He told me that he hadn't been sure it was such a good idea when I left the first time and that he had continued to work my farm along with his while I was gone. He figured when I came of age he'd send me a letter and ask me what I wanted to do with it. In the meantime, he had been sort of renting my farm from me without me knowing it and just putting the money in the bank for me. He gave me the bankbook and it had a nice amount in it. He said since I wasn't planning on coming back I should sell the farm to him so I would have money for a good start when I got to Texas. So I sold him my little farm and now I'm headed to Texas. What's your story?"

"Well, my parents were Irish immigrants. My brother and I were born in New York City. By the time I was fifteen and my brother was thirteen they had passed away and we made our way as best we could. Our parents had been poor in Ireland and they were poor in New York too. My brother and I stuck together and it wasn't long before I figured out how to keep us fed while he made sure no one hurt me. It was a hard life but I worked my way up from walking the streets to the point that I had some regular clients who were well heeled and well connected. They appreciated my discretion as well as my other talents and I was able to limit myself to them and referrals they would send to me.

"The referrals led to other wealthy businessmen and politicians who in turn would call on me to entertain their visiting clients and dignitaries. My brother and I had a nice little house and I was able to get him into college by having some of my clients recommend him.

When he graduated college we bought a general store and were doing quite well.

"Frenchy started working for us in the store. Then a client of mine asked me to bring a friend because he had two clients to entertain. That's when Frenchy got into this side of the business. We've been together six years now.

"One night a diplomat from somewhere in Europe wanted Frenchy to do some strange things and when she refused he beat her very badly. For a while we didn't know if she would live. My brother found that gentleman and during their conversation the gentleman had a fatal accident. Since he was a diplomat the police had been unable and unwilling to do anything about him beating Frenchy but when he had his accident they questioned my brother pretty hard. By the time the police came to arrest my brother, one of my clients had given him letters of introduction to a business acquaintance in Texas and put him on a clipper ship to Galveston.

"When the story hit the papers saying my brother was wanted for murder but nowhere to be found, my escort business dropped to almost nothing and so did business in the store. Frenchy and I were in the process of selling the house and the store with plans to join my brother in Texas but the war broke out and we were unable to do so.

"A couple of my clients stuck with me and gave me letters of reference to business associates in Cincinnati. We went there and bought another store and ran our escort service on the side. We did well.

"When the war ended, I sent a letter to my brother's last known address in Texas inquiring of him. I received a letter from him in return. Then in February, he sent a telegram saying he had opened a saloon in Dallas and he discovered that the army was going to build several forts on the Texas frontier. He asked us to come and bring some girls so here we are."

About this time Luke climbed up on the wagon seat with them. "Why hello Luke," Joshua said quietly. "Have you come to keep watch with us?"

"Uhum," responded Luke as he squeezed in between them on the wagon seat. He allowed Luella to put her arm around him and he leaned his head against her. Five minutes later he was snoring softly. Joshua and Luella smiled at each other in the dark.

Over the next few days Joshua took some of the girls one at a time during their noon breaks and after evening chores to teach them how to use a gun. First he showed Matilda how to handle the Sharps and put her riding with Slim. The next day he taught Helga how to use a shotgun and put her riding with Luella. Finally he taught Ruth how to use a Spencer and put her riding with Nathan.

Joshua felt better with each wagon having an armed driver and a shotgun rider but putting Ruth with Nathan left no room for Luke. While three people might sit on the wagon seat while the wagon was parked, the bouncing around that happened when it was rolling down the trail made that impossible.

The day after Ruth started riding with Nathan; Luke went up to Joshua and said, "I want to ride." So Joshua saddled up the mule for Luke. The mule was shorter and thinner than the horses even though his ribs didn't show any more. Being shorter would make it easier for Luke to mount and dismount. Being thinner would minimize the amount and intensity of the saddle soreness that Luke would experience since he hadn't ridden before.

The first day, Joshua saddled the mule and led it with a rope around his saddle horn while Luke rode. The second day, Joshua bridled the mule but kept the lead line around his saddle horn. By the fourth day, Luke said he was ready to ride by himself. As a safety precaution Joshua left the lead line on the halter and attached it to Luke's saddle in a manner that gave the mule enough freedom to move his head without slack to get tangled in. Joshua could pull the end of the lead line and take control of the mule in an emergency.

Luke rode with Joshua and watched him closely copying his actions. By the end of his first week riding, Luke was taking full care of the mule. He wasn't quite tall enough to saddle the mule by himself but the mule would lower his head so Luke could put the bridle on him. Then it occurred to Joshua to teach the mule to stretch out like one of his saddle horses. That would lower the mule's back so Luke could saddle the mule by himself and make it easier for him to get on. The stretching, called parking out, was taught to tall horses in the Midwest and south so short people could get on tall horses without having to climb a fence.

On Saturday evening Joshua stopped the wagons after crossing a stream. With plenty of water, grass, and wood for a fire, Joshua decided this would be a good place to rest on Sunday.

After supper Nathan took some food scraps for bait, fish hooks and line and set a small trot line hoping to catch some fish. He discovered a pool downstream and told the ladies that it would be a good spot for bathing. Joshua told them to post a guard while they bathed. The girls went downstream to the pool and had their baths. When they returned, the men took a turn.

The next morning after breakfast, Nathan took Luke with him and checked the trot line. Out of six lines they found four bass and a snapping turtle. They took them all back to camp and Nathan cleaned them. The turtle was hard to clean. The girls were amazed that the turtle's legs still clawed at Nathan hands while he was cutting open the shell even though he had cut off the turtle's head. Just for fun Nathan poked a stick at the turtle's head. When the severed turtle head snapped at the stick, Frenchy screamed and ran to the other end of the camp. Nathan and Teresa had a good laugh at that.

Teresa explained that turtles are just like that. Some folks said a turtle won't die until the sun goes down, but they sure do taste good when you fry them up. Teresa went on to tell about how in the mountains of West Virginia where she was from, people ate lots of things that folks elsewhere wouldn't consider food animals. She took the lead with the cooking and showed Slim and Ruth the best way to cook the fish and turtle. She seasoned them with wild onions, salt and pepper, and rolled the turtle pieces in flour before she fried them up.

When the turtle was done she made gravy with the grease, flour, and canned milk. The gravy would go good with the biscuits Ruth made in the Dutch oven. Usually she made enough in the morning to have some left over for lunch but today she fixed a fresh batch for lunch since they weren't traveling. Meanwhile, Slim fixed the staple of their meals; a pot of rice and beans seasoned with salt pork.

Joshua suggested that they all take time to rest after they finished with the meals and daily horse care chores which today meant watering the horses in the stream and making sure the hobbles were secure before letting them loose to graze.

After the horses were watered and turned loose, Joshua, Nathan, and Luke spent an hour looking them over for anything that might indicate a problem.

When they finished with the other horses, Joshua got a curry comb out of his saddlebags, gave the stud a nosebag of corn and brushed him down while he finished the corn. Joshua's stud was picketed away from the rest of the horses so he wouldn't beat up the geldings or breed the mares. He was a well-mannered and well trained stud, but a stud none the less and no need to take unnecessary chances.

Luke watched intently. When Joshua was done and put away the nosebag and currycomb, Luke got them back out and caught the mule. He gave the mule a nosebag of corn and brushed him down too.

After lunch Joshua found a nice shady spot under the Studebaker and stretched out for a nap. With his saddle for a pillow, his boots and gunbelt next to him, he put his hat over his face and was just drifting off when he heard someone come up and sit beside him. The sweet perfume told him it is one of the ladies. Hoping she would go away he began to snore softly.

"Mr. Granger," said a feminine voice with a French accent. Joshua snored a little louder hoping she would take the hint. "Mr. Granger," she said a little louder.

"Yes?" Joshua answered from under his hat.

"Will you teach me to shoot zee peestol?" she asked.

"I suppose I could," Joshua responded without moving his hat. "When would you like to learn?"

"Well," she said timidly, "now seems like a good time to me, if you don't mind."

Joshua sighed under his hat, disappointed that he wasn't going to get his nap. "I was afraid you were going to say that." Joshua squinted as he took his hat off his face, stretched, and groaned. "Let me get my boots on."

"Thank you, Mr. Granger," Frenchy said with a smile and flutter of eyelashes.

Joshua got up and pulled on his boots. He buckled on his guns and dug around in the Studebaker until he found the .36 caliber Colt Navy Model pistol they took from one of the dead outlaws in Tennessee. The Colt Navy was the finest pointing, easiest to shoot pistol made. Pointing a Navy Colt was like pointing your finger. For teaching a novice to shoot, Joshua couldn't think of a better pistol than the Colt Navy.

Joshua handed Frenchy the gunbelt and told her to put it on. She strapped it around her waist and grinned big at Luella who was watching from the shade of one of the other wagons. Joshua walked off toward the stream. Frenchy caught up to him and took his arm as if he were escorting her to a dance instead of target practice on a creek bank.

Joshua and Nathan had emptied and cleaned all the outlaws' guns before putting them away. When they got to the creek bank, Joshua picked a good sized tree and cut a five inch square in the tree bark with his belt knife. He stepped off ten paces and took the Colt from Frenchy. She watched closely as he loaded it. First he put the paper cartridge from the cartridge box on the belt into the chamber from the front and seated it with the loading lever from under the barrel of the gun. He did that for five out of six chambers. Then he took percussion caps from the cap box on the belt and put the caps on the nipples. Next he lowered the hammer on the one chamber of the cylinder that he left empty explaining that it was not safe to load all six chambers and have the hammer resting on the percussion cap. A slight bump could set it off, so load five and set the hammer down on the empty. Cocking the pistol he pointed at the square on the tree and put all five bullets into one ragged hole. "That's how you do it," he said. "Any questions?"

Frenchy shook her head no and Joshua watched her load the pistol giving her pointers as she went. With the pistol loaded he stepped behind her as she faced the target and he gave her some aiming tips. He explained that the pistol would recoil some and not to fight it. Just let it roll in her hand and then put it back on target before she shot again. She slowly fired all five shots. Three out of five hit the square.

"Not bad for your first time," Joshua told her.

Smiling like a child with a new toy she said, "I want to do it again."

"OK, one more time then you get to clean it."

Frenchy carefully loaded the Colt and took her time with the next five rounds. This time four out of five rounds hit the target. Joshua thought to himself that smiling as big as Frenchy was smiling must hurt her pretty face. "That's good," he told her. "I've seen men who shoot regularly who couldn't do that well. Now it's time to clean it," and he started back to camp. Frenchy caught up and took his arm again. She was still beaming when they walked back into camp.

Joshua put some water on the fire to heat and explained that hot water would dissolve the black powder residue which was corrosive and would rust the gun if not cleaned. Cleaning the gun was a fairly simple process; knock out the wedge pin under the barrel that holds the barrel to the frame then pull off the barrel. Next, pull off the cylinder. Then clean and dry the major parts, oil or grease the parts, and put the gun back together in reverse order.

With the gun cleaned and back in the holster, Frenchy said, "That was fun. I hate to give it back."

"Well, I suppose you can keep it until we get to Dallas, but I'll want it back when we get there."

"Thank you," she said and leaned over and kissed his cheek.

Blushing hard and trying to hide his discomfort he said, "If you're going to carry it, you better load it. It's a mighty short club if it ain't loaded. Remember, hammer down on an empty chamber and don't point that thing at anything you don't want to shoot."

"Yes Sir!" She said playfully as she sacheted away patting the pistol on her well rounded hip.

"That's a dangerous woman," Joshua mumbled to himself as the scent of her perfume lingered in his nostrils and imbedded itself in his memory.

A few days later they reached Boston, Texas just south of the Texas state line. It was a small town with a saloon, a general store, stable, church, and some homes. It was early evening so the general store was still open and of course the saloon. They made camp north of town. Luella took the girls into town to buy them some men's clothes like Joshua suggested for the rest of the trip. Nathan and Luke stayed in camp while Slim and Joshua headed for the saloon to see if they could find a game of cards. On the south side of town was a soldier camp so there was bound to be a game close by. Sure enough there were a couple of games going on in the saloon.

Slim and Joshua sat in on a game with a couple of privates, a Sergeant named Titus, and a civilian named Cullen Baker. The stakes were low compared to Joshua's last game with only a couple of dollars in each pot but as the game went on, Baker started winning the bigger pots regularly and never failed to have the best hand when it was his turn to deal. The privates were cleaned out early and Sgt. Titus began to grumble.

When it came time for Baker to deal again, Slim who was sitting across from him pulled out a new deck of cards and his pepperbox. Laying them both on the table he said to Baker, "Let's use these for a change and I'd like mine off the top this time if it's all the same to you."

"You mean this Reb bastard has been cheating?" yelled Sgt. Titus.

"All night," said Slim, his eyes locked with Baker who was considering his odds of getting out of there in one piece.

"Why you son-of-a-bitch!" yelled Titus as he backhanded Baker out his chair and jumped to his feet.

"Yankee bastards," yelled Baker as he pulled his pistol. He shot Titus dead center of his chest and dove for the door, shooting as he went. Joshua and Slim returned fire. One of them hit him in the arm and spun him out the door. As they ran out the door themselves they saw Baker swing up on a horse. He snapped off a couple of shots at them as he spurred the horse out of town. They returned fire but didn't hit anything in the dark.

Back inside one of the privates who'd lost his money was sitting on the floor with Sgt. Titus. "Hang on Sergeant. The surgeon's coming. You made it through the war; you can make it through this."

Wheezing and coughing up blood Sgt. Titus said in a raspy voice, "I'm done for son. The cheatin' Reb bastard's killed me. Make sure you boys get your money back." With that he closed his eyes and died.

The town sheriff who also owned the general store came in and the soldiers told him what happened. Joshua and Slim joined the posse that went after Baker. They rode hard all night but lost the trail in the dark. Baker made it into Arkansas.

Due to Joshua and Slim riding all night with the posse they stayed another day in Boston. Late in the day, Captain Wales, Company Commander of the army unit that Sgt. Titus was part of rode into their camp. He was cordial and thanked them for riding with the posse the night before. He told them that Cullen Baker had a bad reputation before last night, both in Arkansas and North East Texas. Now he had a thousand dollar bounty on his head dead or alive for killing Sgt. Titus.

Looking over Joshua's horses he offered to buy Joshua's stud. "No, sir," Joshua replied, "he's not for sale. But I thank you for the offer."

Captain Wales walked over to the stud and took a closer look. "Officers are required to provide their own mounts, you know."

"Yes, sir, I know. I received a battlefield commission to second lieutenant of the 12th Kentucky Volunteer Cavalry U.S. at the battle of Wildcat Mountain in Eastern Kentucky. Fortunately for me, my family has raised horses in central Kentucky for three generations. Thanks to my brother, I was always well mounted during the war."

"That's a fine animal son, at sixteen hands he's a little taller than most I've had. Looking at him I'd guess he ain't no slow poke either. I'll give you two hundred dollars for him right now. We're headed to Waco, Texas and expect to be chasing Indians. I'd like to be well mounted for it."

"That's a real nice offer sir, but I have to say no. Him and those fillies are my breeding stock. I picked up this other mare along the way though. She's nice, 15.2 and about seven years old. I'll see what kind of foal she throws unless you want to buy her now. I'll take a reasonable offer on her but my brother bred and raised the stud and I just can't part with him."

"Thanks, but I'll pass on the mare. I really like the stud and mares are as temperamental as a woman. One day she'll nuzzle you for a treat and the next she'll kick you for no apparent reason. I suppose the gelding I'm riding now will have to do. He's alright. He's even-tempered and calm but he's past ten now. I lost the best horse I ever had at Gettysburg. He was a Morgan. The damned Rebs shot him out from under me. He took two Minnie balls and only grunted. The third one put him down. He was a brave lad. I finished him off with my pistol rather than let him suffer.

"We'll be stationed in Waco. If you change your mind, the offer stands."

"Well, sir, I'm headed south of Waco about four days ride. My family down there has been crossing Kentucky Saddlehorses like these with the local mustangs for ten years. They make a fine cross especially for this kind of country and what's west and south of here.

67

The mustangs give them stamina and make them pine knot tough. The Saddlehorse gives them some size, refinement, willing attitude, and a smooth ride. If you're interested, I imagine I can round up a few and bring them to Waco. You can pick the one you like best and we'll settle on a fair price then."

"That sounds good to me Mr. Granger. I expect there may be some other officers there who would be interested in good mounts and maybe a cavalry buyer too."

"I'll bring a ten head sample of what we can offer and see what you think. I know the regulation requirements. It generally comes down to geldings, well broke to saddle and solid color, five to nine years old, good size and conformation. That's not the regulation word for word but it sums it up pretty good. Acceptable size is usually 15 to16 hands but I've seen horses accepted as small as 14.3. Late in the war I think some of the state volunteer units from the North East were buying big ponies," Joshua laughs.

"Most Army horse buyers will take a 14.3 horse if he meets the rest of the qualifications." said Captain Wales as he stepped into his saddle. "I look forward to seeing you in Waco. Good day, sir."

"Via con Dios, Captain, I'll see you in Waco."

That night on watch with Luella and Luke, sitting near the dying campfire, Joshua pulled out his tobacco and pipe and had a smoke. "I've never seen you smoke before," Luella commented.

"I don't smoke a lot, but it helps me relax and think sometimes," Joshua replied.

"What's on your mind?" asked Luella as Luke laid his head in her lap.

"I'm thinking about the future."

"I think you're going to be fine. From what I've seen you lead a charmed life. You have the Midas touch," Luella told him.

"What's the Midas touch," asked Joshua a bit embarrassed that he didn't know.

"Midas was a king in a children's story my mother read to me when I was a little girl. A fairy granted him one wish. He wished for everything he touched to turn to gold."

"Sounds good to me," Joshua said.

"It didn't turn out too well for Midas. He touched his wife and she became a gold statue. He couldn't eat because his food turned to gold," Luella continued.

"Hum, I guess the moral to the story is money ain't everything."

"Yes, it helps to have some but it isn't everything. But having the Midas touch is another way of saying things seem to work out well for you."

"I suppose. But I'm still gonna be careful," said Joshua thoughtfully.

"What is it that has you so concerned about the future?" Luella asked. Over the last week she had been able to get Joshua to open up and talk to her. She had an almost sisterly feeling for him except for the part of her that wished she could find a man like him for herself and settle down.

"It occurred to me that I'm probably not going to be as welcomed by her family this time as I was before. I fought for the North and her brothers fought for the South. I know she wants me to come but I expect there will be problems with her brothers. I'll probably have to whip them. I wish we could just be friends but I expect a fight is pretty certain. I hope it doesn't come down to a killing. She would never marry me if I killed one of her brothers and I'd have to leave Texas in a hurry and never go back. I don't want that. They'll be angry with me that I fought for the Union. But, I did what I thought was right and I'll not apologize for it."

"Do you really think it could come to a killing? Would you really kill one of her brothers?" Luella asked in surprise.

"Sometimes tempers flare. If they forced me into it; yeah I'd kill'em." Then quietly, almost to himself, he said, "I've killed enough men that one more wouldn't matter." Luella shivered at the cold, matter of fact way he said that, no bravado, just a resigned tiredness with a hint of remorse, as though he knew he'd be called to account on judgment day and wasn't looking forward to it. "I'd rather we could just be friends again but I don't know if they will let that happen."

"You know," Luella began hesitantly, "there are other women in the world that you wouldn't have to go through all of that to marry them. If you want a wife, any one of my girls, except maybe Rachel, would skip out on their contract with me and be thrilled to marry a

69

man like you. Hell, I might even marry you myself if you were to ask. Are you sure she's worth the trouble?"

"She's worth it," replied Joshua with a smile. "You see when I was young and my father took us on that first trip to Texas, I was the youngest son. I was small for my age and shy. My brother was my mother and father's favorite. They never came right out and said it but I could tell. They didn't mistreat me and they did love me but it was plain to me that he was number one and I was runner up.

"But when she looked at me, she didn't see the runner up. She's always made it plain that she thought I was great. I was her first choice and she didn't want anyone else. I had never been first choice before. But to her I've always been first choice and knowing that has given me the strength and confidence to do the things I've done. It's good to be first choice. So, I'm going to her and I'll take whatever comes because I'm her first choice."

"Is she your first choice?" asked Luella.

"Oh, yeah. I remember the first time I saw her. She was the prettiest girl I'd ever seen. We laughed and played together for the whole two weeks we stayed with her family that first trip to Texas. I told her I wanted to raise horses like my Daddy when I grew up. She said she liked horses too and she wanted to be a rancher's wife like her mother and raise lots of babies. She said if the rancher she married also happened to have the best horses in all of Texas she reckoned that would be fine.

"We rode our horses by ourselves a lot those two weeks. She's a hell of a rider." He chuckled to himself as he thought back. "She had this palomino mustang. She's always loved a palomino. She gets that from her Uncle Fernando. That mustang was mean but she rode him anyway. One day we were riding together when he threw her into a cactus plant and headed home without her. We rode my mare double back to the house. She was skinned up and bleeding a little bit but she never cried. She was too mad to cry. I didn't know Spanish back then but she did. She mumbled, grumbled, and fussed in Spanish all the way back to the house.

"Her Uncle Fernando heard her as we rode up to the barn. He helped her down from behind me and told her she better not let her mother hear her talking like that or she'd wash Sarah's mouth out with lye soap and take a switch to her too. That was no way for a lady to be talking he told her. All I remember is cabillo Diablo. It means devil horse. She said it over and over among other things. I asked Uncle Fernando what all she said and he told me it was best that I didn't know.

"Diablo had run into an open corral and was munching hay. Our fathers and brothers were saddling up to come look for her. Her father saw her and ran over, picked her up and gave her a hug and a kiss. She assured him that she was alright. When he set her down she walked into that corral and closed the gate.

"When she swung up on that mustang he went to bucking again and she let him have it. She rode him like one of Uncle Fernando's vaqueros spurring him with every jump. She was wearing a pair of silver spurs that Uncle Fernando had special made for her in San Antone. That pony was snorting and blowing and squealing and she was yelling at him in Spanish the whole time. She rode him to a standstill and he just stood there shaking. He was wore out. She let him catch his breath and then put him through his paces, backing him up, making him spin, walk, trot and canter before she got off. She unsaddled him, brushed him down and turned him loose.

"When she came out of that corral her Papa was waiting for her with a switch. He told her it was damned good ride but he better not ever hear her talking like that again whether it was in English, Spanish, Comanche, or any other language. Then he took her by the hand and led her in the barn to give her a whipping. Uncle Fernando was standing there. He crossed himself and asked God to forgive him for teaching her those words. He said it wasn't nearly as funny as he thought it would be.

"I snuck into the barn and hid in one of the stalls to watch. Her Papa thought nobody else was around and told her to scream, yell, and cry like he was beating her to death or her mother would come out to the barn and take the switch to both of them. So he hit her a couple of times on her backside with the switch and she put on quite a show crying, screaming, and begging him to stop. She had tears, snotty nose and all. I've seen professional actors in San Francisco who couldn't put on a show like that. It was a first rate performance. It couldn't have hurt too bad; she had boy's britches on under her dress. It was the only way her mother would let her ride astride and they didn't have a sidesaddle small enough for her.

71

"She saw me watching and when her Papa left she came over and sat down by me in the stall. I asked her if she was alright and she said "Yeah, I'm fine. I just had to teach that cabillo Diablo who was boss." We sat there and talked for a while then went to the house and got a couple of cookies from Mary Louise. She's their Negro cook and housekeeper. I hope she's still with'em. That woman sure knows how to cook.

"Later on that week a circuit riding preacher came to town. Sarah's mother said we were all going to the camp meeting Sunday even if he wasn't Catholic and there are some things you just don't argue with that woman about. So come Sunday we all got cleaned up and headed to town early in the morning. Sarah wore a light blue dress and her mother had curled her hair and put it up in ribbons. She rode in the wagon and was the perfect little lady all day. It was an all-day affair too. There was a sermon in the morning, followed by dinner on the ground, and another sermon that afternoon. When the grownups were all saying good-bye and getting ready to leave, Sarah walked up to me and asked if I was mad at her. I told her no and she asked, 'then why have you been staring at me all day?' I was a little embarrassed and told her I couldn't help it because she was the prettiest girl in the whole world. She blushed and smiled and ran off giggling. We've known we wanted to get married ever since.

"Later on when I was living with them, I guess I was fifteen. Her brother Jesse caught us kissing in the barn. We fought for fifteen minutes straight before her Papa came along and broke it up. That boy fights harder than anyone else I've ever fought. Two months later her Papa announced at supper one night that Sarah would be going away to a finishing school in New Orleans for a couple of years. She would come home for holidays."

"So they sent her to school to keep her away from you," Luella said.

"I never thought of it that way but looking back on it I guess so. That night she cried and cried. She made me promise to write and come see her. Her father drove cattle to New Orleans a couple of times a year and I went every time. The last time I went, the school head mistress told me if I ever came back to the school she would have me arrested."

"Why in the world would she do that?" Luella asked.

"Well, it was just before Christmas and her school had a dance with a boys school there in New Orleans. We had brought a herd of cattle to market and were going to take Sarah Lynn back home with us for Christmas. Since I came to visit regularly the head mistress said I could come to the dance if I wore a suit and left my spurs and pistol behind. So I bought a suit and went. I was on my best behavior until I overheard two of them city boys make a crude remark about Sarah. So I snatched them both by the scruff of the neck and escorted them outside.

"When we got outside, I let'em go and told them I was going to whip them for what they said about Sarah. Then I lit into them. By the time the head mistress got out there and pulled me off the last one, I looked about as bad as they did. But, since it was one of me and two of them and we were about the same size and age I didn't feel too bad about it. I told the head mistress that I whipped them for something they said about Sarah but wouldn't tell her what. Then I looked at those two boys and told them that if they repeated it I would whip'em again. They didn't repeat it and they got sent home but the head mistress told me if I ever came back that she would have the sheriff come and arrest me. So I left and went back to my hotel room so as not to embarrass Sarah any further.

"The next day Sarah's father brought her over to the hotel before we all left to take her home for Christmas. She made her father wait until she had a chance to patch me up to her satisfaction. One of the boys had pulled a knife and cut me pretty good across my arm. She washed out the cut real good then took a needle and thread and sewed it shut. That hurt worse than getting cut.
All the while I was apologizing for embarrassing her and said I wouldn't blame her if she didn't want to see me again. She told me to hush up that foolishness because she was proud as punch that I took up for her, it just made her love me more and she didn't want to hear any more about it. I guess I was sixteen and she was fourteen at the time.

"Since I wasn't welcome at the school anymore and I didn't want to cause her trouble, I hired on with a cattle drive going north the next spring. When we finished the drive I rode over to St. Joseph and hired on with the Pony Express. I figured I could make some money until she was old enough to marry then I'd go back to Texas and we'd

73

start our ranch as husband and wife. But, the war came along and here we are.

"Now I'm worried about what her family will think of me and then I've taken on the responsibility of Luke here too. She's not expecting a ready-made family."

"Well," Luella said, "from what you've told me I think you'll hold your own if it comes to a fight with her brothers. As for Luke, he's a sweet boy and I can't imagine a woman, especially one like you've described, putting him out. It may take her some getting used to but I think she'll come around pretty quick. I'm already dreading the day we have to part company. I'm going to miss him.

"Maybe that is the answer," she continued. "You could leave him with me in Dallas and I'll raise him."

"No offense but I really don't think a saloon and sporting house is a good place to raise a child, especially one who is different from most folks. It's a nice offer and I don't want to hurt your feelings but I don't think his Mama would approve." They spent the rest of the watch in silence. Joshua slowly and thoughtfully puffed on his pipe, while Luella stroked Luke's hair as he snored softly with his head in her lap.

Chapter Eight; Unexpected Opportunity

When they reached Dallas without incident, they set up camp in the wagon yard. Joshua, Luella, and Luke went into town looking for her brother. Slim stayed in camp with the girls and Nathan went into town alone looking for his brother. It was late in the day but Dallas was fairly busy. Soldiers, teamsters, cowboys, and farmers shared the streets with businessmen, gamblers and salesmen. Joshua and Luella decided to stop at the sheriff's office to ask where they might find Dan Jones. Dan had thought a new place might call for a new name given the reason he came to Texas in the first place.

The sheriff's eyes lit up with interest when the three of them walked in. He stood and shook hands all around as Luella took the lead and introduced them to the sheriff. The sheriff was about five feet eleven inches tall and of medium build. His shoulder length black hair was sprinkled with gray, as was his long mustache. He was neatly groomed and modestly dressed in a dark frock coat. He wore a

Colt Dragoon .44 in a simple cross-draw holster under his coat. In his late thirties, his weathered good looks and his calm polite manner inspired almost instant confidence in his abilities.

"I'm looking for my brother, Dan Jones," said Luella after the introductions. She made it a point to say that Joshua was her guide and Luke was with him hoping the handsome sheriff would understand that she was not married. "He owns a saloon here in Dallas and we're hoping you might be able to direct us to him sheriff…" she paused, "I didn't get your name."

"Charles Nathanial Palmer, at your service," he replied with a chivalrous bow. "My friends call me Nate."

"Are we to be friends sheriff?" she asked in cautious flirtation.

"I certainly hope so," he replied. "Your brother told me you were coming. He's a fine man. He did some good work for The Cause during the war. He asked me to help you find him if you came here looking for him. What he didn't tell me was just how pretty you are. I shall have to speak with him about that," he said smiling.

"Why thank you sheriff," said Luella blushing just slightly.

"Please, call me Nate. Now let's go see your brother." He grabbed his hat and escorted them out the door. Outside, he offered Luella his arm. She smiled and took it as he led them down the street.

That evening the five of them had supper together at Dan's favorite restaurant, his treat. Dan told them that there was money to be made setting up stores and saloons around the forts the army would be building. "The army will buy supplies, the soldiers will spend their money, and the settlers will follow. Then the towns will spring up and we will already be there to service the settlers and towns. The time to move is now," he said passionately.

"Are you going to haul all that freight yourself?" asked Joshua seeing a possible opportunity.

"I will if I have to," Dan said, "but I'd rather contract with someone to do it for me. I want to run the stores and saloons. I had my fill of freighting during the war."

"Dan worked with a gentleman, a Señor Yturria, down on the border bringing supplies up from Mexico during the war when the blockade shut off Texas ports," Nate volunteered. "He's not one to brag on himself so I'll brag for him. He did Texas and the Confederacy quite a service. That was some rough country to be freighting through what with the banditos, deserters, and Indians all over the country. What ever happened to Señor Yturria?"

"Nate you make it out to be more than it was," Dan said modestly. "Señor Yturria took a ship to France immediately following the War. It seems the Federals had lots of questions for him about his finances and his activities during the war that he didn't feel like answering. The Mexican government wasn't happy with him either. All I know is he gave me a break when I needed one; he paid in gold and treated me well. I have nothing but respect for the man. It's because of him that I was able to buy my nice saloon. But let's get back to talking about our business."

"Well," said Joshua, "I've got one wagon and a driver. Luella, why don't you sell me your wagons and teams? You're done with'em. I'll give you $600 for horses, harness, and wagons."

"Make it $800 and you can have them," she replied. "That's still a fair price."

"$650," Joshua countered.

"$800," Luella held firm.

"I'll go $700 but no more. Freighting is hard work. I don't like hard work that much," said Joshua with a grin.

"Deal, and still a good one for you," said Luella.

Joshua turned to Dan, "Well, I got three wagons what do you want hauled?" After a few minutes of discussion they agreed that Joshua would leave the two wagons in Dallas and come back for them in about two months. That way he could go to Georgetown and take care of his business there. Then he'd come back up to Waco to sell his horses and from there on up to Dallas. Then they would discuss what they were going to do and how they would go about it.

That night back at camp, Joshua and Nathan discussed their days. Nathan was excited because he met a man who thought he might know Nathan's brother. Nathan was going to meet him tomorrow. Joshua told Nathan that the girls would be moving into town tomorrow and that he bought the wagons and teams from Luella with plans to haul freight for Dan Jones.

Nathan was optimistic about meeting his brother tomorrow. Dallas had a large population of freedmen who naturally gravitated to the largest city in the area looking for work after Juneteenth. Juneteenth was what the freedmen of Texas called June 19th 1865, the day they finally heard about Mr. Lincoln's emancipation proclamation.

The next day Joshua and Luke helped the girls get settled into their new quarters. Frenchy gave Joshua back the Colt and asked him to take her trunk to her room for her. When Joshua got the trunk in the room, Frenchy closed the door and offered to clean his pistol for him at no charge and she wasn't talking about his Colt or Remington. Joshua blushed furiously and then politely declined. He thanked her for the offer but he'd waited this long for Sarah, he reckoned he could wait a little longer. Looking at him with a demure pout she said, "I thought you would say something like that." She kissed him hard and long on the mouth then whispered in his ear, "If you ever change your mind, you know where to find me."

"Yes, ma'am," said Joshua quickly and dashed out the door.

After helping the girls settle in, Joshua made arrangements at the wagon yard for the horses and wagons for two months and paid in advance. He expected to be back to pick them up before the second month was over.

That night back in camp, Nathan was disappointed. The man he met was not his brother and he didn't get any more leads. They agreed to head for Georgetown in the morning. Nathan believed that freighting all over Texas would give him a lot of opportunity to look for his brother and consoled himself with that.

Chapter Nine; Not Quite Welcome Home

The rest of the trip to Georgetown was uneventful. When they got to Georgetown, they camped on the west side of town upstream on the San Gabriel River. The next morning was May 27, 1866. After shaving, bathing in the river and putting on the new black suit he bought in Memphis, Joshua told Nathan and Luke to stay put and he'd be back that night. Then he saddled up and headed for the Smith's ranch alone.

At the Smith ranch the men were off building a new pen for working cattle and the women were working in the garden. Mary Louise looked up from her hoeing and shading her eyes with her hand stared northeast at the rider in the distance. "Miss Sarah," she said, "you best go on in the house and clean up a bit. You might put on one of your better dresses too."

"Why would I do that when there's work to be done?" Sarah asked without looking up from her planting.

"There's a rider coming up pretty quick. He's riding a gaited horse and I recognize the way he sits it. You best hurry child. Your man Master Joshua will be here in about ten minutes. Oops, better make it five minutes. He's seen us and put spurs to his horse."

Sarah looked up with a start. "Joshua?! Oh My Goodness! I'm a mess. I can't let him see me like this." Dropping her hoe and lifting her skirts she sprinted for the house.

By the time Joshua brought the stud back to a walk and stopped him in front of the house, Juanita and Mary Louise had taken seats on the porch and were waiting for him.

"Good morning, Joshua," said Juanita. "Get down and have a seat on the porch."

"Yes, ma'am, thank you kindly, good morning," Joshua said timidly. "I've come to see Sarah." Stepping off his horse he loosened the girth to make the horse more comfortable.

"Yes, we know why you're here," Juanita replied. "You'll just have to wait out here with us for a bit. I'm afraid you caught us unprepared and Sarah has gone in to make herself presentable. Have a seat she'll be out shortly."

Joshua took a seat on the porch step and nervously turned his hat in his hands not knowing what to do or say. Seeing how nervous he was, Mary Louise tried to lighten the mood. "Mrs. Smith did you ever think that skinny boy what used to live with us would ever grow up to be such a handsome young man? Who'd a thunk it? Now here he is all growed up."

"Thank you, Mary Louise," said Joshua.

"Oh, you're welcome Master Joshua. I guess I ought to call you Mister Joshua now. I'm so glad you made it through the war alright. Miss Sarah and me, we prayed for all three of you boys every night without fail all through the war. I guess our prayers was answered. Mrs. Smith, you remember when them Comanche raided the ranch back in '57? I saw Mr. Joshua jump off this very porch and knock a Comanche off Miss Sarah's palomino. You know that mean one she calls Diablo that she likes so much. Then Mr. Joshua come up off the ground with a knife in his hand and fought that Comanche for Miss Sarah's horse. I prayed for him right then too. I prayed Dear Jesus protect this child 'cause he ain't got a lick of sense when it comes to that girl. I guess God answered that prayer too. How are your ribs Mr. Joshua?"

"My left side gets a little stiff on me from time to time. My ribs only hurt me when it's wet and cold, but I reckon they healed up as well as could be expected. You did a good job patching me up. Thanks again for doing it."

"Oh, you're welcome. It weren't no trouble at all," said Mary Louise.

"Mrs. Smith, about the war," Joshua started but she cut him off.

"Joshua, just let that subject lie," she said coldly. "Frank says the war is over and you are welcome in our home so just leave it be."

"Yes, ma'am," he said quietly.

After a short uncomfortable pause, Juanita broke the silence. "That's a fine horse you're riding Joshua. Did your brother raise him?"

"Yes ma'am," Joshua said proudly brightening up a bit. "I've brought a couple of fillies he raised too that are just as nice as this fella and I picked up a nice mare along the way too."

"You'll be happy to know that Sarah took good care of the horses you left her. She's built up a nice herd crossing the stud with our best stock and keeping one third of the foals for herself. Of course we all know Frank has a hard time telling her no, so he let her keep whichever one she wanted, which means she always kept the best ones. I think she's got about fifty head now.

"Mary Louise, will you go see what's taking her so long? We'll have to start lunch for the men soon."

"Yes, ma'am," said Mary Louise. She excused herself and went inside shutting the door behind her.

"Joshua, I'll be expecting you to stay for lunch. Frank, Fernando, and the boys will be in shortly. They're building a new pen for working cattle. Some of the local men are putting together herds to drive north to market. We don't even know for sure that there is a market anymore. We only hear rumors. But these men have borrowed money from the bank and mortgaged their souls it seems to make this drive. They're paying six to eight dollars a head for cattle here and claim they'll get twenty dollars a head up north.

"Frank says we'll sell them our steers this year and if they do well we might make our own drive next year, though we won't do it on borrowed money. It says right there in the Good Book that borrowing money is bad and we are a Christian family."

"Yes, ma'am," said Joshua in agreement.

At this point the door opened and Mary Louise stepped back outside. Behind her in the doorway was Sarah. Joshua jumped to his feet and caught his breath. The pretty child of his memory had blossomed into a woman of breath-taking beauty and he was stunned.

Sarah stepped shyly through the door, her heart pounding. She had waited for this moment for years and now she didn't know what to say. All the wonderful things she'd rehearsed in her head had vanished. She could only stand there and pray that Joshua liked what he saw. She had chosen the simple dark green dress knowing that it set off her full figure, green eyes, and auburn hair to their best advantage. Her fair skinned face had a light tan and a few scattered freckles. Her long auburn hair was pulled back into a modest bun at the nape of her neck with a couple of wispy curls in front framing the aristocratic features of her face.

Before her stood a ruggedly handsome young man with brown hair, blue eyes, and a scar on his cheek that didn't use to be there. He stood two inches taller than her own five foot seven inches. He looked fit in his obviously new black suit. She noticed that the two pistols he was wearing didn't quite go with the suit but they seemed to fit the man. She slowly reached out with her right hand. Joshua, overcame his shock, took her hand in his and with a gallant bow placed his lips firmly on the back of her hand. Looking up into her eyes, he said softly, "Sarah."

"Joshua," she replied and the formality fell away as they embraced and both of them gushed words like fountains. It's so good to see you, and I've missed you so much, and good to have you home and be home poured from both of them at the same time. Then all was quiet and they kissed longingly. Mrs. Smith, not really as shocked and put out by this display as she was going to act, gave them a moment then cleared her throat loudly and gave them "the look." They blushingly stepped apart still holding hands.

"You're so beautiful," said Joshua, "even more than before. The years have been good to you."

"Thank you. Do you really think so?" she asked pleased that he said it.

"Yes, I do," he answered softly.

Mrs. Smith cut in. "Mary Louise and I are going to go in and fix lunch. We'll leave the door open," she said pointedly and they went inside.

Sarah took a seat on the bench where her mother had been sitting. She patted the spot beside her and Joshua joined her on the bench. For the next hour they sat and talked, catching up briefly on what had happened to them over the years. "How'd you get that scar?" she asked touching his cheek.

"A saber fight in Tennessee," he replied, deciding not to tell her that Jesse had given it to him just before he shot Jesse's horse out from under him.

"Was it terrible? The war I mean."

"Yes, I saw a lot of death and had a few close calls myself. My horse was shot out from under me at the Battle of Stones River. He went down at a full gallop and rolled over top of me. I thought I was a goner. But tell me about you."

"Well," she said, "after I came home from school most of the young men were either off fighting the war or chasing Comanche and Mexican bandits. It was a hard time. I helped Papa on the ranch as much as he would let me. Then the blockade shut off a lot of supplies. Everything had to come up from Mexico and most of that went east for the war. We didn't go hungry but Uncle Fernando went to Mexico and brought back a herd of sheep and a Mexican family to take care of them along with a spinning wheel and a loom. The Mexican woman made homespun cloth for us out of wool from Uncle Fernando's sheep and local cotton that we bartered for. We took that and made our own clothes. Uncle Fernando still has the sheep.

"The Indian raids got worse as the war went on. Papa finally took us women to town in the spring of '64 and stayed out here with a couple of vaqueros that Uncle Fernando sent over to help him since John and Jesse were off to war.

"I taught school in town while we were there. I discovered that I enjoyed the teaching and the children but I hated living in town. It was noisy and dirty with someone always coming and going. The banker's son from Austin, and the mayor of Georgetown, proposed but as you can see I turned them down to wait for you.

"I supported our soldiers during the war Joshua. I supported Texas. I'll not be apologizing for it."

"We all did what we thought was best, honey. I won't ask you to apologize because I won't either. I'm glad it's over and I want to get on with our lives. I have some money and a wagon load of supplies. I intend to homestead a ranch. I also have two more wagons and teams in Dallas and a freighting contract to go with them. There is an army Captain waiting at Waco for me to bring ten head of horses for him to choose from with the possibility of selling more horses to the army. Why the sad look?"

"If you are going to be freighting you won't be here much. I want you here. I want our own ranch. I can't run it alone and the Comanche are still a threat," she said.

"I thought it was a good idea and the opportunity was right there. We'll just have to figure out a way to make it work. I'm glad to hear you like children."

"Why, do you want to have a bunch of them? I think I would like that," she said excitedly.

"I think maybe that would be alright, but there is something else I need to tell you," he said.

"What is it?" she asked hesitantly.

Joshua told her about Luke and Nathan conveniently leaving out the part about his other companions on the trip since in his mind they weren't relevant to the topic at hand. During Joshua's telling of the story Sarah's beautiful face showed a whole series of emotions from uncertain concern, to relief, followed by sorrow, and then anger as Joshua related how he came to Luke's aide, to a loving concern by the end of the story. "If you don't want to keep him, there is a woman in Dallas who offered to raise him and I can take him back with me when I go get the wagons."

"Why Joshua Yerby Granger!" she began as her Spanish temper flared and blazed bright in her green eyes. "I can't believe you would even suggest such a thing! You will bring that young man into our home and we will raise him as our own! We have the means! It is the

Christian thing to do and I will not hear any more about it! This matter is closed!"

"Yes, ma'am," Joshua said with relief.

As they continued to talk, she told him about the thousand acres of land that her father was giving her for a dowry and how he had promised to build them a cabin and dig a well. She told him about the land next to it that she wanted him to homestead.

He told her about the Norman horses and the supplies he had in the wagon. He told her how he hoped to sell horses to the army and he was sure they could sell horses to settlers, and stage lines, and maybe even other freighting companies. They went on and on back and forth sharing their dreams of the future.

Before they realized it there was a group of riders dismounting by the corral and heading to the house. All six men were wearing broad brimmed hats, open vests, neckerchiefs, pistols, boots and spurs. Joshua stood and taking Sarah by the hand walked out to meet them. "Mr. Smith," said Joshua, extending his hand.

"Why, hello Joshua," said Mr. Smith shaking hands. "My, my, what happened to the boy I used to know?" He clapped Joshua on the back. "Looks like you've grown into a man! Welcome son. Welcome. It's good to see you."

Joshua shook hands all around with Fernando, John, Jesse, and the two hired men. John and Jesse were stiffly polite but no more earning them a stern look from their father that only they saw.

Going inside after washing up they found that lunch was ready. The long table was loaded down with the bounty of the land. The fare was simple but there was plenty of it. There were fresh green onions and early peas from the garden, tortillas, refried beans, venison, ham, jalapenos, tomatoes, rice, fresh bread, butter, cheese and honey. Mr. Smith sat at one end of the table and Mrs. Smith sat at the other end. Everyone else took a seat except Mary Louise. It was her job to keep the glasses filled with cool water or buttermilk. She customarily ate when the others had finished.

One of the hired men reached for the platter of venison and Mary Louise whacked him on the hand with a wooden spoon giving him a dirty look. There were smiles and suppressed chuckles around the table. Mrs. Smith silenced them with a look then said sweetly to Mr.

Smith. "Mr. Smith would you lead us in a prayer of thanks to Our Lord for His gifts we are about to receive?"

"I'd be happy to my dear." Looking around the table he said, "Shall we pray?" Every head bowed and Frank asked the blessing of the food, of the ones who prepared it, thanked God for Joshua's safe return, and asked His blessing on all their futures. "Amen"

Several around the table crossed themselves. The hired man who had his hand whacked looked cautiously over his shoulder at Mary Louise. She reached past him and handed him the venison. The plates were passed around the table.

The conversation was minimal as the hardworking, hungry men did justice to the food in front of them. When they finished, the men one by one excused themselves to the porch thanking Mrs. Smith for such a fine meal and complimenting Mary Louise on her cooking. Mr. Smith, Fernando, and Joshua were the last men sitting at the table.

Mr. Smith said, "Fernando, if you don't mind, I'm going to take a ride with young Joshua this afternoon. I believe we have some things to discuss. Do you mind taking charge of the corral building?"

"It will be my pleasure," he said standing up from the table. "I will look forward to your company in the coming days Joshua, but it is fitting that you discuss the purpose of your return with my niece's father as soon as possible. Today is a good day for it, I think," he said with a grin. He excused himself and strolled whistling out the door. "Vamanos, muchachos," they heard him say. "We have a corral to finish." They listened to the spurs jingle and boots thud off the porch.

"Joshua," said Mr. Smith, "let's you and I go for a ride."

"Yes sir," Joshua replied a little nervous.

For what seemed like an eternity to Joshua they rode west in silence. In reality it was only ten minutes. Frank Smith was deliberately making Joshua wait. He wanted to see if the years had taught Joshua any patience. He could tell that the silence was working Joshua's nerves but was glad to see Joshua was holding his tongue, respectfully waiting for him to open the conversation. "Well son, it's a beautiful day, we have all of Texas wide open in front of us and a war behind us. What would you like to talk about?"

"I want to talk about marrying your daughter," Joshua said getting straight to the point. "I've come home to marry Sarah and I'm asking you for your blessing."

"Suppose I say no?" Frank responded, "then what?"

Feeling like he'd been kicked in the gut by a bronc, Joshua swallowed hard and replied slowly, "I'd never really thought about that. I thought I might have to fight her brothers but I never dreamed you would say no. It would hurt us both to have to leave here and start life new without our family. I would rather not have to do that but I can't imagine my life without her in it. She's all I've ever wanted."

"Do you really think you can take care of her if you have to do it alone? She's had some fine offers of marriage and turned them down to wait for you. What have you got to offer her?"

Joshua swallowed hard again. His mouth had gone dry. This was something totally unexpected. He figured he would just ride in and they'd get married as a foregone conclusion and live happily ever after. "Well, sir, I have money from selling my farm in Kentucky. I've saved my wages over the years and have a pretty good stake. I have three wagons and teams and a freighting contract to go with them. I intend to homestead a place of my own. I've brought some good breeding stock horses with me to cross with the local stock and I've got an army officer at Waco waiting for me to bring him ten head of horses for him and his fellow officers. I hope to get a contract selling horses to the army that way. There are wild horses I can catch to cross with my blooded stock. There are wild cattle to be caught and branded to make up my own herd," he said getting excited at all the possibilities open to him. "Yes, sir, I'm still young, reasonably smart, and in good health. Yes, I can take care of her by myself!"

"That's good," said Frank. "That's what I wanted to hear. You can take care of her on your own but you won't have to. You have my and her mother's blessing. Grudgingly on her mother's part but still you have it none-the-less. You fought against her boys and she has a problem with that.

"Now, here is how this is going to work. You two have never been together for more than eight or nine months at a time. She has missed out on being courted by other men because she's been waiting for you. She deserves the respect and romance and all the other things that come with a proper courtship. Don't you agree?

"Well, yes sir."

"Good then you will have no objections to this stipulation on the blessing of her mother and I that you will only marry Sarah after a courtship of one full year. That's three hundred and sixty-five days; not a day less. You will live on your own during that year. You will not live with us. If you can't take care of yourself for a year how will you take care of my daughter for the rest of her life? Are you in agreement?"

Realizing that he had been played into a trap with only one acceptable answer, he said, "Yes sir."

"Good," said Frank pleasantly. "Do you have any questions?"

"Does today count?" he asked.

Frank laughed and said, "Yes, today counts."

The two of them rode on discussing the land Frank would give them and the cabin. Frank told Joshua that Sarah had picked out a half section next to the land he was going to give them that she wanted him to homestead.

Joshua told Frank about Luke and Nathan and how he thought he would have to hire some drivers for his wagons because Sarah wanted him here. Frank agreed that it was something he would have to work out but offered no solution. They agreed that tomorrow Joshua would bring Nathan, Luke, the horses and wagon and they would ride out to the land. Joshua could set up his camp and file his claim the following day.

By the time they got back to the house it was beginning to get dark. Sarah was pacing back and forth on the porch in the twilight waiting for them on pins and needles. "Well?" she asked as they stepped off their horses in front of the house.

"Well, what?" asked her father teasing her.

"Did you have a good talk?" she asked in obvious frustration.

"I'll let Joshua tell you about it. I'm going to put away my horse. Joshua, we'll see you tomorrow," said Frank as he led his horse toward the barn.

"I'll be here," said Joshua as he loosened his saddle to give the stud a chance to relax a few minutes before he had to leave.

"What's tomorrow?" asked Sarah. "It's getting late. Aren't you staying the night?"

"No," he said. "But, I'll be back tomorrow." Stepping up on the porch he pulled her to him. Looking into her eyes he said, "I have a question for you."

"Yes?" she asked with her heart pounding.

Taking her hand in his he stepped back and knelt taking off his hat. Looking up into her beautiful face he asked, "Will you marry me?"

"Oh Joshua!" she said. "Yes, yes, yes, I'll marry you!"

Standing, Joshua reached in his coat pocket and pulled out a small box. Sarah gasped with tears of joy streaming down her face as Joshua pulled out an emerald necklace and said, "My mother never met you but she told me that if we ever did really get married she wanted you to have this. My father gave it to her for their twentieth anniversary."

"Oh, Joshua!" she said as she wrapped her arms around his neck and pulled his face to hers for a kiss.

After a blissful moment, Joshua pulled away and whispered, "I have to go but I'll be back tomorrow." He turned away and stepped to his horse.

As he tightened the girth for his ride back to his camp she said, "Joshua, you've made me the happiest girl in the world. This is the best day of my life."

Turning to look at her in the gathering darkness he froze the image of her in his mind and said softly. "Mine too."

Swinging into the saddle he turned the horse broadside to the porch. Taking his hat in his hand he cued the stud to rear. "Until tomorrow my love," he said with a sweeping bow. Then he spurred his horse and was gone.

In the distance he heard Sarah calling as she ran into the house, "Mother, Mary Louise, Come see!" The rest was lost to the wind in his face as his stud settled into a gentle ground covering lope under the full moon and endless stars of the clear Texas night sky.

Chapter Ten; Meet the Family

When Joshua rode into camp very late that night, Luke was asleep in the wagon and Nathan was sitting by the fire studying his letters and sums as had become his habit at night. Working on it diligently each night by firelight with the assistance of Joshua and sometimes Luella or Slim he had reached the point over the weeks on the trail to where he could read some words; write his name in block letters and put simple sentences together. His spelling left something to be desired but the numbers came easier for him as counting was something he had always had to do. Addition and subtraction he could manage but multiplication tables and long division were not yet within his grasp.

"Mr. Joshua, I don't know if I'll ever be able to read and write enough to do any good," Nathan said as Joshua pulled the saddle and bridle off his weary stud and hobbled him before turning him loose to graze.

"It just takes time," Joshua replied. "The more you work at it the better you'll get until it just seems natural and you won't even have to think much about it."

"I sure do hope you're right," said Nathan. "How'd it go at the Smiths?" he asked as he poured Joshua a cup of coffee from the pot by the fire.

Joshua took the cup of coffee, "Thanks, I'm beat. It went well I think. We have her father and mother's blessing. I asked her to marry me and she said yes. Her father is giving us a thousand acres of his ranch for a dowry and she has picked out a half section next to it that she wants me to homestead. That will give us 1,360 deeded acres all together and there is plenty of open range we can use.

"None of them are opposed to Luke. We'll have to figure out something about the freighting because Sarah wants me to be home and not traipsing all over Texas with a freight wagon. We'll figure out something. Her mother was a little cold but I expected that, the same with her brothers. Her father and uncle were glad to see me though.

"We should probably both turn in. We're all heading back out there at first light. We'll have lunch at the Smith ranch and then ride out to the place I'll be homesteading."

"Yes, suh," said Nathan and he put his primer and notepad away.

The next morning, Luke was anxious. He could feel the excitement in the moods of the men. He acted out his anxiety by being rough with the mule. Seeing this and realizing something was wrong, Joshua went over to him and pulled him away from the mule. He knelt down to Luke's level. "Luke, what's wrong?" he asked. Luke didn't say anything; he just stared off into space with his mouth clinched shut. "We're going to go see Miss Sarah today. I am going to marry her and we will be a family." Tears started rolling down Luke's silent face. "What's wrong son?" asked Joshua again.

"When you make a family with her I won't have a family again. You are my family. I'm a good boy. What did I do to make you leave?" the boy said haltingly through his tears.

Joshua realized then that Luke thought he was going to be abandoned when Joshua married Sarah. Joshua hugged the boy and told him, "Luke, it's going to be alright. I'm not leaving you. When I marry Sarah she will come live with us. It will be you and me and her. I'm not leaving you son. Sarah wants to meet you. She wants you to like her and she wants to like you. Sarah is going to be part of our family. We are going to stay together Luke."

"You promise?" asked the boy snuffling his runny nose and wiping his hands across his eyes.

"I promise," Joshua told him and hugged him again. "Let's get the mule saddled for you," he said as he stood. He picked up the McClellan saddle and blanket, put them on the mule and tightened the girth. Luke took over from there, and this time he was gentle with the mule.

"You alright?" asked Nathan concerned as Joshua walked past him dabbing at his eyes with his neckerchief.

"Yeah," says Joshua. "Wind blew some dust in my eyes."

Nathan went back to hitching the team realizing that the wind wasn't blowing very hard but he didn't bring it up. Joshua saddled the Thoroughbred mare to give his stud a little rest.

It was about an hour before lunch when they arrived at the Smith ranch. Everyone was there; Mr. and Mrs. Smith, Sarah, her brothers, Uncle Fernando and Mary Louise. The hired men from yesterday were out on the range working cattle. Joshua introduced everyone to

Luke and Nathan out on the porch. Sarah knelt down and took Luke by both hands. It was hard for him to look her in the eyes and he looked past her into space.

"What a handsome boy you are," she said with a smile. She gave Joshua a questioning look when Luke didn't respond.

"He's just shy," Joshua said quietly. "He'll be fine when he warms up to you a little. You just need to give him some time," Joshua said not wanting to make a big deal about it. "He understands you. Talking ain't easy for him."

Sarah looked at the boy and told him, "You and I will be good friends in no time. I like you already. Joshua has told me what a good boy you are. Let's go see if we can find you a cookie. Mary Louise made a special batch just for you," she said standing and continuing to hold one of his hands, she led him toward the kitchen.

Luke stopped and looked back at Joshua. "It's alright. You can go with her. I'll still be here," he told the boy. Luke walked into the kitchen with Sarah still holding his hand.

Everyone went in the house and had a seat in the parlor but Mary Louise and Nathan. Mary Louise looked up at Nathan who was still sitting on the wagon seat. "Well," she said, "you look healthy enough to make yourself useful. You reckon you could bring me some firewood in the kitchen around back or has driving a wagon made you lazy like them town nigga's I seen?"

"You looks right healthy yourself," said Nathan giving her an appraising look. "But I reckon I could bring myself to help you out anyway."

"Well, I'm right glad to hear it," she said. "I'd hate to think I had to feed a shiftless no-account. You got something against a woman bein' full growed?"

"Lordy, I do hope you're cookies is sweeter than your conversation or poor Luke's gonna get lockjaw. Just so's you know, I wouldn't have a woman that weren't full growed." Nathan retorted with a grin.

"Humph! Ain't nothing wrong with my cookies and you prob'ly wouldn't know what to do with a full growed woman anyway," Mary Louise grumbled just loud enough for him to hear as she turned and went back into the house.

Chapter Eleven; The Homestead

After lunch, Joshua went out to the wagon and pulled out the things he brought for the women. Mr. Smith instructed his two sons to give Joshua a hand. They did but never said a word. The women were thrilled with the material, thread, and so forth. Even Mrs. Smith smiled which was uncommon for her unless she was looking at Mr. Smith or her children.

Joshua remembered that Sarah's birthday was right around the corner and kept the perfume and silver hairbrush set hidden. He asked Jesse and John if they would like one of the extra guns, but they acted like they didn't hear him. Joshua just let it go and left the guns in the wagon.

With the gifts passed out and the wagon repacked, Frank, Sarah, Joshua, Nathan, and Luke headed out for the land that Joshua would be homesteading. By the time they got there it was late in the day. Joshua and Nathan set up camp and put up the tent. Sarah and her father would sleep in the tent since it was late and they would be staying the night. They had supper around the campfire and traded stories of the past and hopes for the future. Sarah talked Mr. Smith into telling one of her favorite stories; the story of how he and Juanita met, fell in love, and got married.

Frank Smith had arrived in Texas in the spring of 1834 at the age of twenty-one. He was looking for something to do to build his fortune and make a place for himself in the world. One day he rode into San Antonio. There was a celebration of some sort going on and the city was crowded. Everyone who was anyone was in San Antonio. When he rode up to the small hotel to see about a room he saw a young señorita of such beauty that he stopped his horse in the street and just stared at her. He couldn't help it. She was just that beautiful. She and her family went into the same hotel that he had planned to enter. He quickly dismounted and went inside. While the clerk waited on the family he listened and waited his turn. He was a little self-conscious of his rugged appearance in his trail clothes.

Diego Nava, the young lady's father, was a respected rancher in the area who had brought his family to town for the celebration. Frank only knew a few words of Spanish at the time and those words were not the kind used in polite company. He did know a little French from working with the French trappers though. So, he learned his information from the clerk who also spoke French and a little English after the family retired to their rooms. The young lady was Señor Nava's only daughter and considered to be one of the most eligible young ladies in Texas. Her Grandfather had come to Texas and established a hacienda on a Spanish land grant. He had brought his household servants, cattle, horses and vaqueros with him from Mexico. They were of old Spanish nobility sent to Texas with huge land grants after they came up short in a political squabble in Spain. They would be attending the fiesta that evening. Frank made up his mind to attend the fiesta and find the beautiful señorita.

After he checked into his room, he bathed, shaved, put on his clean set of town clothes and made his way to the hotel lobby. There he asked about the fiesta and where the clerk thought the Nava family might be found. At first the clerk didn't want to tell the gringo where to find the Navas. It didn't set well with him that the gringo wanted to meet the young and beautiful Señorita Nava. With a little backwoods Kentucky persuasion that healed up just fine in a day or two, the clerk agreed to tell Frank where the family would probably be.

The start was rocky but Señorita Nava had been educated in Mexico City and spoke fluent French and a bit of English. Frank, trying to be discreet had directed his conversation to Señor Nava and the beautiful Señorita was kind enough to translate for her father. Before the night was over Frank found out where the Navas lived and informed Señor Nava he would be settling in the area on some land allotted to immigrants. Frank had no idea at the time how he was going to manage that but he kept that concern to himself. He managed one dance with Señorita Nava. She was reserved but polite and gave him a single smile with a flutter of eyelashes from behind her fan for encouragement. Frank went back to his room happy with visions of the brown-eyed beauty swirling through his memory and a plan to make her his wife forming in his mind.

It was a full month before he saw her again. It took some doing but Frank managed to get hold of a piece of land next to the Nava's and started building his ranch. The Mexican government at the time wanted Texas settled as a buffer against the Comanche and granted five thousand acres to each immigrant. By the time Texas declared independence Frank had become a good neighbor. Señor Nava was in favor of Texas independence and when Santa Anna came north, Señor Nava and Frank rode side by side to meet him. They fought Santa Anna's Army at San Jacinto under Sam Houston. After the war, the two men returned home good friends and Señor Nava allowed Frank to court the lovely Juanita. Frank found that Juanita was intelligent, articulate, a very devout Catholic, and a warm wonderful person in addition to her stunning beauty. Her reserved manner in public was taught to her by her mother as the proper way for a lady to act. He would never have to worry about her embarrassing him in public. He on the other hand had to put some polish on his manners and as Juanita pointed out to him in the Bible, bridle his tongue. A year later they married. The wedding and reception was the social event of the year and even Sam Houston showed up.

Frank didn't tell them that Juanita's dowry had consisted of another five thousand acres, five hundred head of cattle and one hundred head of horses. All he had wanted was to marry the beautiful and devoutly Christian Juanita. The pursuit of her led him to be a substantial rancher.

Yet even with ten thousand deeded acres, the horses and cattle, they were still cash poor at the present time. They had lost all their cash when Confederate money became worthless. That part of the story he kept to himself. He knew that it was only a matter of time until they recovered. In the meantime they could provide most of what they needed for themselves and they didn't need a lot of cash. When he sold his two hundred head of steers to the cattle buyer at seven dollars a head next week the family would be back on the road to financial recovery.

The next morning, Sarah and Joshua decided they wanted the cabin facing the South East to get the most sunlight in the house. They would dig the well about forty feet in front of the house on the south side of what would be the front yard of the cabin. Sarah suggested they plow a garden patch close to the river, which was south of the cabin. She and Mary Louise would come back and plant it. She quietly told Joshua when no one else could hear, that tending the garden would be a good excuse for her to come visit often.

Nathan wasted no time in harnessing the mule and began plowing the virgin ground for the garden and the corn crop for winter feed.

Sarah was impressed with the variety of vegetable seeds Joshua bought. There were black-eyed peas, squash, cucumbers, purple hull peas, Irish potatoes, sweet potatoes, corn, pinto beans, black beans, green beans, butter beans, carrots, pumpkins, watermelon, and even okra. She was also pleased that he thought enough of her to buy flower seeds too. Joshua smiled at her pleasure and kept it to himself that he had gotten carried away and bought some of every kind of seeds the store had. He'd also bought extra seed corn thinking that he would put in a few acres of corn to feed his saddle stock through the winter.

After lunch, Sarah, her father, Joshua and Luke saddled up and returned to the Smith ranch. It was half a day's ride so they should get there just in time for supper. Nathan stayed at the camp. Luke stuck to Joshua like a shadow and refused to be left behind.

When they arrived, Mary Louise commented that she was expecting to feed one more. She seemed a little put out but didn't say anything else about Nathan not being there. That night Joshua and Luke slept in the small bunk house with the ranch hands.

Chapter Twelve; Damned Yankee

The next morning, after a breakfast of venison, biscuits, eggs, grits and gravy they rode the rest of the way into Georgetown and Joshua filed his claim on the three hundred and twenty acres as the head of household because he had Luke. After he filed his claim Joshua and Luke went to a general store and looked around. Joshua noticed that Luke hit a growing spurt and the pants that Nathan bought him in Arkansas were already getting short. So Joshua bought Luke two new sets of clothes, new shoes and a hat of his own. The new hat brought Luke's hair to Joshua's attention, which led to haircuts for both of them.

After the haircut and a bath, they went back to the store and Luke got a stick of candy. The lady behind the counter said to Joshua, "Don't I know you?" as he paid for the candy.

"Yes, Mrs. Parker you do," he responded with a grin. "I'm Joshua Granger. I used to come in here and get stick candy when I was younger. I lived with the Smiths out west of here before the war. It's been a long time and I'm glad to be home."

"I remember now," she said with a frown. "I heard you was coming back. You should of stayed up North. Sarah Lynn is a sweet Christian girl. It's a shame she's set on marrying a Yankee. It's her only fault. My Jessica is marrying her brother Jesse in September. He's a fine young man. You mistreat Sarah Lynn in any way and her brothers will see you to your grave."

"Yes ma'am, I expect they would, just like I'd see them to their graves if they were to mistreat her. Mrs. Parker, I've loved Sarah Lynn since the first time we met and I have nothing but the most honorable intentions toward her. I asked her father for her hand two days ago. We will marry next year. I'm sorry you're mad that I fought for the Yankees but I did what I thought was right and I'll not be apologizing for it. I'd like to forget about the war and all of us be friends like we were before."

"You can forget about it if you want to but that don't mean the rest of us will," Mrs. Parker said as she turned and walked into the back room. Joshua took Luke and they went to the hotel to get a room for the night.

News travels fast in a small town and Georgetown, Texas was no exception. By morning everyone in town knew that Joshua Granger, the damned Yankee, and Sarah Lynn, the local sweetheart, were getting married. At the hotel dining room Joshua and Luke were greeted with cold stares, burned biscuits, undercooked bacon, runny eggs, and lukewarm coffee full of grounds. Luke didn't seem to notice and Joshua held his tongue remembering that his Mama used to tell him that killing folks with kindness was the right thing to do. Then he smiled remembering that shortly after that conversation with his mother, his Daddy had pulled him aside and quietly showed him a Bible verse that said praying for your enemies was like heaping hot coals from hell on their head in the hereafter unless they changed their ways. He said a quiet prayer for the folks in the room and finished his breakfast.

When they went to pick up their mounts at the livery Joshua was charged twice the regular price but their mounts were grained and groomed. Apparently the animosity didn't extend to Yankee horses and mules, just the Yankees riding them. He prayed for the livery man, too.

Joshua and Luke rode straight back to camp without going to the Smith ranch. It was a shorter trip total distance but it took them all day. It was after sundown when they rode into camp. Nathan was sitting by the fire with his Primer and notepad working on his letters. He put the Primer and notepad away and fixed them a couple of plates of rice and beans, seasoned with salt pork, and poured them each a cup of coffee. He'd already eaten but he kept the food and coffee warm in case they came in late.

After they unsaddled, Joshua told Nathan about their experience in Georgetown. "Now you know kinda know what it feels like being a Negro sometimes," Nathan told him.

Chapter Thirteen; Partners

Late the next morning, May 28th, Uncle Fernando rode into camp. Joshua had always been amazed that Uncle Fernando would work as hard as anyone else but never seemed to get as dirty as everyone else. Joshua on the other hand could just walk past a corral and get horse sweat and cow manure on himself.

If Joshua ever had a hero besides his father, Fernando Nava was it. Fernando was a dashing figure, in his mid-forties. He rode a high stepping, gaited palomino mare that he pampered like a high class girlfriend. He dressed her up in a flashy, black, silver mounted Mexican saddle and matching bridle. Fernando once explained to Joshua that he was all Texan with a Mexican flavor. Fernando's uncle died at the Alamo and his father fought Santa Anna at San Jacinto right alongside Frank Smith. Fernando was born and raised in Texas.

Fernando was too young for his father to let him fight in the War for Texas Independence and made him stay home to protect the hacienda but he fought in the Mexican War and then fought the Comanche with the Texas Rangers after his wife and son were killed in a raid the summer of '51. He never remarried.

A very capable man, he was educated at the Mexican Military Academy before the war for Texas Independence. He was fluent in English, Spanish, French, and Comanche. He was a consummate horseman who had taught much to his niece and nephews. He considered Joshua an adopted nephew. His medium height and broad shoulders with narrow hips and darkly handsome face combined with his mild mannered suave demeanor and the fact that he bathed regularly made him very appealing to the ladies. His impeccable manners, quick wit, and ready smile made him a welcome guest wherever he went. He treated all women as if they were the Queen of Spain regardless of their station in life.

Yet the man had a dark side. His Achilles heel was his hatred of the Comanche. Normally he would go out of his way to avoid a confrontation but after his wife and son were brutally tortured, then murdered and scalped in '51, he would rather kill Comanche than breathe. Whenever he cut loose, he was hell-on-wheels with his fists, knife, pistol, rifle, it didn't matter. He preferred brandy and wine over whiskey and beer because they didn't bring out the dark side of his suppressed anger over his wife and son, but he would drink one whiskey or one beer when offered, just to be polite.

"Hola Tio," said Joshua exercising his limited Spanish vocabulary. "Hello Uncle".

"Hola Joshua," Fernando responded as he stepped down from his mare. He rubbed her face with his black-gloved hand. "My girlfriend is getting old. I shall have to retire her soon. Maybe we should put her with that big sorrel stud you rode in on and see if she gives me another pet to take her place. Fickle woman," he said with a smile as the mare nuzzled his hands. "She would forget me tomorrow if I turned her out with that big fellow today. She was a Christmas gift from my Sweet Maria in '50, you know.

"My Maria, she smiled at me on Christmas Morning and led me to the stable. She showed me this most beautiful yearling filly. I can still hear her musical laughter when she told me, 'I am a free thinking woman and realize that a man as handsome and charming as my husband will have many opportunities to have a girlfriend as well as a wife. So I am giving you this filly. She is young, she is beautiful, and she is the only girlfriend I will allow you to have.' My Maria had a sense of humor.

"Chiquita and I have chased many Comanche, banditos, and even a few cows together over the years," he continued calling the horse by name. "I think she enjoys chasing Comanche almost as much as I do, if not for the same reasons. The only way they can outrun her is to switch horses for a fresh one.

"But that is not why I am here nephew. I am here to find out where you have been, all you have seen, what you plan for the future, and how I may help you."

Over the next few hours Joshua and Fernando talked about the last six years and all they'd seen and done. Joshua told Fernando about the wonders of the Rocky Mountains, the beauty of California, and the horror of war. Fernando told Joshua about fighting the Comanche and Kiowa and how they became bolder the longer the war went on. With most of the fighting men gone off to war the Indians pushed the frontier back a hundred miles. The Indian raids now were worse than when the war began. Then they got down to the present and plans for the future.

"I plan to build a herd of my own," Joshua told Fernando. "The cattle and horses are wild and free for the taking but I have some things I need to take care of first. I have promised to take ten head of horses to Waco to sell to an Army officer. Then I have two more wagons and a freighting contract waiting for me in Dallas. I suppose I will have to hire some men to drive the wagons and hope they are good enough to handle the business at each end of the trip. Sarah wants me here and not traipsing all over Texas with a freight wagon. I can appreciate that but at the same time this freighting deal is just too good to pass up."

"Nephew, you should start building your own herds of cattle and horses as soon as possible. There is always a market for cattle. Sometimes the market is good and sometimes the market is bad. Sometimes it is far away. But there is always a market. In the '50's we drove herds as far as California to get a good price.

"Your hired man is not a cowboy and you will need some help. I will bring a couple of my vaqueros to help you. Many of them worked for my father before me and they have raised families on our hacienda. I have more people to care for than I have work for them to do. I will bring a couple to work for you. They are all good vaqueros and will be honest and loyal. If you treat them right they will stay with you until death.

"My Segundo worked for my father before me and can run the hacienda without me. His father came from Mexico with my grandfather when Grandpapa was given the land grant from Spain. The hacienda is his home, his pride, his life. That is why I am free to do other things like working with the Rangers. But now the new Yankee government has disbanded the Rangers so I have plenty of time on my hands. It is good to have the freedom but a man should have something to do.

"This freighting interests me. Since I got the sheep during the war, I noticed that the Comanche are not interested in sheep, wool is marketable, and mutton tastes pretty good, so I have allowed my herd of sheep to grow. This freighting could be another good thing. People will always need to move freight, much as they will always eat beef and wear wool. Yes, I like this idea.

"How would you like to have a partner Joshua?" asked Fernando. "You have the contract, the wagons and horses. I have the time and the men. I propose a partnership. I will run the freighting business for you and provide three drivers. The first year you will receive two thirds of the profit and I will receive one third. The second year we can review and see where we want to go from there."

"That sounds like a good idea to me," Joshua replied, "but you only need to provide two drivers. Nathan will be driving the big wagon. I'm paying him thirteen dollars a month and found. He's a good man, I won't put him aside and like you said he's not a cowboy. The freighting will also give him a chance to continue his search for his brother. His brother was sold off as a slave to a family moving to Texas before the war."

"You have a deal Joshua. I'm heading home in the morning. I shall return in a few days and I'll bring four men with me," Fernando said.

They spent the rest of the afternoon discussing who they would be freighting for, the equipment, and the arrangements. Fernando knew of Dan Jones who worked for Señor Yturria. He also knew that Jones was not the name the gentleman was born with. But, Texas had always been a land of new beginnings even in the time of his grandfather and a new name in a new place could be helpful if one wished to leave the past in the past and not have it follow you around.

Fernando said he would bring four more horses so that all the wagons would have a six-horse hitch. He'd purchase the extra harness in Dallas. They also talked about Joshua building a herd and the design of his brand. Joshua asked how it worked between the vaqueros and Fernando. How much should he pay them and so forth. Fernando told him that he had always provided everything for them and made sure they were fed, clothed, and housed much like a feudal lord and paid them when and what he was able. Drawing a regular wage would be a new thing to the vaqueros he would bring Joshua. It's not that they were not free to leave Fernando and seek employment elsewhere but family ties were strong and they had grown up on the hacienda. Most didn't wish to leave. The numbers had grown as they married and raised families of their own on the hacienda. Some ventured off but most chose to stay where they were familiar, they were provided for, they had some work to do and life was comfortable.

Joshua wondered if they would want to work for him. Fernando thought it wouldn't be a problem if he presented it to them as if they were doing him a great service by helping the future husband of his niece whom they all adored. Then when they got paid and Joshua treated them well, staying with him should not be a problem. They would be close enough to their families that they could visit from time to time when the work allowed.

The next morning after breakfast Fernando saddled his mare to head for his hacienda which was a two day ride to the southwest.

"Aren't you worried about the Comanche catching you riding alone?" asked Joshua.

Fernando smiled in a way that sent chills down Joshua's spine as he patted the big .44 Walker Colt in a cross-draw holster on his belt and slung the five shot .56 caliber Colt Revolving Rifle across his back. "I would welcome the opportunity to escort the heathens to hell on my way to meet my Sweet Maria and Juanito at Saint Peters gate. What a wonderful day that will be." Swinging effortlessly into the saddle he said, "Adios Nephew. I will see you in a week." Touching his spurs lightly to the flanks of his mare she stepped out at a smooth ground eating rack, which is a four beat gait that is very smooth and easy on horse and rider. When Fernando returned, he would stay for a few days, helping Joshua get the vaqueros started on gathering cattle. Then Joshua, Nathan, Luke, Fernando and the freight drivers would go to Waco and from there on to Dallas.

Chapter Fourteen; Visitors

Joshua, Nathan, and Luke saddled up and rode down the river looking for trees big enough to make house logs. Joshua was pleased that there seemed to be enough for a decent size two-room cabin with a loft. By the end of the day they had found almost enough for the cabin. The sun was setting as they returned to camp.

First thing in the morning right after breakfast, Luke and Joshua saddled up, went down the river and started cutting trees. Luke tried to help and gave Joshua a break with the axe from time to time. His enthusiasm and effort were appreciated and Joshua let him "help" but it was more of an educational experience for Luke than a help for Joshua. Nathan came along behind them with one of the Norman horses and started snaking the logs out of the river bottom and up to the campsite.

Joshua and Luke worked diligently with their shirts off and dripped with sweat from their exertions. They didn't see the approaching rider until Joshua stuck the axe in the tree he was working on and stepped back to take a break. Luke was trimming the smaller branches off the trees with a hatchet and content to be helping. Joshua hadn't swung an axe this much in a long time and knew that he would be sore tomorrow. Turning around he saw Sarah sitting sidesaddle on Diablo, her palomino gelding. She was beautiful as could be in a yellow dress watching him. He was pleased to notice the pistol strapped to her waist over her dress. Being unarmed in this wild country was not a good thing. It was better to have a gun and not need it than to need one and not have it. Sarah had a mischievous grin on her face. Joshua embarrassed by his half nakedness reached for his shirt. "No hurry," said Sarah as she let her eyes wander over his stocky muscular physique, appreciative of the bulging muscles of his arms, shoulders, chest and even the ugly scar on his ribs. "I'm enjoying the view."

"What would your Mama say?" asked Joshua as he put his shirt back down.

"She'd probably say I was shameless and not let me out of her sight until our wedding was over. But I don't think I'll tell her," Sarah responded as she let Joshua lift her down from the sidesaddle.

She stood there on the ground feeling her pulse race as he wrapped his sweaty arms around her and she lifted her face to his for a much wanted kiss. She enjoyed the feel of his strong hands caressing her back for a moment then she reluctantly pushed out of his arms and said breathlessly, "Mary Louise and I brought you men some lunch and I thought we'd spend an hour or so working the garden before we head home. I left Mary Louise at the camp and followed the sound of the axe."

Joshua and Luke put on their shirts then rode back to camp with Sarah.

Mary Louise made herself to home and set up the food on the tailgate of the wagon. Nathan had just finished unhooking the Norman gelding from the log he brought in. "It ain't much but come and get it before I throws it out!" Mary Louise yelled in his direction.

"It looks like plenty to me," said Nathan as he walked up to the wagon and looked at the fried chicken and biscuits with the dried apple pie. "You jest might make some man a fine wife one day if'n you keep working at it," he said with a wink as he finished filling his plate.

"Why you uppity…" and Mary Louise threw a biscuit at him. Nathan caught it with ease and a grin. He went around the side of the wagon and had a seat in the shade. She filled her plate and sat down beside him.

"Good biscuit," said Nathan as he took another bite. "I'll have to tell Miss Sarah how good I think her cooking is."

"That's my cooking and you knows it," said Mary Louise with a huff. "But you're right about me making a fine wife. All I gots to do is find me the right man. I'll make him as fine a wife as a man could want."

"Is that a fact?" asked Nathan.

"That's gospel you can count on but I ain't gonna settle for a shiftless no account just to say I got a husband. No sir! I can stay with the Smiths until the Good Lord calls me home to Glory if I wants too. But someday maybe I'll find me a good man. I still got some good years left in me before I won't be able to bear children for him. But if'n he was of the marrying notion it wouldn't be good for him to waste much time."

"Well just for the sake of somethin' to talk about," Nathan said, "What exactly makes a man a 'good man' and 'good 'nough' to marry the likes of you?"

"I was hoping you'd ask," said Mary Louise with a smile. "He'd have to be fit and able to work. Like I said, I ain't marrying no bum. He should be a good Christian man. If he was young and handsome that would help." Then grinning she looked at Nathan and said, "If he was young enough I figure I could teach him what he needs to know about being my husband without some other woman done taught him bad habits."

"Is that so?" replied Nathan.

"It is."

"And why would you be telling me all this?" asked Nathan.

"Lord, child if you has to have it explained to you then you's too slow for me to worry about it. Here come Miss Sarah, and Mister Joshua with young Luke. Ain't they gonna make a fine family?" she said as she sat her plate on the ground and got up to fill plates for Sarah, Luke, and Joshua.

"When do you plan to head back to Dallas?" asked Sarah after they've gotten their plates and were seated.

"I'm not sure yet," replied Joshua. "I made arrangements for the teams and paid two months in advance. I need to get things going here. Then I need to gather some horses to take to Waco for Captain Wales on my way back to Dallas. I'm not sure how long it will all take."

"The reason I asked is Mother is having a birthday party for me on my birthday and I would like for you to be there. We can officially announce our engagement. It should be a big event."

"I'll be there," he said. "June 11th is your birthday right?"

"Yes it is. I'm glad you remembered. Most men don't remember things like that. I'll give you the horses you need to take to the Captain. You said you want ten head? If we're going to get a contract with the Army we better put our best foot forward."

"Thanks Honey, I was counting on you or your father having some I could buy from you."

"Joshua Granger, you are not going to pay me for those horses. You are my man and I'm your woman and as far as I'm concerned the

103

wedding is just a formality that we have to wait on, although I do want a nice wedding mind you. So you take those horses and sell them. If it makes you feel better then you can bring the money home and I'll hold it for us until we're married."

"Are you sure?"

"Yes, I'm sure. I'll ask Papa to have the boys bring in my ten best geldings and take the edge off of them. I'll have them ready for you at the party. Now what about this freighting contract? Are you going to be able to run it and still be home at all?"

"Well, Fernando came by and we talked about it. He likes the idea so we are going to be partners. He's basically bored since the Reconstruction Government disbanded the Rangers and his Segundo can run his ranch without him. He's going to run the freighting business for a year for a third of the profit. He's going to provide two drivers and four more horses so each team will be a six-up. After a year we'll take a look at it and see where we want to go from there. He'll be back in a few days. He's bringing a couple of his vaqueros to work for us here on our ranch in addition to the drivers for the wagons."

"That sounds wonderful," said Sarah. "The Lord is smiling on us Joshua. You know that don't you? All these years we've waited and God is blessing us for our patience. I'm so excited."

For the next couple of days Joshua, Nathan, and Luke cut logs for the cabin and dragged them to the building site where they let them season. It took a while because they had to go farther down the river every day for the trees. By the end of the week they had cut enough logs for the cabin and they rested on Sunday.

Chapter Fifteen; The Crew

It was late afternoon on June 2nd, when Fernando and his men rode into camp. Fernando had five men with him and four horses for the hitch. Joshua, Nathan, and Luke stopped work to welcome them.

Fernando introduced them around. Javier Garcia was a short young man in his late teens that stood about five foot two inches and was excited to be working away from home. He was a smiling, likable fellow wearing hand-me-down clothes that didn't fit well, a big straw sombrero, and simple brogan shoes. He was riding a black Mustang gelding about 14.1 hands tall with a Mexican style saddle. He carried a braided leather rope called a riata. Joshua noticed that he was armed with a belt knife and a smoothbore musket that looked like it dated back to Texas Independence strapped to his back.

Javier's brother, Pablo was in his mid-teens, also short, and just as excited as Javier about being away from home. He was similarly dressed and armed. His saddle was also Mexican style with a huge horn and his horse was a Mustang pinto gelding with a brown and white body and black mane and tail that stood 14.2.

Ramon Hernandez was an older gentleman age fifty-five and recently widowed. Javier and Pablo were his grandsons by his oldest daughter. He said he came along to keep them on the straight and narrow path of good Catholic boys and cook for them. He promised their mother he would not let them get into trouble. "I think something new to do will be good for me," he said. "At home I sit around and miss my dear wife. That is not good so if you don't mind I will cook for you and help the boys learn to be good vaqueros." He was riding a bay (brown with black mane and tail) Mustang that stood 14.3. It was easy to tell where the boys got their height. He had a trimmed gray beard with an air of dignity about him. His clothes were homemade but his brogans were store bought. He had a knife and a .36 caliber Patterson Colt on his belt.

Carlos and Pedro Sanchez were also brothers. They were in their twenties and dressed like the others but were riding horses a little larger standing 15 and 15.1 hands. These horses were harness broke to be used in the teams when they got to Dallas. Carlos and Pedro were armed with belt knives and single shot muzzle loading pistols in their belts.

Later that evening Joshua and Fernando talked about their plans for the freighting and the ranch. "I have some extra guns that I acquired along the trip down here from Kentucky," Joshua told him. "Would you mind if I gave them to these men?"

"It wouldn't bother me," said Fernando. "Traveling around the country or gathering cattle alone or in pairs in Indian country, it would be good if they were armed better."

Ramon took it upon himself to have supper ready about thirty minutes before sundown. "Come and get it," he yelled.

After a supper of some pretty impressive beans and jalapeno cornbread, the men sat around drinking coffee and smoking. Joshua figured this would be a good time to pass out the guns. "Gather round everybody," Joshua said as he climbed up into the wagon. "I have some gifts for you to thank you all for coming to work for me," he said. He pulled out the guns taken from the outlaws and the .44 Dragoon given to him by his brother years ago. Each of the pistols had a belt with holster, cap box for percussion caps, and cartridge box for the paper cartridges used by the cap and ball pistols.

"Señor Hernandez, since you already have a pistol, I have for you this Sharps carbine."

"Gracias Señor, I hope I use it more against deer than Comanche," he said.

"You're welcome Ramon. Now my vaqueros; step up men. Pick one Javier," Joshua said pointing to the pistols.

"Gracious Patron," Javier said, grinning from ear to ear, as he picked a brass framed Spiller and Burr Company copy of a Remington revolver in .36 caliber.

"Pablo, your turn," Joshua told the younger brother.

"Ah, Patron, I know nothing of pistols. Will you pick one for me?" asked the young vaquero.

"Sure, I think you will like this one. It shoots the same bullets as your Grandfather's and brother's pistols," Joshua told him as he handed him the Colt Navy. He felt his face and ears warm up at the memory of Frenchy. He hoped no one noticed.

"Now my drivers; Carlos, Pedro, come on up. The oldest brother gets first choice."

Pedro stepped forward and took a look at the two pistols that were left. They were both .44's. One was Joshua's Dragoon that his brother gave him all those years ago. The other pistol was a brass framed copy of the Colt 1860 Army produced by Griswold and Gunnison Company for the Confederate government. Pedro picked the Griswold and Gunnison. "Gracias, Señor," he said.

Carlos stepped forward, hefted the big Dragoon and smiled. "If I run out of bullets I can use it as a club. I like it," he said grinning.

Joshua felt better knowing that everyone was better armed. He decided to keep the shotgun and the Enfield at the camp. Everyone had received a gun as a gift and all were happy.

Later that night, Joshua decided to carry one of his Remington .44's in his saddlebags. He'd discovered over the last few days that wearing two guns while working got in the way. He liked having two guns handy considering where he was but after thinking about it for a while he decided that one on the hip and one in the saddlebags was a good compromise.

The next morning Joshua called Fernando over to look at a drawing he had made on the ground. "I think this would be a good brand for my cattle and horses." It was a simple J-G (pronounced J bar G). They agreed it would be difficult to alter and Joshua decided to use it.

"I guess I should go into town and register it," Joshua said to Fernando. "Since I paid Nathan a month in advance, I think I'll do that with these men and take them to town with me. We can take the wagon and pick up some supplies while we're at it. What do you think?"

"I think it sounds like a good idea," Fernando agreed.

"Men gather round," Joshua said. "I'm going to give you a month's wages in advance. Then we will saddle up and ride to Georgetown. I need to register my brand and buy some more grub. I'll get another tent for us if I can find one. You men can get what you like for yourselves."

The men gathered round and Joshua passed out thirteen dollars in gold and silver to each of them. He was aware that some Southerners didn't like the new paper money being printed by the government. Many of them lost everything when they took Confederate paper money that turned out to be worthless after the war. Some of them also didn't like Mexicans, or Negros, or Damned Yankees either for that matter, but they would accept gold or silver no matter who it came from. Joshua decided to give the men coin instead of the paper money he had in order to avoid the whole problem for his men.

They saddled up and harnessed the team. The group arrived at Georgetown just before sundown.

Stabling the horses they headed for a diner. Joshua said he'd buy supper. There were uneasy looks at the group as they sat at a table toward the back of the room. The owner walked over and said, "We don't feed nigga's heaya. He'll have to leave."

Joshua looked at the gentleman and said, "Sir, I'm buying supper for all of us or none us. Now I count nine meals here. We'd like to have your best meal and I'm paying with gold. We don't want trouble, just supper."

"I don't feed nigga's in heaya," the man repeated. "He'll have to go."

"Come my friends," said Fernando getting to his feet. "I know a lady who will feed us all a feast." They all stood with him and headed for the door.

"Now wait a minute," the owner stammered. "I ain't running all of you out, jest the nigga."

"Sir," Fernando responded as he stepped out the door, "my nephew told you we will all eat here or none of us will eat here. You have made your choice," and he closed the door behind him.

Outside, Joshua looked at Fernando. "Where to?" he asked.

"Follow me," Fernando told them and he strode off down the street. He led them to the edge of town where a single story building had a sign over the door that simply said, "Meals". The building was unpainted and in every way unimpressive but there was light coming from the single front window and the murmur of conversation inside. Fernando opened the door and led the men inside.

The room was dim and the place was full of a wide spectrum of humanity. There were teamsters, vaqueros, Anglo cowboys, salesmen, and farmers lined up on the benches at the long tables in the room. The furnishings were simple but sturdy and clean. A young Spanish looking girl in her teens came from the kitchen carrying a platter with a large bowl of refried beans and a stack of tortillas on it. Behind her was another woman who was an older version of the young one. She was carrying a platter of roast beef. She had the strong arms and shoulders of a woman who had worked all her life with the tired look of a long day behind her. Yet the work and years had not stolen the womanly curves of her figure, or her smile, or the light from her eyes. When the ladies set their burdens on one of the tables the young girl headed back to the kitchen without looking at the door or saying a word. The older of the two had her back to the door and welcomed them in Spanish and English as she was turning around.

When she was facing the group of men who had just come through her door, she brightened the room with her smile and said, "Fernando Nava, for what do I owe the pleasure of your visit to my humble establishment?" She walked up to him, brushed a stray strand of hair behind her ear and curtseyed.

Fernando removed his hat and bowed gallantly, as he took her calloused hand and kissed the back of it. "Consuela, you are as lovely as the Texas moon. It is always my pleasure to see you. My young nephew and I have joined together in a business venture and brought our men to town for supplies. We are hungry and wish to dine at your sumptuous table."

"Fernando, you old devil, it's good to see you and hear your compliments even if I don't believe them," Consuela responded with a laugh. "Nine of you? Give me a moment to clear one of these tables so you can all sit together."

After a few minutes she returned and led them to a table all to themselves where they spread out and seated themselves on the benches. "Señors, we have roast beef, refried beans, fresh hot tortillas, rice of my own recipe, and jalapenos for the main course. We have donuts for desert. To wash it down we have water, beer, coffee, and fresh buttermilk. The beer is fresh from the Germans in Austin today."

"Set us up and we'll all have a beer to toast our new ventures together," Joshua said.

"Coming right up, I'll tell my daughter Patricia to make sure you are well taken care of. I would serve you myself but I must be in the kitchen cooking," Consuela told them as she headed for the kitchen.

"I like this place," Joshua said as Consuela went back to the kitchen.

"You'll like it even better when you try her cooking," Fernando told him.

109

For the next hour the men sat and enjoyed the meal laughing and joking with each other.

They teased Pablo when they caught him and young Patricia watching each other. When their meal was finished, they paid their hostess with gold and compliments and Joshua left a nice tip for Patricia.

Javier and Pablo had never had beer before and were a little tipsy as they headed for the wagon yard at the stable where they would stay the night. They began discussing the beauty of Patricia and ended up in an argument over which one of them would marry her. The argument continued at the wagon yard and one thing led to another until they came to blows as brothers are liable to do from time to time.

Joshua started to get between them and Fernando stopped him. "Let them go nephew," he said. "They will not hurt each other too badly. But a man who steps between two fighting brothers will find himself fighting them both. Tomorrow they will still be brothers and they will laugh about this." Joshua stepped back as the two aspiring young vaqueros continued to pound each other over the affections of a young woman that neither of them had had the nerve to speak to yet. Joshua flinched involuntarily as Pablo bloodied Javier's nose.

"Boys will be boys," Ramon said.

The next morning Javier and Pablo cleaned up as best they could before the crew headed to Consuela's for breakfast. Patricia brightened noticeably as they came through the door but then she frowned. "Oh, you poor things," she said to Pablo and Javier as she set coffee down on the table for the crew. "What happened to you two? Such handsome men and now so bruised and skinned up. Who did this to you?" She demanded.

Javier and Pablo looked at each other sheepishly; pointed at each other, and in unison said, "He did."

"Oh my goodness," Patricia said. "What on earth would cause brothers to hurt each other so? Why were you fighting?" she asked like a mother scolding her boys.

"It was over a woman," Javier said with pride.

"A woman of great beauty," young Pablo chimed in with grave sincerity. The rest of the crew was doing their best not to laugh.

Understanding dawned in Patricia's eyes and she turned red lowering her eyes to the table and the coffee she was pouring for them. "I suppose this beautiful woman should be flattered that such gallant men wish to seek her affection. Maybe such brave men would do better discussing their intentions with this woman rather than beating each other senseless. Surely you are not afraid to talk with her?" Pedro the teamster choked on his coffee and excused himself. The door was hardly closed before they heard his laughter outside.

After breakfast, Joshua went to the blacksmith shop and ordered a branding iron made for his J-G brand. While the branding iron was being made he went to the courthouse and registered his brand. Joshua met his crew at Parker's General store. Mrs. Parker scowled at Joshua but still took his money as he paid for a stick of candy for Luke. The four young men eagerly bought new clothes and felt hats. The two vaqueros bought a pair of inexpensive spurs from the limited selection that Mrs. Parker had on her shelves. Then they went to the cobbler shop to order a pair of boots. Fernando bought a box of .44 paper cartridges for his Walker and a box of .56 paper cartridges for his revolving rifle. The rifle wasn't terribly common and Mrs. Parker ordered the cartridges especially for Fernando. After he made his purchases he looked around and talked with Mrs. Parker about the upcoming wedding of Jesse and Jessica. They also talked about Sarah's birthday party which Mrs. Parker confirmed her family would attend. He then casually told her that he had gone into the freighting business with Joshua. She didn't say anything but her frown said it all for her.

Nathan didn't really need anything and waited on the bench in front of the store lost in thought. A feisty older woman who was a good cook had him thinking of the comforts of a good woman and a home of his own. That was a possibility that he had never given much thought to before. Hanging on to his money wouldn't hurt anything and it might come in handy later should he decide to settle down.

Joshua and Ramon gathered up flour and corn meal, baking soda, a side of bacon and a sugar cured ham, salt, sugar, coffee, seasonings, more rice and beans, some molasses, and another tent. By the time Joshua got back to the blacksmith shop his branding iron was done.

The J-G crew had lunch at Consuela's. Javier and Pablo were spic and span after a bath, a shave, a haircut, and wearing their new clothes. Patricia commented on the improvement. After lunch they decided to head back toward the ranch and camp for the night along the river. On the way out of town Pablo told them he had to do something and that he'd catch up. He rode away at trot. Pulling up in front of Consuela's, Pablo dismounted and went inside.

"It's a little early for supper," Patricia said from her dishwashing as Pablo stepped timidly into the kitchen.

"Si, I wanted to ask if I might call on you when I come back to town," he replied hurriedly with his new hat held tightly in his hands.

Pulling her hands from the dishwater she wiped them on her apron. Taking Pablo's hand she looked him in the eye and said, "I would like that."

"Alright, then. I'll see you when I come back to town," Pablo replied nervously. He quickly kissed her cheek and bolted for the door. As he swung into the saddle, his loud "Yippee!" startled his mount and the rest of the town as he put his new spurs to his pony and raced out of town. Patricia smiled and went back to washing her dishes humming a happy tune.

Chapter Sixteen; Building a Herd

June 5th, found them back at the ranch. They spent the 5th and 6th cutting more logs along the river to build a bunkhouse for the vaqueros. They would let these logs season also. The bunkhouse would have to be built in picket fashion because all the big logs had been harvested for the main cabin. Picket style construction was putting the logs upright in the ground side by side like a picket fence. The logs were shaved flat on two sides and put flat side to flat side as close together as possible and then chinked with rocks, sticks, and mud. Making one side of the building taller than the other gave a slant to the roof. For added stability Joshua agreed to buy some board lumber from the sawmill in Georgetown so they could have a seal board across the bottom of the pickets and a board roof when the time came to put up the building. This style of construction allowed the use of logs that were smaller in diameter and shorter than what would be required for a forty foot by forty foot cabin with the logs laid on top of each other horizontally.

When they had enough for the bunkhouse, they cut poles for and built two corrals to hold the saddle and wagon horses at night. Summer had come and the Comanche would be raiding anytime. It would be good to have the horses close and secure, especially at night. With the corral finished they took the remainder of the afternoon to rest.

Lounging in the shade of the wagon, Joshua looked around and thought to himself that he'd come a long way already with the help of Fernando. "Uncle, I never could have gotten this much done without the help of you and your men. Gracias."

"De nada nephew," Fernando replied from under his hat. He was lying under the wagon with his saddle for a pillow. His hat was over his face with his boots and gunbelt next to him. "I enjoy helping you because you work so hard yourself. Besides, you are going to marry my only niece and I want it to go well for you both.

"The young vaqueros make me proud; they work hard for you and never complain. You know they would only do that for a man they respect. They are good men. With good men and good equipment we shall surely do well in our ranching and our freighting." The rest of the day was uneventful as the men and horses rested. Pablo worked on showing Luke how to use a rope.

The next day, June 7th, they started digging the well. It was just past noon when John and Jesse rode into camp. "Hola Tio," Jesse said with respect to Fernando. Purposely ignoring Joshua he said to Fernando, "Papa sent us to help the Yankee get this place ready for Sarah. What do you need done?"

"Thank you for coming," replied Fernando sensing the tension between his blood and adopted nephews. "Joshua is in charge here. Today we are digging a well and gathering cattle. Joshua, what would you have them do?"

"Thanks for coming," said Joshua. "I've got Javier and Pedro doing the digging for the moment. Nathan and Luke are bringing up rocks from the river to line the walls of the well to help keep it from caving in. The rest of us were getting ready to saddle up and see what we can find in the way of cows and start branding. You're welcome to ride along. We figure we'll go west along the San Gabriel today and see what we can find. We'll push whatever we find toward the camp and tomorrow we'll start branding. We'll brand whatever is full grown and not branded and any calves that are with unbranded mothers."

The day went on and by dark the men had pushed around forty head of cattle to the camp. That night around the fire, the men commented on the work accomplished. Jesse and John were sullen and didn't say much although they had worked as hard as any of the other riders. They stood their shift on night guard with no complaints.

The next morning they started branding. The cattle were pushed into a tight herd and held by some of the men while two others cut cattle from the herd, roped and threw them for branding. John and Jesse were cutting the herd, roping and throwing the cattle. John roped the head and drug them to the fire where Jesse roped the back feet and pulled them out from under them stretching them out on the ground and holding them there.

Joshua was taking his turn with the branding iron and had branded ten head of cows and two calves when John and Jesse brought in a young bull. Joshua branded the bull but before he could step out of the way, the bull's feet came loose of the back rope and he kicked Joshua in the stomach knocking him flat. John put spurs to his horse and drug the bull away as it scrambled to its feet and tried to go after Joshua with its horns.

"Sorry, my rope must have slipped," said Jesse, grinning from the saddle as Joshua got up off the ground. His chest heaved as he regained the breath the bull knocked out of him.

"Get off that horse," rasped Joshua.

"What?" asked Jesse?

"Get off that horse or I'll drag you off," Joshua said. "I've worked cattle with you before and your rope don't slip unless you want it to. Now get off the damned horse. You've wanted a fight since I came home. I could see it in your eyes. We're going to settle this right now."

"Alright Yank," said Jesse softly as he stepped to the ground. "I should have run you off like a stray dog when you got here. Reckon I'll make up for that now."

"Shut up and fight damn you," said Joshua and he hit Jesse square in the mouth smashing his lips and bringing blood. Jesse staggered back ducking Joshua's next swing and landed a punch of his own to Joshua's stomach that lifted Joshua onto his toes. As his feet touched

114

the ground Joshua landed a round house to the side of Jesse's head that spun him half way around. The two men closed in and began hammering each other with short hard punches. The rest of the men had left the cattle and formed a circle around Joshua and Jesse with the vaqueros cheering for Joshua and John cheering for Jesse. Fernando looked on quietly with a frown as they pounded each other to pulp. Jesse knocked Joshua to the ground and Joshua kicked Jesse's feet out from under him before Jesse had a chance to kick him. They scrambled up and closed in again. After a moment they stepped back and traded blow for blow like boxers in a ring, both men with eyes so swollen they could barely see, their faces bruised and puffy. Joshua landed a punch to Jesse's chin that knocked him flat on his back. Joshua fell face first into the dirt with the momentum of the punch and neither of them was able to get up.

"You give?" asked Joshua lying on the ground with one side of his face in the dirt.

"I'll let you rest up before we finish," responded Jesse staring blankly at the sky.

"Very nice," said Fernando with disgust as he pulled the exhausted brawlers to their feet. His voice rose as his anger boiled over. "You should be ashamed of yourselves; grown men brawling like a couple savages. Both of you go to camp! Clean yourselves up and tend to your wounds! The rest of us will continue with the work! Now go!" he yelled at them. "Madre de Dios! The war is over damn it! We must continue our lives in peace! We are a family for the love of Christ! If you want to fight, go find Comanche and they will give you all the fight you want! What the Hell?!! This damned foolishness is over! Do you understand me?!! Finished!!"

Cowed by Fernando's rage, Joshua and Jesse murmured "Yes Sir, Tio" as they climbed stiffly into their saddles and headed for camp. They had never heard Fernando curse like that before. John and the vaqueros went quietly back to work. When they finished the forty head they had, they spread out bringing in twenty more by dark.

Later that night sitting on the riverbank with Fernando, Joshua asked, "Tio, why is it OK for Javier and Pablo to fight but not Jesse and me? I don't understand."

115

"Joshua, Javier and Pablo are still boys and they are workers not owners. You and Jesse are grown men from a family with royal heritage. You are both educated, well brought up and seasoned in the ways of the world. You both have wealth and position in life. You should be able to settle your differences like civilized men without resorting to your fists."

"Are you saying we are better men than Javier and Pablo?" asked Joshua.

"No, we are equal in the sight of God. But as in the parable of the talents, he who is given more has more expected of him. Do you understand now?"

"Yes, Sir, I'm sorry I disappointed you."

"God forgives and so do I Nephew," said Fernando. Then with a grin he continued. "That kick from the bull had to hurt but you still put up one hell of a fight. If you had fought Jesse before you were kicked I think maybe you would have won. But I hope that the lesson has been learned and a draw is acceptable to you both."

"It suits me Uncle," Joshua said.

"Bueno."

One thing you can count on when your in-laws live half a day's ride away, is that they will usually show up in time for lunch and either leave shortly after lunch or spend the night. So, no one was too surprised when the branding was interrupted the next morning by the arrival of three visitors who intended to spend the night. The identity of one of the visitors however did surprise them all; Juanita Smith. Mrs. Smith, Sarah, and Mary Louise rode into camp just in time for lunch. Jesse and Joshua looked at each other and groaned when the riders were close enough to be recognized. Both of them had black eyes, busted lips, bruised cheeks, and skinned knuckles. By mutual agreement they both headed for the far side of the herd.

Fernando, John, and Nathan assisted the ladies with dismounting and Ramon took the lead rope of a buckskin gelding that Sarah was leading. Mary Louise rode an ancient Mexican saddle with her leg wrapped around the horn so she could be ladylike and sidesaddle along with Mrs. Smith and Sarah. Mrs. Smith looked around the camp and at the work that had been done along with the branding in progress. "Well, I'm impressed," she told Fernando. "A lot has been accomplished in a short time. Where are Joshua and Jesse?" she asked looking around.

"Joshua! Jesse! Come on in. Juanita wants to see you," yelled Fernando.

"John, what is so funny?" asked Mrs. Smith as Joshua and Jesse came riding up slowly. Then as they got close, "Oh my, what happened to you two?"

They looked at each other but before they could say anything, Fernando said, "It's these wild cattle. This bull charged Joshua's horse and spooked him. He threw Joshua into the rocks along the river. So Jesse went to help him and the bull tried to gore Jesse's horse but only brushed the girth which spooked Jesse's horse and he threw Jesse into the same pile of rocks alongside Joshua."

"It seems strange that two riders like these, who were riding before they could walk, would be thrown face first into the same pile of rocks at the same time. They must have tried to catch themselves with their fists," she said sternly looking at their hands.

"Honest, Mother. It happened just the way Tio said it did," John confirmed.

"Well, get down and go in the tent. Take your shirts off so I can look you over. I want to make sure nothing was broken by those fist sized river rocks. Well, go on," she said as they hesitated. "You won't be the first brawling, I mean fallen cowboys I've ever doctored. Mary Louise if you'll help me with this, I know with this many men around there must to be a bottle of whiskey somewhere. Please find it for me so I can make sure their wounds are clean." she continued. "Sarah Lynn you go see if you can help with lunch we'll be out shortly."

"Yes, Ma'am," said Sarah Lynn.

Mary Louise followed Mrs. Smith into the tent with the whiskey bottle Ramon kept on hand for medicinal purposes and lowered the flap behind them. For the next fifteen minutes they heard, "Ow! Does it hurt when I push here? Oh! Yes Ma'am. Ugh! Hold still I want to make sure those rocks didn't break any ribs. Ow! Hold still I need to clean out the cut over your eye. Agh! Does the whiskey burn? I'm so sorry." Then Mrs. Smith exited the tent with a smile.

"I think they are going to be fine," she said with satisfaction. "I hope they do a better job of staying on their horses in the future."

"Yes, Ma'am, I'm sure they will," said Nathan with a grin.

After lunch, Joshua showed Mrs. Smith, Sarah, and Mary Louise all the progress they had made and the plans for the immediate future. Sarah suggested that the bunkhouse should also face the Southeast and should be built north of the cabin. Joshua agreed to build it there. The corral for the horses was behind where the cabin would be. Then he pointed out that it was far enough away from the house that the wind wouldn't blow the smell into the house. The outhouse would go on the far side of the corrals. The branding of the cattle was finished before lunch and Joshua showed them the brand he chose. Mrs. Smith approved of it all including where the well was being dug. Joshua was very pleased with her approval.

"I think you are doing as well as my own husband would," she told him. "Maybe you will make a decent son-in-law after all, if you can learn to stay on your horse," she concluded leaving Joshua speechless. Turning to Sarah she continued, "Mary Louise and I are going to get the hoes and go see how the garden is doing. We'll expect you to join us shortly."

"Yes ma'am," said Sarah as her mother walked away giving her and Joshua a few moments alone but in plain sight of everyone. "Oh, Joshua," Sarah said in an excited half whisper. "Did you hear that?! She gave you a compliment. Come to the corral with me I have something for you." Taking his hand she led him away.

At the corral she leaned on the top rail and pointed to the 15.3 hand buckskin. He probably weighed about eleven hundred and fifty pounds. "I brought him for you. He's four years old out of my best Mustang mare by the stud you left me. Joshua, he is the fastest horse I have. He'll spin and work cattle and he's gaited like you like them. He's got a good mind too. He'll be a walking advertisement for the quality of horses we breed. I want you to have him. Your stud is a wonderful horse but if you keep riding him all the time we won't get the breeding out of him we need. What do you think?"

"I like him. The stud could use a break and you're right, we need him for breeding. Thank you, Honey."

"You're welcome. I guess I better go help Mother."

"Alright, I think I'll saddle up my new horse and try him out."

Out on the range, Joshua and the buckskin got acquainted. The horse was still pretty fresh even though he had followed Sarah on a lead line all morning. He snorted and pranced and danced around when Joshua swung into the saddle. Joshua made him walk out of camp but he could tell the big fellow wanted to run. Once they were away from camp Joshua decided to let the horse have his head and see what happened. Joshua loosened the reins and the horse stepped into a trot. Joshua clucked to him and he stepped into a fast rack that was as smooth as Joshua had ever ridden. Joshua clucked again and the horse broke into a lope. A light touch with the spurs and the horse went into an all-out run. Riding low in the saddle, Joshua enjoyed the adrenaline rush as the horse thundered over the ground so fast the wind made his eyes water. It was the fastest horse he'd ever ridden. After about half a mile Joshua started reining him in and gradually brought him back to a walk. What a horse, he thought to himself. He had the horse to back up and made him spin both ways. Very nice. Riding back to camp the horse was content to walk but Joshua could feel that he'd only just taken the edge off of the buckskin and there was still plenty of horse between his knees. He rode into the herd and picked a cow to cut out. The horse steadily pushed the cow to the edge of the herd where she bolted for wide open spaces. Joshua held the prancing buckskin back with his left hand on the reins and shook out a loop from the rope on his saddle. Joshua made a kissing sound with his mouth and the buckskin was off like a shot after the cow. The horse caught up to the cow with ease and Joshua cast his loop. Just as the loop settled over the cow's horns, the buckskin put his backend to the ground in a stop that jerked the cow off her feet. Joshua dismounted to see what happened. The buckskin backed up just enough to keep the rope tight on the cow. Joshua climbed aboard and touched the buckskin with his spurs. The buckskin stepped forward. Joshua flipped the rope off the cow and started pushing her back toward the herd. She tried to get past the buckskin to the open range but the horse moved so quick to cut her off that Joshua grabbed a handful of mane to steady himself.

With the cow back in the herd, Joshua headed to the garden patch. "Well, what do you think?" asked Sarah even though she knew what the answer would be.

"I think he's the finest horse I've ever been on," Joshua said grinning from ear to ear. "Who put this kind of handle on him? He's really nice."

"I did!" Sarah answered with pride. "Well, me and Papa. I raised him gentle and saddle broke him. Papa taught him the rope and cattle work."

"Is he gun broke?" Joshua asked.

"Of course," Sarah said. "Try him."

Joshua pulled his pistol. The horse's ears perked up when he heard the clicking of the pistol being cocked. Joshua prepared himself for the worst, pointed the pistol safely at the ground and pulled the trigger. The pistol went off and the horse simply shook his head and stomped once. "Wow!"

"His full brother is a sorrel two year old." Sarah told him. "I think I'd like to keep him a stud. He's built just like this boy. The only reason I gelded this one is his color. I know you like buckskins and I like the palominos but most folks want sorrels, bays, or blacks. They think horses with more color are too flashy."

"You did good Sarah," Joshua said with pride. "I agree that we should keep little brother for breeding."

"Good, I'll send a letter to the wrangler from the King ranch down south that we're going to keep the sorrel but I'll still sell him the weanling."

"You mean you have three of these?" asked Joshua in surprise.

"Sure," she said. "I've bred the mare every two years to that bay stud you left me. You're riding the first one, we're keeping the second one for breeding and she's got a bay colt by her side. Captain King offered three hundred dollars for the two year old. I'm going to try to get that for the colt."

Under the wide brimmed hat that she wore to protect herself from the sun, Mrs. Smith was smiling with pride at her daughter's accomplishments. But she wouldn't brag or show her pride in a boastful manner. That would be immodest and sinful. So like Mary of old she kept all these things and pondered them in her heart.

That afternoon they hit water in the well. Ramon fixed a special meal and Mary Louise baked a cake in the Dutch oven for celebration. After supper, Luke presented a handful of wildflowers to Sarah. She was appropriately surprised and thankful and Luke bashfully sat quietly beside her. When dark settled, Joshua, Luke, and Fernando moved their bedrolls out of their tent and let the ladies sleep there. The vaqueros and teamsters filled up the other tent while Jesse and John slept in the wagon. Luke slept under the wagon. Joshua and Fernando spread out by the fire.

Chapter Seventeen; Indian Raid

Late that night, when everyone was asleep, Frank Smith came galloping into the camp shouting for the men get up and get mounted. Jumping off his horse he told them of the Indian raid just to the south and west of his own ranch. Some settlers were killed and scalped, their cabin burned. A little boy and girl were alive but in shock after hiding in the brush and watching their parents and older siblings get butchered. Their stock was stolen and the Comanche were riding like hell for the Red River and Indian Territory. The smoke of the burning cabin had caused some neighbors to check out the source of the fire. The Comanche rode to the west of the Smith ranch. There was already a group of men trailing them. A rider had reached the Smith ranch to warn them. Frank had loaned him a fresh horse from the saddle stock they kept at the house so he could warn the rest of the countryside. Frank had saddled up and come to warn them then join the chase to catch the heathens before they got clean away.

In a matter of minutes Mrs. Smith had coffee and cold biscuits from last night ready for the men and they stuffed their faces hurriedly chewing while they were strapping on their gunbelts and saddling their horses. Sarah Lynn and Mary Louise saddled theirs and Mrs. Smith's horses to head for the burned homestead in the opposite direction the Comanche were headed. Mrs. Smith said they might be able to help with the children and preparing the dead for burial. Mr. Smith threw his saddle on a fresh horse and fifteen minutes from the time he rode into camp, he led the men galloping due west into the ruggedly beautiful Texas hill country where the Comanche liked to disappear when they were chased.

Joshua was riding the buckskin and was surprised when he looked around and saw Luke right behind him on the mule. In the rush to saddle up and get after the Comanche he hadn't even thought about telling Luke to go with Sarah. Somehow he just took it for granted he would. Nope. "What are you doing here?" he asked.

"I'm coming with you," Luke said simply.

"You should go back and help Sarah," Joshua told the boy. "This is going to be a fight."

"I'm staying with you," Luke replied looking straight ahead.

Unable to make Luke return without leaving the chase himself, Joshua cursed under his breath and rode on. The moon was full and they had no trouble finding the trail of the Comanche. A couple of hundred horses bunched together and being pushed hard left a pretty plain trail. By daylight they were seeing worn out horses that had fallen behind and been left by the Indians. Fernando took the lead and pushed them all hard. Luke nodded in the saddle but was still with them. Joshua made a mental note not to underestimate the boy. They pushed on all day. By sundown Fernando told them they were only an hour behind the Comanche so they stopped to allow the other party to catch up. The other group of men caught up to them and Fernando explained that if they gave the Comanche some room they would think they had outrun the posse and stop for the night. That would give the men the opportunity to surround the camp and kill them all in the morning, as soon as there was light enough for shooting.

The posse stopped to rest. Those who had it shared jerked beef, biscuits, and water from canteens with the others. Very few of them thought to bring anything to eat in their rush to get after the Indians. Fernando had assumed command of the group by mutual consent. His years of Indian fighting and ferocity made him the natural choice. He didn't allow fires or even loud talk. Sentries were posted. Fernando scouted ahead with a man who had chased Indians with him before.

At midnight, Fernando and the other scout returned and the posse rode north for half an hour. Then Fernando silently signaled for a halt and dismounted. He removed his spurs so the sound of their jingling wouldn't alert the Indians and silently signaled the other men to do the same. They chose two men to stay with the horses and Joshua made Luke stay with them even though he didn't want to. They were to bring the horses forward when the shooting stopped. Fernando went forward alone on foot. After a short while Fernando returned.

122

Wiping blood from his Bowie knife he indicated that the Indians on watch wouldn't be a problem. Then he led the men forward on foot until they could see the Comanche by the light of their fire.

The Indian camp was in a ravine. What was left of the horses were bunched at one end in a makeshift brush corral. As tired as the horses were, it was sufficient to hold them. Fernando and the other scout positioned the men around the camp. Fernando would fire the first shot then they would all shoot, no warning, no mercy. Kill them all.

The tension mounted as the morning sky began to brighten with the pre-dawn light. Joshua counted eighteen Comanche. Two of them were women. He hated the thought of killing women even though a Comanche woman would happily torture him to death if she got the chance. Still, he decided to target only men as he laid belly down watching the camp over the sights of the Spencer. There were twenty-five men with rifles, shotguns, and pistols surrounding the camp. It would be a miracle if anyone lived through what was coming. Suddenly, Fernando's big .56 caliber revolving rifle boomed and the buck sitting by the small fire fell over into it. The hills around the camp roared with the boom of rifles and the crack of pistols. The powder smoke made it look like the brushy hills were on fire. The screams of the wounded and the dying were everywhere throughout the camp as Comanche scrambled into the brush. A few grabbed weapons and returned fire at muzzle flashes but with little effect before they were cut down in a rain of hot lead.

One brave bolted for the horses with rifle in hand and swung aboard the nearest one. With a war whoop he put his heels into the horse, jumped the brush corral and charged straight up the side of the ravine toward where young Pablo was positioned. Pablo bravely stood with his pistol held out and emptied it at the oncoming rider. Two of the three shots he fired hit the warrior but were not immediately fatal. Pablo pulled the trigger again and heard the sickening click of the hammer as it dropped on an empty chamber. The warrior was right up on him by then and fired his rifle at point blank range. Pablo took the bullet in the chest and died instantly.

Javier, a few yards from Pablo, screamed as he rammed home a round in his old musket and shot the Comanche in the center of his back knocking the warrior from his horse. Javier had seen Pablo's stand against the Comanche warrior but his guns had been empty too.

He had franticly reloaded as fast as he could but he had been too late to save his little brother.

In the camp the dead and dying were lying all over. One of the women was hiding behind a log screaming, "Americano! Americano!" over and over. Fernando stood as the shooting stopped and reloaded his Walker before walking down into the camp. Coming upon a wounded brave at the edge of the camp he stopped and fired a round into the man's head bringing his groaning to an end. He walked to the woman who was still behind a log by the fire screaming, "Americano! Americano!"

"Stop Screaming! Enough!" he yelled at her.

The screaming stopped and sobbing started as she raised her head from behind the log. "Americano," she repeated again quietly through her tears.

"Who are you?" asked Fernando in English lowering the big pistol. The rest of the men had come into camp and were shooting any wounded Indian they found. Some were taking scalps. Ramon showed Javier how to scalp the Indian who'd killed his brother. One man tenderly held the scalp of a blonde woman with red ribbons still tied in place. He had taken it from an Indian's belt. He was crying and repeating a woman's name over and over. Overcome by grief and rage he emptied his pistol into the already dead Indian then pulled his knife and began to mutilate the body.

"Who are you?" Fernando repeated softly this time, seeing the blue eyes behind the stringy black hair of the woman who was actually a young teenage girl.

"A-Amanda," she stammered. "Amanda Crofton. Pl-Please do-don't kill me. I'm A-American," she managed to say as she gained control of her sobbing.

"You are safe now Amanda Crofton," Fernando told her softly. "You are among civilized people again." He wondered how true that statement really was as he looked over the carnage around him.

Javier and Ramon were kneeling beside Pablo's body. Ramon was shedding silent tears while Javier, less acquainted with death than his grandfather, wailed over the loss of his little brother and asked God "Why?" The rest of the men had started doing a body count to make sure that all the Indians were accounted for. Only sixteen accounted for. Amanda made seventeen. One man found a blood trail and took

124

two others with him following it into the brush with his pistol drawn. A moment later there were two pistol shots followed by a scream. The scream was cut short by a third shot. The men returned to the camp with a grim look of satisfaction on their faces. The leader of the three looked at Fernando and said, "Eighteen."

"Hello the camp," called one of the men bringing up the horses.

"Come on in," someone told him. "We got them all. We lost one and there's a white girl here."

"Mount up!" yelled Fernando. "It is time to leave this place of death. If there is something here you can use, take it. These heathen won't need it. When everyone is mounted we'll take the horses and head for home. We can spread out and pick up the stragglers they left behind."

"Aren't you going to bury them?" asked Amanda.

"Why? It won't get them to hell any faster," replied Fernando.

The rest of the morning they rode in tired silence. Amanda stayed close to Fernando riding bareback on an Indian pony. Fernando gave her the extra pair of trousers from the change of clothes he carried behind his saddle in his bedroll. Some of the younger men had stared at her because her deerskin dress crept up her thighs while she rode.

Ramon led Pablo's horse with Pablo's body wrapped in a blanket and tied belly down to the saddle. When some of the other men wanted to stop and bury Pablo quickly, Ramon refused stating that he would take Pablo home and bury him with family where loved ones would tend his grave. The men began to argue with Ramon but stopped when a wild-eyed Javier silently rode up beside his grandfather and placed his hand on his pistol.

Frank Smith rode near Joshua, Nathan, Luke and his sons. None of them spoke. What was there to say after something like that? Each was lost in his thoughts. Joshua was thankful that their losses weren't more than they were but was still sorry for the loss of Pablo. He was a good boy, a hard worker, and fun to have around. He died bravely. Not much consolation but it was something.

Frank looked forward to getting home to his wife and daughter thankful his boys weren't killed. Hopefully one day the Indian raids would stop and they could live in peace. Until then he had worked and fought too hard for what he had to let them run him off. He hoped the soldiers coming back to Texas would help. Today was Sarah's birthday.

Luke kept watching Pablo's horse and the burden it carried. He understood death. Pablo and Javier had become his friends and had not picked on him for being different. Instead Pablo had been teaching him to use a rope. He was sad and would miss his friend.

He looked down at the small caliber rifle Joshua let him keep from one of the dead Indians. He didn't know about calibers. He just knew that it was a rifle just his size and it was really pretty with all the brass tacks the Indian put in the stock. The bag that held the bullets and powder and stuff had pretty beads on it too. Joshua called it a Kentucky squirrel rifle and promised to teach him to shoot it.

Nathan was in wonder at this frontier that he had come to. It was the third time he had killed. The second time was when he had helped Joshua fight the outlaws at the river crossing in Tennessee. He was glad Joshua never asked him what had happened to his mother or how he had come by the mule and the Colt or why he refused to take the last name of his former master as was the custom of freedmen following the war.

His mind drifted back to the day on a rundown Middle Tennessee farm when Eli Elder had beaten and raped his mother because she wouldn't give him what he wanted. She had told Eli she was a free woman and didn't have to do that anymore. Nathan had been working the fields all day. When he came in that night he had found his mother in bed beaten and bloody with her clothes torn to rags. He had tried to help her but she had given up and decided to die. She made him promise to find his brother and then had closed her swollen eyes and gave her soul to God.

He had cleaned her up as best he could, put her in a clean dress and buried her that same night. After he had put the last shovel full of dirt on her grave he said a silent prayer and walked into old Eli's house without knocking, the shovel still in his hand. He remembered Eli saying, "So you buried the bitch in the dark." The next thing he remembered was Eli dead on the floor and looking at the blood on his hands. He had left Eli lying there. Searching the house for anything he could use he found a little money and the Colt. The rest of the slaves had run off when the Yankee Army came through so no one was around. Nathan had wanted to go with them but his mother wasn't healthy enough to travel so he had stayed with her. Now he was free to go. Nathan had gone to the barn, swung up on the mule and rode off with the rising sun at his back. Two weeks later he had met Joshua.

At noon the group stopped for lunch and decided to rest for the remainder of the day. They would continue home in the morning. One of the men roped a wandering steer and they butchered it. They split up into small groups to cook the meat and rest. They cooked it Ranger style by cutting the meat into strips then wrapping it around a stick and holding it over the fire. Fernando and Amanda joined Frank, Joshua, and their crew. Ramon treated her kindly and saw that she had what she needed.

"How long were you with them?" Ramon asked Amanda.

"Three years I think," she responded.

"Your family will be happy to have you back," he said pleasantly.

"I have no family to go back to," she said quietly. "They were all killed when I was captured."

"I'm sorry," he said sincerely and they sat quietly together for a time. She started to cry again and he put his arm around her. She buried her head on his shoulder and cried while he held her. From that point on Ramon and Amanda were never far apart. The young girl took comfort in the support of the grandfatherly older man while caring for her helped take his mind off his grief over the death of his grandson.

Chapter Eighteen; Back to Dallas

Late afternoon of June 12th found the Smith family and the J-G crew safe and sound back at the Smith ranch. Sarah's birthday party was postponed until the men from the community returned from following the raiding Comanche. The word was sent out that the party would be in two days on the 14th. Ramon and Javier took Pablo's body to Fernando's hacienda so his father and mother could bury him. Joshua returned to his ranch to check on things and pick up one of the gifts he had for Sarah.

Sarah and Mrs. Smith offered to let Amanda stay with them but she wanted to be near Ramon and declined. They did however give her a dress and altered it to fit. She thanked them for their kindness and rode away bathed and dressed like a white woman with her hair washed and put up in a simple bun. She was not beautiful but she was rather pretty with her blue eyes and coal black hair. Her slim figure was just coming into womanhood. She told them she thought she would be sixteen in December.

On the 14th, people started showing up early for Sarah's birthday party. A calf and a hog were being turned on spits behind the house by her brothers, who were spelled from time to time by the guests. There was plenty of food to go around and everyone had a good time. Someone showed up with a fiddle and some dancing took place in the yard. As it started to get dark people prepared to leave. Before anyone actually took off, Frank Smith had them all gather around the porch so that he could make an announcement. He called up Sarah and Joshua and told the crowd that the two were officially engaged. He told the crowd he and his wife had given their blessing. There was scattered applause mingled with a few murmurs but by and large the announcement went over well considering.

After the announcement Jesse walked up to Joshua with Jessica behind him. "Well, go on!" said Jessica.

"Ah, Joshua," Jesse began uncomfortably and stuck out his hand with a look of distaste on his face. Joshua shook his hand. They nodded without saying anything else and Jesse led Jessica away.

"Now that didn't hurt so bad did it?" Joshua heard Jessica ask Jesse as they walked away. Jesse's mumbled response was unintelligible.

"Well, it's a start," commented Sarah as she took Joshua's arm.

"Come with me," he told her, "I've got a present for you." He led her over to his saddle hanging on the corral fence; the buckskin was in the corral. The horse held up amazingly well during the forced march to catch the Comanche. Reaching in his saddlebags he pulled out the silver brush and mirror set. "Happy Birthday, Sarah," he said.

"Joshua it's beautiful," she said.

"Not as beautiful as the face that will be looking into it from now on," he said.

"Thank you," she said and hugged him.

"I'll be leaving for Dallas tomorrow since the horses are ready," he told her. "I'll not be gone any longer than I have to be."

"I know," she said. "I'll still miss you."

"You puts on a good spread," Nathan told Mary Louise as he stuck his head through the backdoor into the kitchen. "Would you like some help cleaning up?"

"Thank you," she said. "I'll do fine with the cleanup. Besides it's woman's work. Why would you want to help me with it?"

"Lord, child," he said in good humored mocking, "If I has to explain it to you, you's too slow for me to worry about it."

"I ain't slow," she said looking down into her dishpan of dirty dishes. "I just wanted to be sure you was thinking along the right track."

"You's had me thinking alright," he said as he brought in more dishes. "A man could live right comfortable with a job and a full growed woman that knows how to cook. I got the job. I been thinking I might want to find me a full growed woman and settle down myself. That is if she could handle me driving freight all over Texas."

"The right woman might be willing to keep up a home for you if you was to treat her nice when you was to home and not be playing foot loose and free while you was gone," she responded still watching her dishes.

129

"Oh, I think one woman is plenty for any man from what I've seen."

"I'm thinking a good woman would be saving herself for her man while he was out making a honest living."

"Well, I suppose we's thinking along the same lines. You know I's leaving tomorrow to go hauling freight. I may not be back for a while. You reckon a good woman could be found in these parts when I get back?" he asked.

"I reckon there will be one here," she said.

The morning of June 15th, Joshua and the J-G crew were saddled up and ready to ride. Ramon, Javier and Amanda headed out to the J-G ranch. Luke rode to Waco with Joshua, Fernando, Nathan, Pedro, and Carlos.

Taking their time and not pushing the horses too hard put them in Waco by the 20th. Joshua looked up Captain Wales who then gathered up some officer acquaintances. They rode outside of town to see the horses Joshua brought in. The ten horses were all bays and sorrels. Each of them was a Mustang and Kentucky Saddlehorse cross. Captain Wales picked out a bay that he wanted to try. Joshua tossed a rope on it and led it over to him. Captain Wales took his saddle off the horse he was riding and put it on the bay. The bay stood quietly for saddling and mounting as Captain Wales swung into the saddle. He put the horse through his paces, walk, trot, canter and back up, left turn, right turn.

"I'll give you one hundred dollars for this one," Captain Wales said as he dismounted.

"One hundred fifty," Joshua responded. "He's already gun broke. They all are." He pulled his pistol and fired into the ground. The horses in the herd jerked their heads up to look around but they stood where they were.

"One hundred fifteen," said Captain Wales

"One hundred thirty," said Joshua.

"Deal. I'll take the sorrel with the blaze and white left hind for that same price if he's broke as good as this one." said Captain Wales.

"He is," said Joshua addressing the other officers, "Gentlemen, anybody else want to buy a horse?"

130

A major picked out one for himself for one hundred thirty dollars and a Lieutenant picked out two. Joshua agreed to one hundred ten dollars each after haggling with the Lieutenant for twenty minutes and telling him he drove a hell of bargain. Captain Nelson told Joshua he was the officer authorized to purchase remounts for the Army. He offered Joshua seventy-five dollars each for the other five. The haggling was intense with Joshua shooting for the one hundred fifty dollar price he knew the Army paid for horses during the war. Joshua finally settled for ninety dollars each when Captain Nelson explained that a stingy Congress had once again cut the Army budget to the bone.

"Mr. Granger," said Captain Nelson, "I would be interested in making regular purchases of horses from you if these are the quality of horses that the Army can expect from you."

"They are," Joshua replied.

"Then I would like to invite you to bid on a contract to provide horses to the Army. We take bids periodically as the needs of the Army require. I prefer to deal in lots of fifty or more preferably one hundred."

"I'd like to do that Sir and hope to in the future but I can't commit to a contract right now. I have to establish my ranch and make good on my homestead. But I'd like to bid on future contracts if the invitation is open."

"It certainly is Mr. Granger. You obviously have an eye for good horses and from your cavalry experience know what will make a good cavalry mount. I trust from looking at these horses and what Captain Wales has told me about you that you know the regulation requirements."

"I do," said Joshua.

"I want to make sure and point out that the regulations say well broke to saddle in addition to the physical requirements and generally 14.3 to 16 hands tall, five to nine years old."

"Yes Sir, I know."

"Very well then, you have an open invitation from me to bid on any upcoming Army remount contracts. It will be refreshing I'm sure to deal with someone who knows the Army and horses both. You would be surprised how many westerners have tried to sell the Army all manner of wild horses of all sizes, colors, and genders. I look forward to your participation in the bidding."

"Thank you Sir, but it may be spring of next year at the earliest that I'll be able to bid on any of those contracts."

"Then I look forward to hearing from you next year sir. From what I understand, we can expect to wear out a lot of horses chasing the Comanche."

Four days later the J-G crew arrived in Dallas. Joshua and Fernando looked up Dan Jones at his saloon. Joshua was pleasantly surprised that Luella had chosen to open a store in Dallas and leave her other profession behind her. Joshua introduced Fernando and told Dan that he and Fernando were partners in the freighting. Dan suggested that the men get a hotel and they could discuss their plans over dinner at a local restaurant. They agreed to meet at 6:00 pm at the restaurant.

That night at the restaurant, Dan showed up with Luella. "Joshua," he said. "You know my sister Miss Luella Johnson."

"Luella, it's good to see you," Joshua responded. "Miss Johnson, I'd like you to meet my uncle, Fernando Nava and you know Luke."

"You've grown Luke. What a handsome boy," she said as she gave him a hug. "It's so nice to meet you Señor Nava," she said offering her hand after hugging Luke.

"The pleasure is all mine," Fernando said sincerely as he bowed and kissed her hand. Their eyes met as he straightened and they held each other's gaze for a moment.

"Fernando, Luella is the lady who sold me the other two teams and wagons." Turning to Luella he said, "I believe Dan was telling us today that you have opened another store?"

"Yes, Joshua," continued Luella, "I've opened a general store. We will be selling a little of everything at first and expand on whatever sells well."

Over dinner the conversation began with the weather, progressed to politics and the growth of Dallas, then they got down to business. "I've been looking into this," Dan began, "and water is the cheapest mode of transport for goods and people. So in order to make this profitable I have decided to have my supplies shipped in by water to Trinidad. That's seventy-five miles southeast of here and as far inland as one can get by water. You will pick up the freight there and take it to its destination.

"Freight charges have been fluctuating between a dollar and twenty cents per hundred pounds per hundred miles and two dollars and thirty cents per hundred pounds per hundred miles depending on the contract and the time of year. I want us to agree to one price all year round so we can both plan accordingly and know what we are dealing with. In that regard I am willing to go five cents above the average in order to get a stable year round figure. I think that is fair and should be profitable to each of us. I believe that comes to one dollar and eighty-five cents per hundred pounds per hundred miles. What do you think?"

"I think it sounds fair," Fernando replied. "I too have looked into freighting rates and what you are saying is true. By keeping the one rate all year you will be able to judge the mark up on your goods in order for you to profit and keep your merchandise prices stable which will help your merchandise sell. Our winter will be a little less profitable but our summers will be more so. Five cents above the average for a year round price is quite reasonable. I think we should accept this proposition Joshua."

"I'll go with it on your say so, Fernando," said Joshua.

"Good, I've got the papers drawn up and we can sign the contract at my office tomorrow. I have a load at Trinidad waiting for pick up as we speak. It will be brought here for my sister's store and my saloon. I have letters of introduction written up for the gentleman you will be dealing with at the warehouse in Trinidad."

That night back in the hotel room they shared, Joshua and Fernando discussed the deal they would be signing in the morning. "We're going to make a fortune on this Fernando!" Joshua said with excitement.

"We will make a profit but we will earn it. We have struck a good bargain, but do not fool yourself into thinking it is better than it is," cautioned Fernando. "If you do that you will be disappointed. We must be realistic."

"Well, the way I figure it each wagon can carry two thousand pounds and the Studebaker can carry at least two thousand five hundred. If it's a full load we will make ninety dollars and nineteen cents on the one trip from Trinidad. Ninety dollars and nineteen cents for a week's work isn't bad at all. That's fifteen dollars and three cents a day! We'll be rich in no time!"

"Alright," said Fernando, "it is time for your first business lesson. Yes, fifteen dollars and three cents a day is nice but it is not all profit. There is the pay and feeding of the drivers, the feeding of horses, and the fact that we can't carry the whole six thousand five hundred pounds of freight.

"We must consider the actual weight of feed, water, and other things like firewood and cooking utensils. I think we can safely figure on dropping down to an actual freight weight of two thousand pounds for the Studebaker and one thousand five hundred for the other two wagons. That gives us a total freight weight of five thousand pounds, which for the seventy-five mile trip from Trinidad will bring us to sixty-nine dollars and thirty-eight cents. At thirteen dollars a month for the drivers, this is average pay these days, which breaks down to forty-three cents a day. At that rate three drivers will cost nine dollars and three cents over seven days. Using the figure of sixty-nine dollars and thirty-eight cents a week, that drops the profit figure down to sixty dollars and thirty-five cents for a week. Then feed for the horses will cost let us say another six bits a day per team. That brings us to forty-four dollars and sixty cents a week which is six dollars and thirty-seven cents per day and an average of two dollars and twelve cents per wagon. You paid seven hundred dollars for two wagons and teams I believe and won one of them in a poker game. At the rate of two dollars and twelve cents per day, the wagons will pay for themselves in about six months. After the wagons have paid for themselves is when the real profit begins. Even when we have to start replacing harness, horses, and wagons we can do it and still make a profit.

Since there is no loan against the wagons we can start banking the money as soon as it comes in. However, the way to make the trip more profitable is to carry freight both ways. Whatever we carry to Trinidad will be pure profit because the trip from Trinidad will cover our expenses. We will do best to carry freight both ways. Driving around with an empty wagon is not the way for a freighting business to make money. We may not get the same rate hauling for other people that we will hauling for Dan, but we can take that as it comes.

134

I think we have a good thing here Joshua. We can probably do better than these figures because horses are faster than oxen and a trip that would take oxen six days at twenty-five miles a day may be made with horses in four or five days depending on the weather. We may also be able to put more weight on the wagons but we will have to wait and see. These numbers are just conservative estimates."

The next morning after breakfast they met Dan Jones in his office and signed a contract for the year-round rate of one dollar and eighty-five cents per hundred pounds per hundred miles. They made the contract good for one year. Fernando talked to Dan about hauling something to Trinidad as well as from Trinidad. Dan introduced Fernando to a man who had a load of hides to ship.

Chapter Nineteen; Money in the Bank

The next morning Joshua and Luke hit the trail again heading back to Georgetown and their ranch. With just the two of them Joshua got Luke to talk a little bit and found that the boy was pretty sharp even though his social skills were lacking. Joshua took the opportunity to teach Luke how to shoot the short Kentucky squirrel rifle he picked up at the Indian fight. It was a percussion .32 caliber and used a .31 patched round ball. The .01 thickness of the patch brought it up to .32. It was old but well-made and just the right size for a boy to learn on. Joshua figured it was probably special made for a short pilgrim who never made it all the way across the plains. After they cleaned it up it was a nice looking little rifle. The bond between the boy and the man grew as they spent time together. Joshua showed Luke how to hunt with his new rifle in addition to just shooting at targets. Luke's confidence grew with the experience and he came out of his shell a little bit more.

By June 28th they were in Austin. Joshua opened a bank account at a private bank since there was no state or national bank any closer than Galveston Bay. In addition to what was left of the money he brought from Kentucky, he put five hundred dollars from the sale of the horses in the account. While they were in the bank, Mr. Carson, the bank president, came out of his office to see Joshua. Mr. Carson was well dressed in a town suit. A well groomed man tending toward heavy but not quite fat, he had the lukewarm smile of someone who smiled whether he felt like it or not.

"Mr. Granger," Mr. Carson said and stuck out his hand. "I heard you were back in the area. What brings you to our little bank?"

"Opening an account Mr. Carson," Joshua replied accepting the handshake.

"I hear that in addition to marrying the prettiest girl in this part of the country you have homesteaded a ranch and gone in partners with Fernando Nava on a freighting venture."

"Yes sir, all that's true. I'll be marrying Sarah Lynn Smith next spring. I've homesteaded a ranch northwest of here on the San Gabriel. I have a three wagon freighting outfit with a one year contract which Fernando is running as a partner. I've also sold some horses to the Army and have a verbal invitation to bid on upcoming remount contracts."

"My but you are an ambitious young man. That is the kind of customer we like to have. Come in my office and chat for a moment," Mr. Carson said leading them back to his office. "If you are ever in need of a loan I'm certain that we can make some arrangements. Have a seat please," as he motioned Joshua and Luke to chairs and had a seat behind a rather imposing desk.

"Thank you sir I appreciate the offer and I'll keep it in mind. I do have some ideas for the future but I'm not ready to move on them at this time. However, I might be inclined to invest in some sound businesses if you happen to come across some."

"I'll keep that in mind Mr. Granger. I understand that you left here on a cattle drive, rode for the Pony Express and then fought for the Yankees in the late unpleasantness."

"Yes sir, I did all that. Is me fighting for the north going to be a problem for us Mr. Carson?" asked Joshua.

"Heavens no!" said Mr. Carson. Joshua couldn't tell if the man was sincere or not. "Mr. Granger, let me be right up front with you. My sympathies were with the Confederacy. However, I am also a practical man. The war is over. It did not turn out to suit me but I must live with it. I am a banker. I loan money. I have to have it before I can loan it. You sir have money which you just deposited in my bank. I can now loan some of that money to some industrious soul who will hopefully make sound decisions with it, then pay it back with interest. You will receive a portion of that interest in return for allowing me the privilege of holding it for you and we both make more money that way.

"I am a businessman Mr. Granger and I don't let my politics get in the way of that. We may never be close friends but I believe we can be trustworthy business associates. I can see that your efforts will be good for the local economy and that will be good for the town which in turn will be good for the bank. Does that sound reasonable to you Mr. Granger?"

"Yes sir it sounds reasonable to me. Well, I have to get on out to my place and see how my hands are doing. I've been gone for a couple of weeks. I'll drop in to see you when I'm in town if you don't mind," Joshua said as he got to his feet with Luke following his lead.

"That would be fine Mr. Granger. I look forward to doing business with you." They shook hands again then Joshua and Luke headed for home by way of the Smith ranch.

Late evening on the 29th they rode into the Smith's ranch. They had to push their mounts to make it but Joshua and Luke were both ready to be home. Sarah came running out to meet them. She kissed Joshua and hugged Luke. Mrs. Smith came out and hugged Luke before whisking him into the house to spoil him some more. It had been a long time since her children were young and she enjoyed having him around. Jesse and John were formal but not hostile in their attitudes toward Joshua.

Over supper Joshua told them about selling the horses, the freighting deal, and that Fernando seemed pleased with it. The men would come home for Christmas and New Years and be home for two weeks. They might drop in if they were on their way through the area.

In turn Frank Smith told him that Micah Benson, the brother of the man whose family was killed by the Comanche in the last raid had decided to give it up. He would be taking his family and his brother's two surviving children and going back east. This was the last straw for him. He was trying to sell his and his brother's property. Between the two of them they had 4,000 acres and estimated 1,000 head of cattle and horses on the range. Jesse and Jessica would be married in September and Frank was adding a room onto the house for them in the meantime.

After supper Joshua and Sarah sat on the porch talking. "I rode out to check on the garden several times while you were gone," Sarah told him. "Amanda was there. I talked with her about her plans and she doesn't have any. Her family was killed when the Comanche captured her and she has nowhere to go. Ramon has taken her under his wing."

"What do you think we should do with her?" Joshua asked a little uncomfortably, not sure what Sarah was leading up to with this conversation.

"I don't know. We can't just throw her out on her own. She's taken to cooking for Ramon and Javier while they work the cattle. She is really the one raising the garden and tending to the corn crop. So she's pulling her weight. I guess as long as she is not a problem then we should let her stay. She seems happy enough considering all she's been through.

"You know that there will be enough work for two women at the ranch. It would be nice to have another woman around too I suppose. Once we start having children it will be nice to have some help around the place. I'd love for Mary Louise to come stay with us but I don't see it happening."

"I guess she can stay as long as she wants too then. We'll have to figure out a place to put her. It wouldn't be right for her to sleep with the men."

"Well, you will need to pay her a decent wage if she is going to continue to work for you." Sarah told him. "You should pay her at least as much as you pay the vaqueros. A man doing the cooking would expect to make twenty-five cents a day more than the cowboys and he wouldn't do anything but cook. She's doing the cooking and tending to the garden and corn. It's only right that if she stays you should pay her."

"Damn, woman, what did they teach you in that finishing school? A woman just doesn't get paid as much as a man."

"Joshua, I'm not going to argue with you about this. She's doing the work. If you don't pay her I will."

"Alright, alright. I'll pay her thirteen dollars a month like I pay the cowboys and teamsters but no more."

"Thank you," said Sarah and she squeezed his hand.

"Changing the subject; I opened an account at Carson's bank in Austin this morning with what I had left from selling the farm in Kentucky. I put half the money from selling the horses in there too. We got a little over a thousand dollars for them. Here's your five hundred."

"That's wonderful Joshua! But you could have put it all in the bank."

"Once we're actually married we will but for now just trust me and keep your half of the money. Putting our money together before we marry would be unseemly. Word would get out and people would talk. I don't want to do anything that would hurt your reputation."

Chapter Twenty; Horses, Cattle, and Cooking

After dark on July the 1st Joshua and Luke rode into their home camp. Ramon was sitting by the fire sipping coffee in the dark. Javier and Amanda were already rolled in their blankets.

"Señor Joshua, Luke, welcome home," he said as he stood. He helped them unsaddle and they talked about what all had happened in the last two weeks. "Amanda has taken over the cooking and is doing a fine job. I have been working with Javier catching and branding cattle where we find them. We have another fifty head branded. It is not a large herd but it is growing steadily Patron.

"Javier and I have spotted two herds of wild horses but we have not been able to get close enough to rope any of them. We have been thinking of how we might catch them."

"That sounds good Ramon. Tomorrow you can show me the horse herds. We'll see if we can figure out a way to catch them. We need more horses."

"Si, Señor."

In the morning, Javier gave Pablo's Colt back to Joshua. "I think Pablo would want to give it back to you Señor." Then he took Luke and introduced him to Pablo's horse. Luke was quiet and gentle around the horse. Javier went on to explain that it was a good horse and not too old. He saddled up the pinto with Pablo's saddle and told Luke to get on. When Luke got in the saddle, Javier adjusted the stirrups to fit Luke. "The horse and saddle are yours my young friend. My brother would approve. Stick with me and I will show you how to be a vaquero." Javier told Luke. "Now we can go find more cattle for Señor Joshua," he said as he swung up onto his own horse. "Follow me," he said to Luke and headed west at a trot. Smiling wide but saying nothing Luke looked at Joshua.

"Go ahead," Joshua told him.

Luke rode away with a huge smile and caught up with Javier.

Ramon showed Joshua where he saw the horse herds. They read the sign on the ground and followed it to a stream that fed into the San Gabriel River. The sign showed that the horses went to a certain spot in the stream to drink regularly. They backed off from the stream and found a spot where they could watch for the horses without being seen. They staked out their own horses another hundred yards behind them. All day they waited. The Texas summer sun was brutal as they laid on the hot ground silently watching for the horses. The sun was sinking in the west when they heard horses coming. They watched silently. This herd was a small bachelor band of seven horses. They approached the water hole cautiously then all of them walked down to the water and drank. The leader was a bay; the other six were sorrels (light brown body with light brown mane and tail). Joshua guessed the average height to be 14 hands. One or two of them might be big enough to sell to the Army. The rest would end up being used to work the ranch or sell to civilians at a modest price. They were not an awe-inspiring lot but they were decent and would be useful. None of them had crippling conformational faults although one of them was noticeably ewe necked (had a thin straight neck like a sheep).

When the band left, Joshua got up to go but Ramon motioned for him to get back down. Another herd of horses was coming in to drink. This time a battle scarred stallion with twelve mares came to drink. The stallion was dark brown, almost black with lighter brown on his muzzle and strong black hooves. He was big for a Mustang. Joshua guessed he stood 15 hands and weighed about eleven hundred pounds. The lead mare was solid black. Most of the mares had foals and there were some yearlings and two year olds in the bunch too. This was a nice bunch of horses. Their average height Joshua guessed to be 14.2. Still a little small for the Army but putting them with his Kentucky Saddlehorse stud should produce some larger foals. The

Army didn't buy mares anyway. There were a couple of pintos but the rest were blacks, bays, and sorrels with one grulla (brownish gray mouse colored with a dorsal stripe down her back and tiger stripes on her lower legs). When the herd moved off Ramon motioned for Joshua to follow him and they went back to their horses.

"Well, patron," Ramon asked, "What do you think?"

"I think we should try to get them all. Are there other herds that come to this place to drink?"

"Maybe, I am not sure. It looks like these two herds come here every day. They don't range far from here. What should we do to catch them?"

"I wonder if there is a canyon close by where we could build a trap corral and run them into it. We'll look for that tomorrow. We won't be able to take both herds at the same time. The stud would try to kill the bachelor band if we ran them in together. We'll have to take one bunch at a time. I think we'll take the last bunch that comes to water on the night we take them. If we take the first bunch it could scare off the second bunch and we might not get another chance. Tomorrow we'll scout for a place to build a trap and figure out a plan from there."

Back at camp Amanda had food and coffee waiting for them. She had taken to wearing men's clothes even though she had a dress. Joshua decided she had been through enough and if she wanted to wear men's clothes, that was her choice. Amanda didn't say much and seemed a little nervous. Ramon never asked if she could stay, she just came along and nobody told her not too. It seemed to be working out so Joshua left it alone. He figured come payday he'd pay her the same wage he paid the men like he promised Sarah. Joshua tried the beans and rice and they were delicious. When he mentioned it Amanda simply smiled nervously.

The next morning Amanda was up before them all and had breakfast ready by first light, coffee, bacon and biscuits. As they were eating she looked at Joshua and said, "I miss fried potatoes."

"Huh?" said Joshua caught off guard.

"I know we have potatoes in the garden but they aren't ready yet," Amanda continued, "I was wondering if the next time someone goes to town if we could get some potatoes. The Comanche don't eat potatoes so I haven't had them for a couple of years. It would be a nice change from the rice. I was also thinking too that if you don't mind I might take the shotgun or rifle and see if I can get us some doves or rabbits or deer or something. I'm not complaining about the beans and rice every meal. We have plenty to eat and we don't go hungry. I was just thinking that if you like my cooking, I can add some variety. That is if you don't mind."

"Well," Joshua began a little surprised. "I don't see any harm in it. What do you think Ramon?"

"I enjoy a woman's cooking much better than my own. I think it would be wise to allow her the freedom to cook what she wants. I think we will all benefit from it," Ramon commented.

"Do you know how to use the guns, Amanda?" Joshua asked.

"Yes, sir, before the Comanche came, my father taught me to use them. He loaded them light for me and showed me how to do it. I hunted for the table when I had free time. We were poor but we ate good."

"In that case I guess it will be fine with me and the next time someone goes to town we will see about getting a sack of potatoes and whatever else our new cook wants. Looks like you're on the payroll," Joshua told her with a smile.

That evening when everyone returned to camp for supper, Amanda had a pot of prairie chicken and dumplings waiting for them. Everyone was pleased including Amanda. Joshua thought to himself that this kind of cooking was worth every bit of thirteen dollars a month.

Over the next week, Javier continued to ride the range with Luke looking for unbranded cattle to add to the herd and teaching Luke what he knew. They usually added one or two head a day to the total. Ramon and Joshua built a trap corral upstream about a mile from the water hole the Mustangs used. The corral was fairly large and had grass and water so they could keep the horses there for a day or two if need be.

The night came when they were going to gather the wild ones. Everyone including Amanda was in the saddle that night. The canyon was to the north of the water hole and Joshua spread the crew out on the south and west of the water hole far enough away that they wouldn't spook the Mustangs. Javier and Luke were on the west side

142

with Joshua, Ramon, and Amanda to the south. This time the Stallion and his mares came to the water before the bachelor band. Joshua and the J-G crew let them go. When the bachelor band came down to the water Joshua let them drink before sending Amanda and Ramon around behind them on the east side. Once they were in position Joshua moved north. The horses heard him coming and started to move away retreating to the east where they came from.

Ramon and Amanda hazed them back the other way as Javier and Luke moved in from the west. The only place left to go was north. The Mustangs broke into a run and all the horsemen followed alongside with Joshua behind them. The first horses balked at the mouth of the trap but bolted through it when the riders closed in on them. Joshua jumped down and slid the poles into the makeshift gate, happy with the night's work.

"We'll let them settle down tonight and tomorrow we'll start working with them," Joshua told the crew.

The next morning, Joshua, Ramon, Javier, and Luke returned to the trap corral with the branding iron. The Mustangs were in good shape and ran around the trap looking for a way out when the men showed up. Finding no way out they gathered at the far end of the corral.

"I don't see any of them that I'd want breeding my mares," Joshua said matter-of-factly. "That means all these boys get gelded. That will be the first order of business. Javier, I'll rope the front feet. You rope the back feet. Ramon you do the cutting and branding. Luke, when the horses go down I want you to rope their head so they won't thrash around and hurt themselves. Can you do that?" Luke took his rope from his saddle and nodded quietly.

Joshua and Javier took down their ropes and shook out loops as Ramon opened the gate and let them in. Then he built a small fire and laid the branding iron in it to get hot. The next three hours were hard on men and horses both as the gelding and branding took place. The wild ones fought for all they were worth and the cowboys earned their pay. The screams of the horses split the air as Ramon's razor sharp knife changed their lives forever. Joshua felt sorry for them in a way but not sorry enough to stop the job. It was a simple economic decision to geld these horses. They would be better mounts and

143

useful as calm geldings instead of runty studs too ornery to ride and not good enough to breed. While they had them down they also put hobbles on them so they could walk but not run. When it was over Joshua decided that now would be a good time to drive them back to the ranch. The mustangs were tired from fighting, sore from being cut, and with the hobbles on, they weren't going to be in a big hurry to take off for the far horizon. That afternoon they drove the seven geldings back to the ranch.

Chapter Twenty One; Breaking Horses

For the next two weeks Joshua worked with gentling the horses. His father taught him to gentle a horse down before getting on it. Joshua had watched Texas cowboys rope a horse and throw it to the ground to get a saddle on it then let the horse up to buck itself into exhaustion with a cowboy in the saddle spurring away the whole time. While that method would work, it was hard on the horse and hard on the cowboy. So he took the gentler approach his father, who was a horseman and not a cowboy, showed him. Some horses would still buck when the rider got in the saddle, especially Mustangs, but they usually didn't buck as much after some gentle handling and they waited until the rider was on before they tried to kill them. One of the hardest parts of breaking a horse was being able to catch him first and then get in the saddle without getting kicked, bit or both. The rider could do that by roping and tying a horse but if a horse was broke that way, it wouldn't sell for much.

Joshua worked with all the horses every day but one became his favorite. The bay gelding who was the leader of the bachelor band was just barely tall enough to sell to the Army at 14.3 hands tall and his conformation was good. He was a tough and smart animal. Joshua liked the horse. The first few times Joshua roped him the bay fought the rope. By the fourth time the rope dropped over his neck he submitted having learned that fighting the rope was painful. At that point Joshua took a saddle blanket and got the horse used to it touching him. This was called sacking out because some people used an old feed sack for this purpose. When the horse would stand tied and accept the blanket being thrown over his back without throwing a fit Joshua brought out the saddle. For this particular part of the training Joshua used the McClellan saddle with the stirrups removed. The McClellan saddle didn't have a horn for roping so it was less likely to injure the horse if he reared up and flipped over. It took a couple more days of working with the horse before the saddle could be cinched without a bucking fit. Once the bay learned that the saddle wouldn't eat him he calmed down a little. Then the stirrups were put back on the saddle and their flopping around resulted in more bucking. Finally it was time for the bridle. Joshua used a bridle with a bosal to start with because there was no bit to injure the horse's mouth. He learned about the bosal by watching Fernando's vaqueros break horses. The bosal worked through pressure on the nose and jawbone of the horse. The bit would come later in the horse's training after he would accept a rider without a fight. A couple of days with that and the bay was still nervous but could be saddled and bridled without trying to kill himself or those around him.

Sarah and Mary Louise had been coming by every few days to work the garden and see the progress with the horses. Sarah was there when Joshua saddled the bay for his first ride. With Javier holding the horse's head Joshua swung into the saddle. Javier let go of the bay and the horse blew up, straight up. Joshua had the reins of the bosal in his left hand and his right arm stretched out behind and above him using it for balance while he rode the bucking horse. The gentling method only went so far. Horses are prey animals and their instinctive defense to something on their back trying to eat them is to buck it off. Generally speaking a horse raised in the wild is more likely to buck than one raised and gentled in captivity from birth. And the bay bucked. He bucked his way around the pen with Joshua sticking to him like a cocklebur. Sarah was hanging onto the corral fence yelling encouragement to Joshua as the bay snorted, blew, and squealed his discontent. After a bucking lap around the pen, the horse spun to the right then went straight up into the air to come down on all four feet at once, stiff legged with his head down and his back bowed jarring Joshua from his ankles to his clenched teeth. Then the bay spun the other way bucking at the same time. Joshua groaned as the bay did three more stiff legged jumps in a row spinning this way and that with each jump. The last one shook Joshua loose and the bay put his head between his front feet and reached for the sun with his back feet. Joshua slammed into the rocky Texas ground and slid to a stop with dirt in his mouth.

The bay stopped bucking in time to watch Joshua hit the ground. Joshua sat up and shook his head to gather his senses. Then he stood slowly trying to draw the breath back into his lungs. The bay snorted and rolled his eyes but let Javier catch him. Shaking the stars from his eyes, spitting out dirt and brushing himself off, Joshua picked up his hat and pulled it down tight on his head. With the reins in his hand he took a deep breath and let it out then jammed his boot in the stirrup while Javier held the bay's head. "Turn us loose," Joshua said as his backside hit the saddle. Joshua and the bay gave their audience quite a show until the horse stopped bucking and began to run around the pen. Gradually he slowed to a walk and then stopped with his sides heaving. Joshua squeezed the horse a little with his legs and the horse flinched into a trot. After a couple more laps around the pen Joshua brought the horse to a stop and stepped down from the saddle. He rubbed the bay's neck and talked gently to him as he led him around the pen at a slow walk for a few minutes to cool him off before unsaddling and turning him back into the other pen with the rest of the horses.

"How was that for a first ride?" Joshua asked as he walked over to the water bucket by the tent and took a sip from the dipper. He rinsed the dirt out of his mouth and spat. Then he took a long drink.

"For a first ride I think it went well," Ramon responded. "Personally, if a wild horse didn't buck the first few times I got on him I would never trust him. He is not an honest horse. But a wild one who bucks the first few times or even several times is honest about the fact that he does not like it. Such a horse you can trust. When he no longer bucks you know that he is no longer afraid and you can then begin to teach him what you want him to know."

"I think you did pretty good," Sarah told him. "I still think you should let me get in there and work with him."

"I've told you before," Joshua began testily as he stretched a kink out of his back. "It's one thing for you to work with the horses you raise. It's something altogether different for you to be working with these wild ones. I'm not going to have you getting hurt. Now I'm telling you. Leave the wild ones to me."

Sarah's face turned red with anger more at his condescending tone than what he said. Snatching the hoe from where she had leaned it against the pen, she stomped off toward the garden grumbling about high and mighty, hard headed men and she hoped he ate fifty pounds of dirt before he got those horses broke. She couldn't wait until women got the right to vote.

"A firm hand should also be gentle to get the best result from spirited horses. It is not good to break the spirit or to spur them when it is not needed. Women can be like horses sometimes." Ramon commented softly without looking up from sharpening his knife.

Joshua gave him a hard look but Ramon never looked up from the long slow strokes of the knife on the stone. Joshua turned back to the corral where Javier was saddling another Mustang for him to ride. By the end of the day Joshua had given each of the seven geldings their first ride. He was tired to the bone and aching in places he hadn't even known he had. Sarah had returned home without saying another word to him. What a day.

By August the seven geldings were rideable by someone with experience. Joshua, Ramon, and Javier each rode two a day while they continued to search for more cattle to brand. Luke rode the broke horses.

Joshua decided that the geldings were broke well enough that they could gather in the other herd of wild horses. He had Javier and Luke stay away from the area where the herd was so they wouldn't get spooked and change their range or watering habits. In the meantime Joshua had been riding the range watching the herd from a distance and reading their sign.

The day came when they were going to gather the horses. The plan was the same as the last time. Get in position in early afternoon and wait for the herd to come to the water. After they'd had a chance to water, the riders would move in and push the horses to the trap corral at the head of the creek.

Late that morning, Sarah and her brothers rode into camp. She wore a divided skirt and rode astride. All of them were leading an extra horse. Joshua invited them to get down and have some lunch. Over lunch, Sarah informed him that they'd come to help catch the wild ones that evening.

"I've told you I don't want you messing with the wild ones," Joshua told her.

"I helped Papa work cattle and horses both while all you boys were off soldiering and I can out ride any of you. Papa said I could come if Jesse and John would come with me. So you get three extra hands, mister. With about twenty head in the herd you'll need all the help you can get."

"Joshua," Jesse cut in quietly when he saw Joshua working himself up to argue with Sarah, "Don't waste your breath. She's got her mind made up. I tried to talk her out of this. Papa tried to talk her out of it too and we're still here. She'll come whether you tell her she can or not. So you might as well just accept it and figure out the best place to put her."

Joshua closed his mouth from where he had started to say something and shook his head in agreement. "Alright. Alright. She had the same look on her face the day she rode Diablo to a standstill. I reckon you can come along."

Sarah smiled and her whole face beamed with satisfaction and anticipation.

That afternoon with everyone mounted on a fresh horse they rode out and Joshua put them all in position. Jesse, Javier, and Luke were on the south west side of the water hole about seven hundred yards away and spread out. John, Ramon, and Amanda were to the east with Joshua and Sarah due south. The herd came in from the northwest. While they were drinking, John, Ramon, and Amanda swung wide and rode north into position. When everyone was in position and the horses had had their drink, Joshua and Sarah spread out and moved north slowly. Everyone else closed in at a walk.

The wild ones saw riders on all sides but one and turned north. The riders kept pace with them and closed in tighter. In a couple of minutes the Mustangs broke into a run and the riders chased them upstream toward the corral at an all-out run that sent the adrenaline pounding through everyone's veins. At the gate the lead mare balked but the horses in the rear were still running and pushed her and the other lead horses into the corral. The stud followed with Joshua and Jesse closing in on him yelling and swinging their ropes in the air. Finding no way out the horses began to mill around and call out to each other. The stud put himself between the mares and the riders. He charged the gate with ears laid back and teeth bared, snaking his head. Joshua, John and Jesse jumped off their horses and slid the gate poles into place just in time. The stud slid to a stop just short of the poles and reared, pawing at the air calling out a challenge.

"I count twelve mares, nine foals, five yearlings and two year olds; with the stud that comes to twenty-seven horses. Woo, Hoo! That's a good catch!" yelled Sarah. "Look at that stud Joshua," she continued excitedly. "He's nice enough to keep intact. We can put him on any of the mares and still get good foals I'll bet. Look at those mares; two pintos, three bays, five sorrels, two blacks and only one of the foals is a pinto."

"It's a nice bunch of horses. We'll leave them here for the night," Joshua told them. "They have grass and water in there so they'll be fine. It will give them time to calm down. We'll come back and check on them in the morning and decide what we're going to do and how we're going to do it.

Riding back to camp Sarah rode beside Joshua. "I know how some people who just want broodmares cut the muscles in the back legs of wild mares. They can still carry a foal but they'll never run again or be useful for anything else. I don't want you to do that to these mares Joshua. It's cruel. Some of these mares could make good mounts too."

"I don't like that either, Sarah so you don't have to worry about that. I'm a horseman. I'm not going to cripple any horse on purpose." Joshua replied.

"We'll brand them here, hobble them of course and herd them back to the ranch. I'll start working with them the next day. I don't know about keeping the stud intact. Between us we have two Kentucky studs and a young Kentucky/Mustang cross coming on. I think I'll see if I can gentle the stud down and break him to ride. If I can't then I'll geld him for sure. We don't need to be breeding bad attitudes into our herd. If he's got a good mind and he's trainable then we'll keep him a stud. We'll have to divide our mares into three herds. With the sorrel two year old that you left intact that will mean four herds in the next year or two or somebody gets gelded or sold.

149

The more I think about it Honey, the more I think we just don't need another stud."

"But he's just so proud, and he's a nice horse. He's got good conformation. You can look at those foals and see that he throws some nice babies. I know you're not going to want to put him with the Kentucky mares but what if we put him with the culled mustang mares and Kentucky cross mares that aren't exactly what we want? If we breed them to him and they throw better foals than what they are we will have improved the herd and not lost any mares in the process. We're going to need all the mares we can get for a while. With four studs we can keep a good mix in bloodlines. We can maintain four separate herds on the range we have."

"Alright, if I can gentle him down and ride him in thirty days we'll keep him a stud. If I can't ride him as a stud in thirty days he gets gelded. We're not going to have an ornery stud putting a mean streak in our bloodlines. Fair enough?"

"Fair enough," said Sarah. "You should hold the mares to the same standard. If they can't be ridden in thirty days then they should be sold for whatever they bring. We don't need ornery mares putting meanness into the herds either."

"So you want me to break these mares to ride too? You know that most folks in these parts don't ride mares and just use them for breeding. The only reason Fernando rides a mare is because his late wife gave her to him and he doesn't give a damn what other people think. You just said we need all the mares we can get for a while so we won't be selling any of them no matter whether they're small, knock-kneed, ewe-necked or what until we get enough to sustain a decent foal crop every year. So why should I ride them all?" he asked.

"It was your idea to keep mean streaks out of our bloodlines," she said with a smile. "I'm just agreeing with you. If you choose not to sell the mares you can't ride that is up to you."

"My idea? And what do you mean by the mares I can't ride? If I get on it, you know I'll ride it." Joshua said with pride, a bit put out that she would suggest he couldn't ride them all.

"Of course it was your idea, and if you say you can ride them all, then I believe you. So it really isn't a problem is it?" Sarah said grinning in the darkness. "You just now said we can't have ornery

150

horses putting a mean streak in our bloodlines and that you can ride them all. The only way to see if they're mean is to break them to ride. So, it really was your idea and you just said you can do it. You're so smart. That's one of the reasons I love you."

"Ahuh," said Joshua. "I'm smart enough to know you just conned me into riding thirteen broncs instead of one. That was smooth using my own words against me like that. But you made your point and I'll ride the mares too. If they're broke to ride maybe they'll bring more if we do wind up selling them later on. Some pilgrim might buy a mare for riding or pulling a plow. Folks back east don't think anything about riding a mare. I've rode them, Confederate General John Hunt Morgan rode a mare and I heard that one of General Lee's favorite horses was a mare too. I just don't want you thinking I don't know that you conned me into it."

"Why Joshua Granger, that is such a mean thing to say to me," said Sarah with feigned hurt in her voice. Then she laughed.

The stud gentled down well enough and by mid-September Joshua was riding him on a regular basis. By then each of the men had a four horse string that made up their regular mounts. Joshua still rode his Kentucky stud once in a while but he also rode the buckskin Sarah gave him, the bay Mustang gelding, and the black Mustang stud with the brown nose. Javier and Ramon took turns riding the rest of the Mustang geldings with Javier taking the rough ones and Ramon putting finishing touches on them when Javier got them to the point that they worked without fighting him. Joshua had started working with the mares to gentle them down before riding them.

In the meantime Luke's riding had improved and for a kid of approximately eleven years old he was helpful with the cattle. He rode the broke horses. Joshua wouldn't let him rope any big stuff yet but had him doing most of the roping of calves and colts.

Whenever Amanda needed to ride she rode the pinto Indian pony she claimed the day she was saved from the Comanche.

Chapter Twenty Two; Building a Home

September 1st was Jesse and Jessica's wedding. It was a very nice affair and the bride was beautiful as she could be. Sarah was the Maid of Honor and she made sure that she didn't outshine the bride. She did however catch the bouquet, which got Joshua a couple of pats on the back and smiles from some of the older men around. Most of the younger men had fought for the Confederacy and still gave him a wide berth. At the reception a gentleman with a little liquid courage in his system got belligerent and insulting with him. Joshua ignored him while John and Fernando quietly escorted the gentleman from the festivities. Joshua's stature went up a bit with the brothers for not disrupting the wedding reception when he had every right to defend his honor and they knew from painful experience that he wasn't afraid to do so.

On September 10th, Sarah had a birthday party for Joshua. It was a small affair with mostly family attending. Most of the locals didn't really know him that well or want anything to do with the Yankee. It didn't bother Joshua too much. He figured they'd come around sooner or later and if not it was more their problem than his. He had a ranch to build and didn't have time to waste worrying about whether the locals liked him or not. He would rather they did but if not, oh well.

Sarah baked him a cake and gave him a new shirt and pair of pants she had made for him out of the material he had given her. Mary Louise knitted him a new pair of socks. She also knitted a pair for Nathan and gave them to him quietly when they had a few minutes alone.

The guests included Fernando, Nathan, and the teamsters. After supper the men were sitting on the porch smoking and talking except for Nathan who helped Mary Louise in the kitchen.

"I have been thinking that change is coming," said Fernando, "and those who are prepared for it will be the ones who are successful. Farmers are coming from the east. They are doing most of their farming with oxen right now because they are cheap and easy to maintain. As they prosper they will want to work more land faster than oxen will do it for them. Generally speaking, farmers like mules better than horses where ranchers like horses better than mules. The

Army also buys mules to pull the Army wagons. Mules can go longer without water than horses and Indians don't like mules as well as they like horses. They will steal them where they find them but it is horses they really want. I think a man could do well raising mules as well as horses. Besides all that, we will need to replace our harness horses in a few years and I think mules would be the best choice. A mule will pull more freight than a horse on the same amount of feed. What do you think, Joshua?"

"I think it's an idea worth considering. Right now I have my hands full with horses and cattle. Maybe next year I can think about raising mules too. I still have a cabin and a bunkhouse to build and now I need another cabin for Amanda. I can't put her in the bunkhouse with the men and I can't put her in the cabin with Luke and me and I can't leave any of them in tents for the winter. So I think I'll build a separate kitchen and put a good sized room on one end of it for her. That way she will be right there to do the cooking and have her own space at the same time."

"What is she going to cook on?" asked Fernando. "If you are going to build a cabin, a bunkhouse, and a separate kitchen you are going to need four stoves unless you intend to heat and cook with fireplaces. A fireplace is pretty and romantic but they are not practical unless you have no money to buy a stove. You have money to buy stoves. Stoves use less wood and heat better in the winter too. It is also easier to build a nice cabin without trying to put a fireplace in it. We should build your cabins and then go to town and buy four stoves.

"I think the logs have seasoned enough and you should look to getting your buildings up before it gets colder. We will keep the teamsters here and help you. The horses could use the rest anyway. It shouldn't take but a few days to get the buildings up if you know where you want them. I think we can do it easily in a week with the men we have."

"That sounds good to me. But why should I buy four stoves when I'm only going to have three buildings?"

"Joshua, a woman appreciates a warm bedroom on a cold winter night. She also appreciates the privacy of a closed door. We will get two large cook stoves for heating and cooking in the kitchen and your cabin. Then we will get a heating stove for the bunkhouse and a small room stove for the bedroom of your cabin. You are still planning to marry Sarita, no?" Fernando concluded with a chuckle.

"Oh. Yeah," Joshua responded, embarrassed that he hadn't thought of that.

A few minutes later Frank Smith came out on the porch to join them. "Joshua, Fernando," he said, "We'll be making our fall roundup the second week of October. It will probably take two weeks. Can we count on you two to help us?"

"Yes, Sir," Joshua said, enthusiastically.

"Of course," said Fernando. "It will do me good to work some cattle. Nathan can handle the freighting for a couple of weeks without me."

"Some of the ranchers say that cattle aren't worth the trouble and money it takes to hire a crew and do a round up this year." Frank said. "But we have ourselves and we have cattle so we are going to have a roundup. We'll find some place to sell them sooner or later."

The next few days were busy leveling the spots for the cabins. Amanda was very excited about the kitchen and the fact that she would have her very own quarters in it. It was proof that she had established a permanent home for herself on the ranch. The big house, as Joshua and Sarah's cabin was being referred to by the rest of the crew, was going to be in the same place it was originally planned. The kitchen would go next door to it on the north side and the bunkhouse would go on the north side of the kitchen. For the time being all the buildings would have dirt floors. Wood or stone floors would come later as the ranch prospered. Joshua would rather have the money in the bank to operate the ranch than luxuries for the time being. With three hired hands it cost him thirty-six dollars a month in wages alone to run the ranch. That didn't include supplies and improvements. At that rate the five hundred dollars he had kept from selling the first ten horses to the Army in June would be gone by spring if not before then. The money from selling his farm in Kentucky wouldn't last forever either.

By mutual agreement the big house went up first followed by the kitchen and finally the bunkhouse. A week and all three buildings were up. The big house was built using traditional horizontal log construction. Because of the shortage of large trees, the other two buildings were built in picket fashion so that smaller logs could be used. Enough lumber was brought in from the lumber mill in Georgetown to make doors and shutters and put plank roofs on the buildings and then shingles on top of those. Some things were worth the money it took to have them and Joshua believed good doors, shutters, and a good roof were worth paying for. He also kept his promise to have a seal board around the bottom and top of the kitchen and bunkhouse to help make the picket construction a little sturdier.

Luke was shown the loft of the cabin and Joshua explained to him that the loft was just for him. He smiled and moved his bedroll into the loft, spread it out and lay there smiling looking at the roof. Everyone else moved their bedrolls into their respective quarters. The tents were taken down and stored in the bunkhouse.

After some thought and encouragement from Fernando, Joshua decided to put stone floors in the cabins to bring his bride home to. He didn't want to bring her home to a dirt floor cabin after what she was used to. The stone was free from the San Gabriel except for the sweat and time it took to get it out. A local man with stone mason experience agreed to lay the stone for him for fifteen dollars per cabin. He helped Joshua select the stones from the river and then Joshua and Ramon used the mule to drag them out of the river and up to the house where the man smoothed them and shaped them and fit them into the floors.

After the cabins were built, Nathan and Joshua rode into Austin in the Studebaker to buy the stoves. Nathan told Joshua about his travels back and forth from Dallas to Trinidad and down to Waco, Austin, and Fredericksburg hauling supplies to the stores Dan had opened in each of those places. There were plans to build more forts further west and Dan was planning on opening a store and saloon at each one. In January he planned to open one in Jacksboro in North Texas. Nathan still hadn't found his brother but was confident that he would.

"I can feel it Mr. Joshua," Nathan told him. "He's around here somewhere I can feel it. I's gonna find him."

"How's the reading and writing coming along?" Joshua asked.

"Mr. Fernando has been helping me. He says I'm getting better all the time."

"I'm glad to hear it. It will be useful for you. I'm sure it already is."

"Yes, suh, it is. I's learning to talk Mexican from the other drivers. That helps too. I been thinking Mr. Joshua. When I finds my brother, if he wants to come with me he can ride right up here with me if he wants to. I got a mule and a hoss and two saddles that I ain't getting no use out of. I gots me this here good job too. I been putting my money in a bank account in Dallas. Mr. Fernando helped me open an account. Oh yeah, that reminds me. I had to have a last name to open the bank account so since I's driving a wagon for a living now I chose the last name of Wagoner. So I's officially Nathan Wagoner. What do you think?"

"It sounds like a good last name to me. I'm glad you picked out one that says something about you." Joshua told him.

"Thank you Mr. Joshua. Getting back to where I was headed before I sidetracked myself, I don't really need those animals. Would you buy my hoss and mule and them saddles and bridles? I wanted to save 'em 'til I found my brother but I can buy more later if I needs to."

"Sure, I'll buy them from you. Luke likes the mule and I can use the gelding too. I'll give you one hundred dollars for mule, horse, and tack."

"I'll take it. It's probably all together worth more than that but considering what I paid for it all, it ain't a bad little profit," Nathan said with a grin.

In Austin, they bought the stoves and got the supplies that Amanda had asked for. Joshua ordered a mattress for Luke and a good solid bed with a good quality mattress, a dresser with mirror, a wardrobe, a wash stand with porcelain bowl and water pitcher for their bedroom. He also ordered a cupboard for the big house and another for the kitchen. Thinking about what Fernando said about women and cold nights, Joshua decided to get another small room stove for Amanda. She could stay warm by using the cook stove for heat but Joshua reasoned that the smaller stove would use less wood to keep Amanda's room warm rather than trying to keep the whole kitchen warm with the cook stove. He and Ramon would make the rest of the furniture they would use in the house and elsewhere on the ranch.

Nathan suggested that Joshua buy sufficient pillow ticking so that the whole crew could use it to make straw or feather mattresses for themselves and Joshua and Luke wouldn't have to sleep on the floor either while they were waiting for the two store bought mattresses to come in. Joshua agreed and reached a little deeper in his pocket to pay for it. Setting up a comfortable home for his future wife and crew was not free. It seemed like he was spending more money every time he turned around and while it was all easily justified he kept thinking about how fortunate he was that he had the money from selling his farm and his Pony Express wages. He'd spent more than he'd made since he'd left Kentucky. The thought came to him too that it seemed like other people could always find more ways to spend his money than he could.

They went home the following day. Along the way they saw a few other settlers moving into the area with everything they owned in an ox cart pulled by a span of oxen or sometimes two or three span for the more prosperous ones. Some were Confederate veterans starting life over with nothing after the war. Others were former tenant farmers from the east looking for land of their own. Some were immigrants from across the sea and still others were leaving the life of city slums behind. Most of them were broke or very close to it having used all the money they had to get there. Joshua counted his blessings and was glad the freighting was bringing in some money because it would be a while before the ranch started paying for itself.

The tales that came back with the drovers who took cattle north in the spring were not encouraging. A few made a good profit. Some barely broke even. Some lost everything to angry settlers who didn't want the herds coming through because of Spanish Fever associated with Texas cattle. Mobs of masked men stampeded some herds to hell and gone. Other folks were swindled out of entire herds by accepting phony bank drafts for payment. Some were simply robbed at gun point before they could make it home with their hard earned money. Some hadn't been heard from since they left going north in the spring. All of them endured hardship and danger whether they made a profit or not.

On the way back from Austin they passed through Georgetown and had a meal at Consuela's. When Patricia asked about Pablo, Joshua told her of his death as gently as he could. Her pretty face went stone cold and her lower lip trembled. Silent tears fell from her eyes until the kitchen door closed behind her. Then they heard her begin to cry. They camped that night along the river rather than pay to stay the night in Georgetown.

Riding into the ranch the next day, Joshua exclaimed, "Wow! It's starting to look like a real ranch. It ain't fancy but by God it's mine!"

"Yes, suh, Mr. Joshua you got yo'self a fine start in life."

Amanda was so excited about having a real stove to cook on that she could hardly contain herself. After it was all set up she started cooking supper immediately. She was thrilled that it was a real cook stove designed for cooking and not just a heat stove that she would have to make do with. It even had a hot water tank on the stovepipe. She began talking excitedly about being able to bake and fry and stew all at the same time. She claimed it was the nicest stove she had ever seen. In the two hours from the time they set it up she had quite a meal ready for them.

The next thing on the agenda was to put up a corn crib, then harvest the garden and the corn. Amanda laid out the beans, peas, and onions on the table in the kitchen for them to dry then put them in bags she saved from the flour and other supplies they had bought. Then she hung the bags of dried vegetables on pegs along the wall of the kitchen. Ramon built a wooden bin along one wall of the kitchen to put the potatoes in. The corn was cut from the stalks and put in the crib. The stalks were left standing to dry out. Joshua figured the saddle stock Mustangs would eat the corn stalks like hay later in the winter. He once watched a Mustang eat a stick the size of his little finger. The corn stalks would be fine fair compared to that and it shouldn't founder them since they'd be working.

The first week of October Joshua and his crew went to town. Amanda hadn't seen a town in years and it had been months since Ramon and Javier had been there. Since his wagons were all being used for freighting they didn't have a wagon to carry supplies back to the ranch. So Joshua took four of the smaller geldings from the bachelor herd to town to trade. He traded the geldings and ten dollars for an ox cart and two span of oxen to pull it. Horse drawn wagons were more expensive and harder to come by as were harness horses and mules. Maybe next year he would graduate to the carriage trade class of society. The carriage trade was how the merchants referred to wealthy people who could afford the luxury of buggies, and carriages used strictly for traveling in comfort. For now the oxen and wagon known as an ox cart were the most hauling power he could get for the fewest dollars without taking his freight wagons away from making money.

Joshua paid for all the supplies and had Amanda pick out what she wanted. She got enough material for making matching curtains and a tablecloth for the kitchen. She picked out a set of candle molds so she could make candles, a hundred pound bag of flour, another of rice, fifty pounds of salt, twenty-five pounds of sugar, fifty pounds of coffee and a new coffee grinder. She also picked out a tin washbasin and water pitcher for the table she'd had Ramon build to set by the kitchen door. She also got a washtub and washboard for washing clothes.

For herself she bought women's undergarments and stockings and a simple pair of shoes to take the place of the deerskin moccasins she had made for herself. She bought a pattern and material to make herself another dress. She also got a winter coat.

Joshua restocked on ammunition for the Enfield and the shotgun that Amanda had put to good use. He picked up some tools, matches, and some tobacco for his pipe.

Ramon and Javier each bought a new set of clothes and a coat. Joshua replenished the ammunition for their pistols.

Luke got a new set of clothes, a coat and some candy and that was enough for him.

Once they made their purchases they headed back to the ranch. As they camped that night along the San Gabriel River Amanda looked up at the stars, "It'll be getting cold soon. I wish I had a couple of buffalo robes for my bed," she said.

"Yes, that would be nice," Ramon agreed. "But where would we get them?"

"Why don't we go on a buffalo hunt?" she asked. "We've got the corn and the garden gathered. The Comanche will soon be heading on to the reservation or deep into the plains to hole up for the winter. They have a huge canyon they use for winter quarters but only they know how to find it. I spent a winter there once but couldn't begin to find it now. I was completely lost when we got there. But we're only a couple of days ride from where we should find plenty of buffalo."

"Maybe we should do that," Joshua replied. "It sounds like fun. We could use the hides and I haven't had buffalo meat since before the war. We might even see a few more horses to catch."

"That would be good too," said Amanda. "I learned a lot in the three years I was with the Comanche. I know the best way to cure the hides and we can dry the meat to use it later."

"We'll plan to go after we help Mr. Smith with the fall round up," said Joshua.

Chapter Twenty Three; Real Freedom at Last

Sunday afternoon the J-G crew gathered at the Smith ranch. The roundup was discussed over supper and Fernando was present as promised. Frank, his boys and Fernando would go south for two day's ride, then work their way north pushing what cattle they found toward the center of the ranch then hold them half a day's ride west of the house. Joshua would take his crew a day's ride north of his homestead and push cattle south toward the Smith ranch. When the two herds met everyone would pitch in and work the cattle. They didn't want to go more than a full day's ride west because of the danger of Indians. Frank told them no amount of cattle was worth getting caught on the plains alone or in a pair by a bunch of bloodthirsty Comanche. If the soldiers were successful in pushing the Indians back on to the reservations they could look for more cattle further west in the spring or even next year.

That night while everyone else was asleep, Mary Louis was alone in her former slave quarters shack bathing from a washtub with flower scented soap she saved for these special occasions. The only light came from her small fireplace. The flames flickered when the door opened and closed swiftly and silently. "Hello," she said softly to her visitor. "I was hoping you wouldn't disappoint me."

"Have I ever failed to come when you left the signal for me my love?" a male voice responded from the shadows by the door.

"No, never, and that makes tonight that much harder," she said sadly. "I have to talk to you about something and it ain't easy."

"I think I know. But I must hear you say it," he said solemnly.

Rinsing the soap from her large naked breasts she stood and wrapped a makeshift towel around her well-made body that usually stayed hidden beneath her baggy servant's clothes. She walked over to him where he leaned against the wall. She laid her head on his shoulder as he wrapped his arms tenderly around her. She thought of how she would miss him after tonight. She breathed deep the smell of horses, leather, sweat, and gun smoke, with a trace of the lye soap he used to bathe every few days.

"I have a chance to marry and be respectable," she told him as silent tears began to fall. "I can't continue to see you like this and be a good wife to him. It would be wrong. What we have had has been wrong enough with our secret love and no hope of marriage. I can live with the memory of our love but I could not live as an adulterous wife. I'm asking you to make this easy for me and let me go knowing that you understand and wish me well."

"Ah, mi amore, we have always known this day would come when we would have to say adieu to our secret love. Though it will hurt my heart to see you with another, you may rest assured that the world will never know. No word or action of mine will ever give you cause for grief or shame. I love you too much to hold you back from this chance at the happiness you so desire. He is a good man and will treat you well or I would not let you go. I have but one request. Let us have this one last night together and you will have my blessing with the dawn. But for tonight, be my woman one last time." He bent his face toward hers as she looked up at him and he kissed away her tears.

"Yes," she whispered hoarsely as her strong fingers undid his gunbelt and the Walker Colt thumped to the dirt floor. "The dawn will come soon enough. Take your woman one last time," she wrapped her arms around his neck and kissed him fiercely as he swept her into his strong arms and carried her to the bed...

She woke before dawn as was her habit. Smiling sweetly with her eyes still closed she reached for him. As always the covers where he laid were still warm but he had gone as silently as he had arrived. She continued to smile as the tears came to her eyes. The combination of joy at her new beginning and the sadness of lost love were overwhelming and while she smiled with happiness, tears of grief streamed down her cheeks. She was a little late getting breakfast ready but if anyone noticed they didn't say anything. Her former lover smiled when she made sure he got the biggest piece of ham and his eggs were just the way he liked them.

The next two weeks were filled with long, dusty days in the saddle as they pushed the cattle together. It was slow work bunching the cattle and moving them in one direction together. The Smith clan worked together and everyone pitched in. When the branding, castrating, and sorting was done, the Smith steers were moved toward the ranch headquarters and the cows, calves, and bulls were left to disperse on their own.

Joshua's cattle were pushed toward his range. He had one hundred ninety head wearing his brand. Thirty-eight were full grown steers that would be ready for market in the spring. The rest were breeding stock or calves. While it paled by comparison to Frank Smith's thousands, it was a long way from what he'd started with in the spring. With natural increase and continuing to brand mavericks, he would do fine in time.

Chapter Twenty Four; Buffalo Hunt

By the time they got back to the J-G ranch, the nights were cold but the days were still warm. Then one night they got a frost. The next morning Amanda was excited and reminded Joshua that he promised them a buffalo hunt after the roundup. She told him that the frost would have most of the Comanche still on the plains headed for their winter home, whether it was their secret canyon or the reservation in the Territory. Now would be the time for their hunt. Joshua told them all to pick their best two horses, clean their guns, and pack the ox cart with a tent and two weeks worth of food. They would also need to rig up six pack saddles to help carry the meat and hides. The ox cart would only hold so much. They would leave in a couple of days when everything was ready. They would return in two weeks or when they had all the hides and meat they could carry. Joshua saddled his Kentucky stud knowing that he wanted to keep the buckskin fresh for the hunt and made a quick ride over to the Smith ranch to let them know he and the crew were going hunting so they wouldn't worry. He was back by nightfall and had Sarah's brother John with him. John said it sounded like fun and wanted to come along. Besides, who couldn't use a buffalo robe for their bedroll and another gun in Indian country was always welcome. Mrs. Smith reminded them that Thanksgiving was a few weeks away and that she would like the whole family together for it. She said even though it was a Yankee idea, taking a special day to give thanks was a good idea. Joshua and John assured her they would be back in time.

Two days later they set out headed northwest. They were all excited but the slow pace of the oxen kept them in check and the pace was easy on them all. Joshua had them spread out with the ox cart in the middle and the rest riding at the four points of the compass from it, but always within sight keeping an eye open for any signs of trouble or buffalo or wild horses. Luke took the responsibility of keeping the spare horses close to Amanda and the ox cart. They passed just southwest of the little community of Liberty Hill, Texas. By the fourth day they saw signs of buffalo. They found them on the fifth day alongside a small stream. Joshua stopped the group and pointed out to Amanda and Ramon where he wanted them to make camp.

The herd was so huge they couldn't see the end of it. Luke had never seen buffalo before and sat his horse wide eyed in wonder. Joshua rode up beside him and told him, "I want you to stay here with Ramon and Amanda and help them set up camp. Buffalo can be dangerous and I don't want you getting hurt," he told the boy. "You'll get your chance to kill buffalo when you get a little older but right now I want you to stay with Ramon and Amanda. That will keep three guns together in case we missed seeing some injun sign. Alright?"

Luke was disappointed and his shoulders slumped but he said, "Yes, Sir." Sometimes it was hard to be a good boy like he promised his mother he would be.

They would take the hunt Indian fashion, riding into the herd and killing as many as they could before their horses played out and the buffalo outran them. While their weapons were large caliber and used respectable powder charges, they had short barrels for use on horseback and were therefore intended for short range. They would need to be close to be the most effective. Taking his Spencer in hand

Joshua led John and Javier toward the herd. As they rode toward the herd he told them they would need to ride in close to the buffalo and shoot down into the space behind the shoulder trying for a heart or lung shot that would be fatal. Otherwise they would just make the buffalo mad resulting in a charging buffalo, which could get them hurt or killed.

The men spread out and rode toward the herd. Joshua was the only one with a repeating rifle so John and Javier would have to reload on the run or use their pistols. Joshua had heard of people killing buffalo with pistols but it usually took every shot in the gun.

Joshua was riding the buckskin gelding Sarah had given him. He touched the gelding lightly with his spurs and sent him right into the herd. John and Javier did the same. Joshua, riding with his knees and feet, steered the galloping gelding toward a big bull buffalo. By now the herd had started running too. Joshua spurred the gelding again and he caught up to the buffalo. Joshua could hear the buffalo breathing and smell him as he took the best aim he could from the running horse and pulled the trigger. The buffalo went down in a sliding heap and Joshua went after another one. This time he saw a cow buffalo. He steered the speeding gelding through the dust and made a poor shot. It was a hit but not where he wanted. The gelding had the idea now and moved in close to the cow buffalo. Joshua put a .50 bullet into her heart and lung cavity. She lumbered on a few more steps and then dropped.

The pounding hooves of the herd on the move almost drowned out the sound of the gunfire from John and Javier. The gelding was breathing hard but steady and Joshua went after another buffalo. The racing herd, the noise, the dust, and the gunfire were exhilarating. He brought down five buffalo with the seven shots from his rifle and decided that was enough for this run. He chose not to empty his pistols trying for more because then he'd be empty and vulnerable. John brought down three buffalo with three shots from the breech loading Sharps carbine he had brought back from the war and didn't use his pistol either. Javier brought down two buffalo; one with his musket and one with his pistol. His pistol was now empty. They were all excited and happy with the kill. Javier was a little sheepish when the two older men commented on the fact that he was now in injun country without a loaded gun. Remembering the death of his brother it was a lesson he took to heart.

The rest of the day was spent skinning and dressing the ten buffalo they had killed. The hides were stretched out and staked to the ground to dry. The choicest meat was carved from the carcasses and cut into thin strips to be cured by drying them over a fire the way Amanda learned to do it from the Comanche. That night they feasted on fresh buffalo tongue and buffalo hump.

They spent the next few days drying the meat and Amanda showed them how to work the hides to make them soft. She scraped them clean of pieces of flesh with a scraper made from a buffalo bone. Then she rubbed a mixture of buffalo brains and fat into them to keep them pliant and soft. She asked Joshua to gather the buffalo horns so she could use them to make spoons and ladles and such out of them when they got home. In a couple of days they started out again looking for more buffalo. They figured one more day like the last hunt and they should be ready to go home.

Two days later they found a smaller herd by following the creek they had camped on. This time Javier borrowed his grandfather's Sharps carbine so he didn't have to use his pistol or try to reload his big muzzle loading musket on horseback. Reloading the Sharps on horseback was easy; work the lever to open the breech, put in the paper cartridge, close the breech with the lever, put the carbine on half cock, put a musket cap on the nipple, bring the hammer to full cock and fire.

As they rode into the herd Joshua noticed there were a lot of prairie dog holes around and thought maybe this was not a good place for a horse and buffalo race. But then Javier cut loose with the Sharps and a buffalo went down. The rest of the herd began to move. Too late to worry about it now, so Joshua picked a buffalo and went after it. Riding with no hands again Joshua brought down the buffalo and went after another one. Just as he leaned into the shot and pulled the trigger, the galloping gelding sidestepped quickly to miss a prairie dog hole. Joshua's shot was poor and before he could regain his balance the gelding jumped another prairie dog hole and Joshua hit the ground with a thump. The gelding kept going caught up in the heat of the moment. Fortunately they were at the tail end of the herd or Joshua would have been trampled. With a shooting pain in his ribs and shoulder he heard a buffalo snort and then pounding hooves getting closer. Scrambling to his feet he saw the wounded buffalo charging straight for him.

"Aw, hell," he said. He had dropped his rifle in his fall and knew the pistol bullets would just bounce off the buffalo's skull making him madder. Joshua had no choice but to race the buffalo to the creek and hope he could get below the bank before the buffalo got him. Literally running for his life Joshua sprinted for the creek as fast as he could go. Joshua was puffing too hard to yell for help and didn't look over his shoulder for fear he'd trip and fall. He didn't see how close the wagon was or the fact that Amanda and Luke both shot at the buffalo chasing him. Feeling the nose of the beast against his back, Joshua made a dive for the creek bank. Barely making it over the edge he scrambled back against the bank. The buffalo followed him over the bank head first and landed in a pile in front of him stone dead.

Amanda and Luke came running up to the edge of the creek. They looked over it cautiously not sure of what they would see. The buffalo was dead in a heap and Joshua was on his hands and knees just trying to catch his breath. Ramon strolled up with a canteen in his hand. He slid down the bank to give Joshua a drink and help him up.

Smiling, he clapped Joshua on the back as he gulped from the canteen. "I had no idea that you were so fast Patron. Maybe you should enter the foot races at the next festival. I will bring the buffalo and we will all bet on you to win," he said with a chuckle. Joshua gave him a dirty look and Ramon laughed out loud.

Examination of the buffalo carcass showed one bullet high behind the ribs where Joshua's shot went when his horse moved out from under him. Another large caliber shot showed high in the shoulder, a third one in the flank. The fourth shot and the one that was fatal was the smaller hole through the heart from Luke's gun. Joshua grabbed the boy and hugged him telling him what a good shot he made and thanked him for saving his life. Luke was embarrassed at the attention. He just smiled and looked away.

John rode up leading Joshua's horse and Javier handed him back his Spencer. "I think that's the first time I've ever seen you run Yank," John said with a grin.

"First time it ever seemed like a good idea," Joshua responded. "How many did y'all get?"

"I got four and Javier got three before we saw you high-tailing it. Then I tried a shot at this one but was too far away to help you. You alright?"

"I'll be fine. My ribs hurt on my right side. I'm a little skinned up and winded but I'll be alright."

"Patron, let me feel your ribs," Ramon told him. After feeling of his ribs Ramon said, "You have a rib out of place señor. Lie face down and I will put it back in place for you. It will hurt for a moment then it will feel better."

Not sure about this, Joshua laid down on the ground and Ramon felt around, then suddenly pushed hard. The rib popped, Joshua grunted, then he felt better.

"What did you do?" asked Joshua.

"It is just something I learned from an old Jesuit priest when I was a young man. I was studying for the priesthood but then I met my wife and well, I didn't go into the priesthood," said Ramon.

That night they feasted again on fresh buffalo and everyone got their jokes in about Joshua outrunning the buffalo. They all complimented Luke on the shot that saved Joshua's bacon. They agreed that when the meat was dried and the hides were ready they would go home. The robes and best cuts of meat from nineteen buffalo should be enough for their needs with plenty left over. Joshua commented that they should be home in time to have Thanksgiving with their families.

Chapter Twenty Five; Hard Times

The Thanksgiving celebration at the Smith ranch was attended by the entire Smith family including the new Mrs. Jessica Smith and of course Luke, Joshua and Fernando. Nathan was there too but he ate in the kitchen with Mary Louise instead of the dining room with the family. Ramon, Amanda, and Javier visited Ramon's family at the Nava hacienda. When everyone was seated around the table, Mrs. Juanita Smith began listing all the things she was thankful for including the addition of Jessica and Luke to the family. She had taken a grandmotherly interest in Luke and made it known to all that she had taken him into her family Joshua or no Joshua. Then she surprised everyone when she good-naturedly commented that Joshua appeared to be making an industrious addition to the family even if he couldn't seem to stay on a horse.

After a huge meal the men retired to the porch to smoke and the talk turned to the politics of Texas. Jesse seemed the most discontented with the situation.

"It's like the damned carpet baggers are just trying to gouge us into doing something that they can put us in jail for. Rubbing our nose in it that they won the war." Jesse said in relation to all the Colored Troops being stationed in Texas. "Why just the other day I was in Georgetown and saw another bunch of them Colored Troops headed up from Austin. Do they really think them niggers is gonna stand up against the Comanche? I don't think so."

Not wanting to ruin a nice evening with an argument Joshua kept his thoughts to himself as he remembered the Colored Troops he saw during the war. They fought just as hard as their white counterparts. He understood why Jesse felt the way he did about the reconstruction government, but he disagreed with him about the Colored Troops. Many of the Union supporters from Texas had gotten into positions of authority with the new reconstruction government and were trying to enact laws and take action against their Confederate supporting neighbors for the way they themselves were hounded, hunted, persecuted, and sometimes killed for their support of the Union during the war. They remembered hiding out in the hills while their homes and crops were burned and their cattle stolen, all in the name of patriotism while the real patriots were off doing the fighting. It was a messed up situation and Joshua could see both sides but neither side was blameless and two wrongs didn't make a right.

Frank diverted the conversation to the current economy saying, "The past is the past and we have to leave it there if we're ever gonna get out of this mess. You're just gonna have to learn to live with the free Negros. What we need to figure out is what we're going to do with these cattle. The northern markets are unsure at best (the great railroad markets in western Kansas wouldn't open until late 1867 and weren't even a rumor at this point) and the local markets are flooded. I don't know if we should sell some of our land to immigrants to get back on our feet or not. What with free land available we won't get much for any land we do sell but we have to figure out something to get by."

"We did alright selling to those cattle buyers in the spring," said John. "We could do that again. It wasn't a lot of money but it helped. I'm not for trailing a herd north or anywhere else when we're as apt to lose it as to sell it. We ain't living high but we ain't hurting bad enough to take those kinds of risks."

"What have you got in the way of horses to sell?" asked Joshua.

"I hadn't really thought about it," Frank replied. "Why?"

"Well, I got that invitation to bid on contracts to sell horses to the army. The officers I sold the last ones to liked our horses. They usually like to buy a hundred or more at a time. I don't have enough to do that but if you have enough that meet the requirements we could go together and make a hundred. I could go to Waco to see the Captain and find out when they're taking bids on the next contract and put in a bid for us. We'd probably make more money per horse than per cow but the horses will take more work. They'd have to be broke to ride if they ain't already. We'll need to bid low to get the contract but I figure if we go for seventy-five or eighty dollars a head we could probably get the bid since they know the quality of our horses."

"That's an idea," said Frank. "What do you boys think?" he asked Jesse and John. "We've got the horses but they'll have to be broke and you'll be the ones doing most of it. My old bones won't take it like they used to."

"I don't like the idea of selling horses to the same army I just spent four years fighting, but if you say we should do it I'll do what you say," Jesse told him. "I reckon if they're going to chase the Comanche or be chased by them, they should be well mounted either way."

"It don't bother me none," John said. "We ain't got much else to do until spring roundup anyway. We might as well break some horses. It'll be something to do. If we don't get the bid we can still use them or sell 'em to a drover or somebody for whatever we can get in the spring."

"What do you think Fernando? Do you want in on it?" asked Frank.

"I think it is a good idea but I am going to stick with the freighting this winter. I have discovered that I enjoy the company I keep in Dallas and I'll probably stay there through the winter. I can throw some horses into the deal but I'm not interested in riding rough stock anymore. That is for younger men than me," said Fernando.

"I'll head out for Waco the day after tomorrow and see what I can find out. If I can get us the contract I'll buy twenty-five head of broke geldings from you at fifty dollars each payable to you when we get paid by the Army." Joshua said.

"Fifty dollars each for twenty-five head is fair enough since you'll be doing all the work and you have the invitation to bid," Fernando replied.

"That leaves seventy-five head for us to put together," Frank said. "Boys, can we put seventy-five head together?"

"I'm sure we can," Jesse responded. "We may have to break a few to get that many but like John said, we ain't got much else to do until spring anyway."

"Frank, Joshua," called Juanita, "Come inside please we need to talk about wedding plans. We've only got six months left and there are arrangements to be made."

"Well, gentlemen," said Frank. "I believe that is a request that is best honored. Joshua," he said standing. "If you'll join me."

"Yes, Sir," Joshua answered with a grin as he stood and followed Frank inside.

Meanwhile, back in the kitchen Mary Louise and Nathan were talking as he helped her with the dishes. "When we finish here," he said, "I got something for you out in the wagon."

"Really?" she asked in genuine surprise.

"Yep," he said. "It ain't much really but I wants you to have it."

"I'm sure it's wonderful. Let's go see it now. These dishes will wait."

Taking her by the hand he led her out the back door and around to the barn where the wagon was. Climbing up, he reached in and pulled out a sidesaddle. "It ain't a new one but I hopes you like it. I sold my hoss and mule to Mr. Joshua to get the money for it."

"Oh Nathan," she said. "I don't know what to say; my own sidesaddle. I...well, I...I never expected to have one."

"I thought 'bout how you was riding that old Mexican saddle with your leg wrapped around the horn and decided that my woman should be able to ride like a real lady since you is one."

"Oh Nathan, I think that is the most thoughtful gift anyone has ever given me. So is that how you think of me; as your woman, as a real lady?"

Placing his hands on her shoulders he looked her in the eyes and said, "Yes Ma'am. I reckon I do. You been on my mind all summer and I want to marry you if you'll have me. Will you?"

"Yes, I'll marry you Nathan Wagoner. I think you'll make a fine respectable husband and I'll make you a fine respectable wife." With that she wrapped her arms around his neck and kissed him like he'd never been kissed before. "You won't be sorry," she said.

"Frank," Juanita said as Frank and Joshua sat on the sofa next to Sarah. "You will have to accompany Sarah and me to San Antonio to see the Padre. Our daughter will be married in a Catholic ceremony by a priest and we need to make the arrangements in advance. I'd love for her to be married in the Catholic Church too but since we don't have one here, we'll have the wedding here at the ranch if we can't get the Presbyterians in Georgetown to let us use their church. It will be easier to bring the priest to the wedding than to take the wedding to the priest. Frank, I'm sure you and the boys can persuade him to make the trip one way or another so I won't worry about that and I'll just plan for the priest to be here. I heard what Joshua said about going to Waco and I approve. It's a good idea. In the meantime, I want us to leave for San Antonio the day after tomorrow."

"Joshua, while you're passing through Georgetown I want you to see about using the Presbyterian Church for the wedding. If you have to join the Church to make it happen it won't hurt you.

"Now let's talk about this courtship young man. I understand that you have been working hard to establish yourself and that is respectable. However, it is my opinion that you have fallen short on the courtship end of this arrangement. She won't tell you that but I will."

"Ma'am?" asked Joshua a little stunned. He looked at Sarah who smiled sweetly but nodded her head in agreement.

"Young man, you only live half a day's ride from here, less than that on a fast horse. You have fast horses if you can stay on them and you have not been making regular visits to see the woman you profess to love. I'll not stand for it any longer. From now until the wedding you will be here bathed and presentable to court my daughter properly every Saturday without fail and you will accompany us to church service on Sunday. Showing up and riding a bronc or hunting with Frank or the boys doesn't count. You will spend this time with Sarah Lynn. Do I make myself plain?"

"Yes, Ma'am," he said.

"You will always be accompanied by me, Jessica, or Mary Louise. You are not to be out of sight alone. We'll not have a repeat of the barn incident. Is that understood?"

"Yes, Ma'am."

"We will expect you to stay for supper on Sunday nights and if riding home in the dark leaves you tired on Monday that is a small price to pay for the love of my daughter."

"Yes, Ma'am."

"Do you have any questions?"

"What day of the week is today?" he asked.

Two days later Joshua, Fernando, and Nathan rode into Georgetown on their way to Waco. Luke stayed at the Smith ranch being spoiled by the women and eating Mary Louise's cookies. Fernando had agreed to wait in Waco with Joshua until he got an answer on his bid. If Joshua got the bid Fernando would send a letter with Joshua to his Segundo telling him to sell twenty-five geldings of Joshua's choice to Joshua for fifty dollars each payable after Joshua sold the horses to the Army.

Since they stayed overnight in Georgetown, Joshua looked up the preacher of the Presbyterian Church and asked him about using the church for a wedding. The pastor was not sure what his congregation would say about a Catholic wedding in their church. After a long discussion it was agreed that if Joshua and the entire Smith family joined the Presbyterian Church they could have the wedding there as a benefit of membership. If Joshua wanted a priest to perform the wedding to keep his bride and in-laws happy, well the pastor understood. However, the Reverend made it plain that he would expect to see Joshua and the Smiths regularly for services.

By late afternoon five days later, Joshua had a reply to his bid. He had a contract for 100 head of horses to be delivered to Captain Nelson in Waco for inspection on or about April 1st at the price of seventy-eight dollars per head for each horse accepted by the Army.

Back at the Smith ranch Jesse and John were glad to get the news and they started planning to round up the horses they had on the range. Most of their ranch bred and raised gelding were green broke as two and three year olds according to the custom of the area. Then they were turned loose and rounded up for use as needed. This method usually meant that someone had to ride the rough off of them to get them in working condition whenever they were to be used. In two weeks they brought in ninety horses to work with. Some of them had been ridden and some hadn't. The idea behind the ninety horses was that they would take more horses with them than the contracted amount in case some of the horses didn't make the cut.

Joshua took Javier and Luke with him to Fernando's. They selected twenty-five broke geldings. It wasn't as easy as Javier thought it would be. While all ranchers had horses and some ranchers had lots of horses, that didn't mean that all those horses fit the Army requirements. The Army wouldn't accept mares, the very young, the old, the too short, the too tall, or pintos, or the spotted Nez Perce horses of the North West. Only about one quarter of Fernando's horses met the Army requirements and Joshua disqualified some of those for conformation, injuries, or attitude. By the time the selection was done Joshua had the cream of Fernando's crop. Joshua assigned six horses each to Ramon, Javier, and Luke. They rotated the horses riding a different one every day so that all six were rode at least one day a week until the time came to sell them. Joshua took the seven roughest horses for himself and turned his J-G horses out for the winter.

Joshua's crew used the horses on their daily rides to check on cattle and the horse herds. Since Joshua had three studs he kept three separate herds of horses. It was a constant task to keep up with the cattle and the horses and keep them from wandering too far from the home range. Sometimes they had to rope a calf and doctor it. This usually required roping the mother cow too to keep her from attacking the cowboy on the ground working with the calf. There were days when they had to pull a cow out of a soft spot in the river. There was always something that needed to be done. Sometimes it was just as simple as pushing the livestock a little closer to home.

Every Saturday without fail Joshua and Luke rose before the sun and went off to the Smith ranch with the first light of dawn. Joshua really enjoyed the time with Sarah and wondered why he didn't think of it himself. One Sunday morning he started chuckling to himself on the way to church.

"Is there something funny about going to church young man?" asked Mrs. Smith.

"No Ma'am. I'm just glad you came to the idea on your own. I was trying to figure out the right time to tell you that I had to commit the whole family to attending on a regular basis in order get the preacher to go along with us using the church and having a Catholic priest involved in the ceremony. The preacher said if we were a large part of the regular congregation that we'd have no trouble having the wedding there and we could do the ceremony however you wanted to do it."

"Well I guess that settles the matter," said Mrs. Smith. "I knew you could talk them into it."

Chapter Twenty Six; Christmas

Christmas at the Smith ranch was celebrated by a large lunch on Christmas Eve attended by all the Smith family including Mr. and Mrs. Smith, Jesse and Jessica, John, Luke, Sarah and Joshua. The gift exchange took place after the meal and young Luke made out like a bandit. Mr. and Mrs. Smith gave Luke a complete new set of clothes. John and Jessica gave him a new hat. Mary Louise knitted him two pair of socks. Sarah gave him a pair of boots she had made for him in San Antonio and Joshua gave him a pair of spurs. "I want you to wear your new clothes when we all go to church together," Mrs. Smith told Luke.

Then it came time for Sarah and Joshua to exchange gifts. Sarah gave Joshua a new pair of decoratively carved open top holsters that she had made for him in San Antonio. He gave her the bottle of perfume that he had bought for her in Memphis. The only chance

174

they had to be alone was when they walked out on the porch after dark with Jessica as their chaperone. Jessica claimed a chill was in the air and went back inside for the time it took to get her coat from her room. Sarah and Joshua were silently grateful as they quickly tasted the fire of long, loving, passionate kisses.

Out behind the house in Mary Louise's quarters, Nathan and Mary Louise had a gift exchange of their own. She had hand stitched him a new set of clothes from the material Joshua gave her. She had become quite the tailor over the years and the fit was close to perfect. Nathan was very pleased. He gave her a new store bought dress. It was the first new store bought anything she had ever owned. All her life she had been adequately dressed but it was either something homemade or a hand-me-down. A new store bought dress was something she had only dreamed about.

"I bought it a little bigger than I thought you really is," Nathan told her nervously. "I thought if I was wrong and it was too big you could take it in but if'n I was wrong and it was too little you wouldn't be able to let it out."

"You did just fine," Mary Louise told him as she smiled. "You did just wonderful."

Later that evening after he had helped her clean the kitchen, Nathan started to leave to go sleep in the wagon like he usually did. Mary Louise took his hand however and silently led him to her quarters.

December 24, 1866, Dallas, Texas

Fernando and Luella were having a quiet dinner at the small house she had built. She was dressed in a dark red, off the shoulder dress with black lace accents. Her long blonde hair was fashionably put up showing her neck and shoulders to full advantage. The dress was tight where it should be while remaining respectably modest.

Fernando was wearing a new black pin stripe suit with a black silk tie, all of which he purchased just for this occasion. The local hatter cleaned and blocked his hat and there was a fresh shine on his boots. His mustache was trimmed and waxed and his hair recently trimmed.

The little house was lit with candles on the table and in the windows as Luella and Fernando enjoyed the meal prepared and served for them by the Negro couple Luella employed for cooking and cleaning. Luella and Fernando had been seeing a lot of each other over the past couple of months. During the course of their business, the attraction that had been immediate the moment they had looked into each other's eyes, had grown. For the first time since the death of his wife, Fernando was seriously considering the idea of marriage. Of course he hadn't said that out loud to anyone.

He wondered where tonight would lead. He'd heard the rumors that Luella had been a high dollar prostitute in Cincinnati and New York. It bothered him a little but he was pleased that she had left that life behind. Her beauty took his breath away. He reluctantly admitted that she was just as beautiful as Maria. Her laughter was like music to his ears. Her smile warmed him inside in places that had been cold and dead for over fifteen years. There had been one woman who had eased his pain and who he had cared for very much, but their forbidden love was a secret memory known only to the two of them.

Luella's conversation was much more interesting than that of most women of the frontier. Being well read and having traveled a bit in high political settings as well as being a business woman, she was able to discuss topics that most frontier women wouldn't begin to know anything about. He could understand why a man who wanted to impress dignitaries and business associates would be willing to pay a princely sum to have her on his arm at an important affair. She fascinated him and made his blood race through his veins.

Luella on the other hand was enjoying the attention. The idea that this man enjoyed her company simply for the sake of her company was new to her. The men in her past had enjoyed her company too, but for them it was all a preliminary to make them feel like they were more than just another paying customer before she gave them what they had really wanted. For her, the dinners, the plays, the social functions, and occasional gifts had been a way for her to feel like she was more than just a whore. But in the end she always knew that the money and the lifestyle would all go away if she didn't take those men to her bed before she sent them home; just as they knew they weren't getting into her bed for free. She had accepted the reality that she'd done what she'd needed to do to survive and provide for her younger brother in a world where a woman's options were limited.

With Fernando things were different. She didn't need his money and could honestly enjoy his company. He made her feel like she really was special. He treated her like a lady and had never asked her for sexual favors even though she could tell that it had been on his mind. She knew he had heard rumors about her past, something like that was hard to keep a secret for very long, but it hadn't run him off and he hadn't treated her like a whore. Looking at him across the table all cleaned up and handsome, she wondered where the night would lead because she really didn't know.

Chapter Twenty Seven; Nathan and Mary Louise

January was cold and rainy in Texas, as usual. Sometimes a hard, cold wind would come out of the North and make it will feel like there was nothing between Texas and the Canadian border but a split rail fence and somebody had kicked it down. Mix that with a driving rain and it made for a wet, nasty, miserable day. It was just that kind of day as Nathan hunched in his coat calling out encouragement to the Norman horses as they plodded their way through the muddy streets of Fredericksburg, Texas. It had been a hard trip and he was looking forward to sitting next to a warm stove as he pulled up in front of the store.

Getting down from the wagon seat he walked up the steps into the store. "What do you want boy?" asked the clerk behind the counter.

"My name is Nathan. I's wagon master for three wagonloads of goods from Mr. Dan Jones for you. Now we's cold, wet, tired, and hungry and so's our hosses. We need some help bringing in the goods or we can set them in the street. Which you want us to do?" asked Nathan with a hard look in his eyes.

"I suppose it would be the Christian thing to do, to have the stock boy help you," the clerk said with a shake in his voice. He was not accustomed to being spoken to that way by a black man or to seeing a black man openly wearing a gun. "But you better watch your mouth boy or it will get you in trouble." Nathan looked him in the eye and the clerk turned nervously away. "Jim Bob, come out here and help unload these wagons." A teenage white boy came out of the back of the store and quietly put on his coat to help Nathan. Thirty minutes later the wagons were unloaded and Nathan drove away to the wagon yard with the other teamsters right behind him.

At the wagon yard they put the horses in stalls with hay and grain after watering them. Then they brushed the horses down, and cleaned out their hooves. Next, they wiped down the harness as best they could. By the time each driver had taken proper care of his six horses they were all beginning to warm up a little. They put their coats and hats back on and had supper at a diner that would serve Mexicans and Negroes. The food was basic but it was hot and filling and the coffee was hot and strong.

Back at the stable the three men shared a half pint of bourbon between them before they replenished the hay and grain for the horses and watered them one more time before turning in for the night. It had been a long day. The warmth of their bedrolls was welcome. Nathan drifted off to sleep with thoughts of a clean one room shack with a warm fire, a good meal, and a strong but tender woman. He slept well.

Three days later Nathan knocked on the door of the little shack that had been in his dream. "Welcome back," Mary Louise said to Nathan as she let him in. "I been worried about you what with all this weather."

"I feel like I been chilled to the bone for a week," Nathan told her. "I was hoping we could stay for a day or two and rest the hosses. I asked Mr. Smith and he said it would be fine with him so we'll be here for a couple of days."

"I'm glad," she said. "I'll build up the fire then make you some hot coffee and something to eat. Pull that chair up close to the fireplace and get out of those wet clothes. I'll get you a blanket to wrap up in."

A few minutes later Nathan was wrapped in a warm blanket sitting next to the fire as Mary Louise was hanging his clothes up to dry. "Lord, Lord," she said. "I see I'm gonna have to do some patching on these clothes. I can't have my man running around with his unmentionables showing through. I'll patch 'em up nice and neat for you. I can't have some other woman thinking you don't have somebody to take care of you. You're gonna be here for a couple of days you said, so I'm gonna wash and mend these clothes for you. Next time you come I want you to bring me some material so I can make you another set of clothes. I figure a working man should have at least three sets of clothes; one on his back, a second clean set in his bedroll, and another set at home waiting on him."

That night she fed him chicken and dumplings with beans and cornbread and insisted on heating water for him to bathe with. When he finished, she went to the well and got fresh water to heat. Then she bathed with her flower scented soap by the firelight and got a quiet thrill from the hungry look in Nathan's eyes as he watched her from his chair by the fire. It was way up into the night before their hunger for each other was satisfied and they slept soundly wrapped in each other's arms. The next morning he was still in bed next to her and she smiled to herself as she watched him sleep.

Chapter Twenty Eight; Educating Luke

Joshua and Luke rode into Georgetown on a Saturday afternoon in February with the Smith clan. Joshua was able to convince Mrs. Smith that they should go into town on Saturday this time and go to church together on Sunday. They got a room at the only hotel in town.

The town folks were a little less hostile now. Joshua had been spending hard currency when he came to town and that went a long way in a cash poor economy. The only time he'd bartered for anything was when he had traded the geldings for the oxen and ox cart. Even then he had put a small amount of cash with it.

He also hadn't rubbed their nose in it that the Union won the war, or used his status as a Union Veteran to get a government job, or position of authority to lord it over them. They all knew he could have with the Reconstruction Government in power. He treated people fairly and only asked the same from them. Having the reputation of a hard bargainer wasn't the same as being a cheat, and while he'd driven some hard bargains, no one doubted his honesty, fairness, or courage. They might not like him, but they were beginning to respect him.

Joshua and Luke went into Parker's General Store to look around. Mrs. Parker was home visiting with the Smith women and Mr. Parker was tending the store. He was not quite as sentimental as Mrs. Parker and didn't let Joshua's war record get in the way of business. A cash paying customer was always welcome.

Mr. Parker took notice of Luke's rifle. The boy kept it with him all the time and was obviously very proud of it. "Can I see your rifle son?" Mr. Parker asked Luke.

Luke looked at Mr. Parker suspiciously but handed him the rifle when Joshua nodded that it was alright. "Hum, nice rifle, well made, handles good too," said Mr. Parker as he put the rifle to his shoulder and sighted in on a spot on the floor, without putting his finger on the trigger. Looking at, but not into the muzzle of the gun he said, "I'd say a .32 caliber by looking. Am I right?"

Luke nodded his head. "Luke, how old are you?" asked Mr. Parker.

"Twelve I think," said the boy.

"Well now," said Mr. Parker glancing at Joshua. "If Mr. Granger doesn't mind, I may have just the thing to go with this fine rifle."

"It depends on what it is whether I'll mind or not," Joshua said cautiously. "What do you have?"

"Well, I took this in on trade the other day for a new Colt revolver," Mr. Parker said as he reached under the counter and pulled out a pistol in a homemade holster. "It's a .32 caliber Allen and Thurber Pepperbox Revolver. I was thinking it would be just the thing to go with a .32 caliber Kentucky rifle. Granted, it's a smoothbore and best at close range but a pistol is a short range gun anyway. What with him riding the range and doing man's work on the ranch it's only fitting that he be armed with a pistol like the other men in case the Comanche, or some of the bandits running loose over in the hill country happen to ride up on him; and this one will use the same size balls as his rifle."

"Let's have a look at it," Joshua told him. Luke watched quietly but with wide eyed interest as Joshua took the revolver from Mr. Parker. The pistol showed wear on the finish from being carried in the holster but the gun functioned well and all six of the five inch long barrels were smooth and rust free. Someone knew how to take care of the gun.

The Allen and Thurber was stamped with a patent date of 1837. In the beginning of the revolver age, there were several makers of pepperbox pistols of various sizes, number of barrels, and calibers. They gave Colt, Remington, and Smith and Wesson some competition. But rotating cylinders eventually became more popular than rotating barrels and production of pepperboxes declined. That didn't make them any less effective though. A .32 caliber bullet was as deadly from a revolving barrel as it was from a revolving cylinder. It would be slow to reload but it would be five more shots than with the rifle alone with the hammer down on an empty barrel.

Joshua reached in the leather shoulder bag, called a possibles bag, on Luke's shoulder. He pulled out a .31 caliber round ball and the .01" thick patch that made up the .32 caliber rifle bullet and tried it on the pepperbox barrels. Since the pepperbox barrels were loaded from the front like the rifle, the patched ball formed a tight fit on all six barrels like it did on the rifle. "You got a ramrod and powder flask along with the holster for this thing?"

"Yes, sir, right here. I even have the bullet mold that came with the gun." Mr. Parker said as he reached under the counter and laid the items out for them.

"What do you think Luke?" asked Joshua as he handed the boy the pistol. Luke handled the pistol for a bit and then shook his head yes. "If I get this for you, you will have to be careful with it. I'll show you how to use it but you only shoot it when you need to protect yourself or someone else. Only practice when a grown up is with you. Understand?"

"Yes, sir," Luke said with a serious look.

"How much do you want for it?" Joshua asked Mr. Parker

"For him I'll cut you a deal. How about six dollars?"

"How about three dollars?" Joshua countered. "My Spencer only cost twelve."

"I'll meet you at five dollars for the whole set up and I'll throw in a belt for the holster." said Mr. Parker.

"You've got a deal."

"A deal it is," said Mr. Parker.

As Mr. Parker was getting a belt to go with the pistol Joshua told Luke, "We'll keep this in your saddlebags while we're in town. You can wear it when we're on the trail or at home. While we're in town you keep it in the saddlebags. We don't want people to think you're looking for trouble."

"Yes, sir," Luke said as he took the bundle from Mr. Parker with a huge smile on his face. "Thank you, Mr. Parker."

"You're welcome Luke," Mr. Parker told him.

Later that evening Joshua and Luke met Sarah and her family at a restaurant for supper. The Smiths were spending the night with the Parkers. They would all meet at church in the morning.

At church the next morning, everyone was in their Sunday best. Joshua and Sarah sat next to each other with her parents on either side. Luke sat next to Mrs. Smith and fell asleep against her during the service. After the service they had lunch at the Parker's house. Mrs. Parker's attitude toward Joshua was still cold but her food was hot and tasty. After lunch Joshua and Luke went to their hotel room and changed into their trail clothes while the Smith clan did the same at the Parker house.

On the way out of town Luke reached into his saddlebags and pulled out the pepperbox. "Mrs. Smith, look what Joshua got me!" he said excitedly as he handed it to her. Mrs. Smith frowned quickly at Joshua from her seat in the buggy. She unwrapped the belt from around the holster to pull out the pepperbox.

"Oh My Goodness," she said. "This is a real pistol. Joshua, are you sure he's old enough for this?"

"Yes, ma'am, he says he's twelve and he handles a man's work on the ranch already. He's proven himself capable and safe with the rifle. Besides that, it shoots the same ammunition as his rifle."

"I agree with Joshua," said Frank. "The boy handles his share of the work and he's good with the rifle. As long as we keep an eye on him and we teach him right he'll be fine."

"Well, I seem to be out-voted," Mrs. Smith said with a cold smile. "It is a nice gun Luke. Please be careful. I'd hate for you to have an accident with it."

"Yes, ma'am," he said happily as she handed it back to him. He wrapped the belt around his waist, blissfully unaware of the hard disapproving looks Mrs. Smith gave Joshua and her husband.

That evening at the Smith ranch Mrs. Smith pulled Joshua off by himself to have a talk with him. "I'm concerned about Luke," she began. "I know this is a rough country and he needs to be proficient with weapons as well as a rope and horses and cattle in order to survive here so I won't even try to talk you out of the pistol you gave him. But the boy needs an education in addition to the things you are teaching him. Your mother taught you to read, write, and do your figures. I taught my children. Who is teaching Luke these things?"

Joshua hung his head. "Nobody," he said. "We've all been so busy working cattle and horses, putting up the buildings and such that it just doesn't get done. It seems like the work never ends. Luke stays right in there with us doing all he can. He's a quick study and a good hand for his size. It's almost like he's a little man even though he still don't talk much. He doesn't have time to be a boy for the all the work that needs doing."

"That's what I thought," Mrs. Smith said softly. "I know you want to do right by the boy so I want you to leave him here with me until after the wedding. That way I can start teaching him to read and write and to do arithmetic. When you and Sarah marry this summer, you can have him back and she can continue his lessons. I've come to care for him and I want the best for him too. I know you mean well giving him the pistol. It just brought home to me how uncivilized his upbringing has been to this point. I don't fault you, mind you. You took him in when he had nothing and no one. I know you're doing your best. You're a man and you do man's work well so that is what you're teaching him. There are just times when a woman needs to step in to make sure the children have a civilizing influence. The Good Lord knows children tend toward being heathens naturally but civilizing takes some help and a woman's touch."

"I'll think on it," said Joshua. "If you don't mind us sleeping in the bunkhouse, we'll stay the night and I'll give you an answer in the morning."

"Fair enough," she said as she laid a hand on his shoulder almost tenderly. Then the firmness that he was used to came back and she squeezed his arm. "Mind you, if I catch you snooping around Sarita's bedroom window I'll shoot you dead myself."

"Yes, ma'am," Joshua said with a chuckle. "I wouldn't expect anything less."

"Now go on and think about how much good it will do Luke to leave him here for me to tend to," she said softly.

The next morning Joshua rode back to his ranch alone. Mrs. Smith convinced Luke to stay by telling him she needed another man around the house when her husband and boys were out and about and then bribed him with Mary Louise's cookies.

The ride back to his ranch was a lonely one. Joshua was surprised how the quiet of the cabin affected him. Luke had been his shadow for so long now that it just didn't feel right when the boy wasn't there. Joshua reflected in the quiet that night about how much Luke had come out of his shell with the work, love, and attention he had received. There had been minor discipline problems but a scolding usually fixed whatever it was. The poor child was so eager to please and seemed to have an underlying fear of being abandoned if he misbehaved.

Joshua was glad that Mrs. Smith had taken to Luke the way she had. He was sure that she would be a good influence on him. She might be hard as a flint arrowhead at times but Joshua knew that she had a fine heart and would give the dress off her back to someone in real need. Luke would be better off for her influence in his life.

Chapter Twenty Nine; Spring

Joshua and the rest of the crew continued to work cattle, hunt, and scout for mustangs. They had seen some mustang sign; they came across occasional tracks of unshod horses. None of the tracks were deep enough to indicate a rider and never more than three or four to a bunch but Joshua was hopeful that they would spot another good sized herd soon. He knew there were more herds further west but he wasn't ready to go west to catch any until after he sold the ones he had to the Army.

One morning when Joshua, Ramon, and Javier were riding the range together, Javier saw a group of five mustangs grazing about five hundred yards away. Rather than try some elaborate plan Joshua shook out a loop in his rope, put spurs to the buckskin and took off toward the mustangs. With nothing to lose Ramon and Javier took off right behind him. As Joshua closed in, he saw there were three mares in foal, a yearling and a stud. They were average sized mustangs in the 13 to 14 hand range with the stud being maybe just a little bigger than the rest.

When the mustangs heard the three cowboys closing in on them they sprinted in the other direction. Joshua was impressed that they went from standing still to full speed in two jumps. The buckskin was breathing hard and strong, showing no signs of slowing down. Joshua yelled over his shoulder to Ramon and Javier, "Catch whatever you can," and touched the spurs to the buckskin again. Joshua wasn't really interested in the stud since all of the mares were in foal, which would be sort of a two for one deal. One of the shorter mares fell behind and Joshua passed her thinking correctly that Javier or Ramon would pick her up. Joshua knew he was riding the best horse of the three of them and he'd push the buckskin as long as he didn't show signs of hurting. Another pregnant mare, this one a little past her prime, fell behind and Joshua passed her too. The buckskin was going strong so he figured he'd take the next one he caught up to. The next one to give out was a sorrel mare about ten years old and barely 14 hands. Joshua tossed his loop around her neck and took three dallies around the saddle horn. The buckskin slid to a stop, that caused the mare to swap ends and she went down but came up fighting the rope.

Joshua knew the buckskin could hold her but he wished he had brought a second loop with him. Without the second loop to rope her feet Joshua didn't know how he would get her hobbled or if he could get her back to the ranch without it. Suddenly the mare went down. She'd choked herself out. Joshua heard her ragged breath and jumped from the saddle sprinting to the end of the rope. Kneeling quickly on the mare's head he loosened the rope enough for her to breathe and jumped back away from her. She got to her feet and fought again. The buckskin squatted and held her. Joshua got the hobbles he kept with him out of the saddlebags. The second time she choked herself to the ground Joshua hobbled her front feet before he loosened the rope.

Joshua rode back to Javier and Ramon who were also leading their mares back to the ranch in hobbles. Everyone was pleased with their catch. Back at the ranch they took the mares into one of the corrals. They quickly built a fire and branded the mares then put hay in the corral for them and filled the water trough.

Not bad for a quick, spur of the moment catch. Three mares in foal, assuming all went well that was six more horses. It was still a good catch, but not a way to increase the herd quickly or with the best stock. Joshua was glad Sarah wasn't there or she'd try to get him to ride these mares too.

The shortest mare was just 13 hands, a bay, with good conformation but she had a head like a brick. She looked to be three or four years old. She still had a couple of years to grow. If Joshua kept her up and poured the feed to her she might get a little taller. That would probably be more trouble than it was worth, he decided.

The second mare they caught was a dun color, reddish tan with a dark line down her back and dark stripes on her legs. She had a nice head and decent conformation but she was probably upwards of fifteen years old. About the only thing she would be good for was breeding because trying to break a mustang that old to ride would be like playing Russian roulette every time you got in the saddle. She might not try to kill you today but there was always tomorrow.

The sorrel mare that Joshua caught was about ten years old and 14 hands. She had a little bit of a ewe neck but the rest of her was fine. At her age he wasn't going to break her either. He smiled to himself remembering how he had told Nathan he'd sell anything under 14 hands. The reality was he needed all the mares he could get regardless of size until he got a substantial foal crop every year. Even though the army wouldn't buy the shorter geldings, he could use those for ranch work and sell them to locals or to drovers taking cattle to market who needed more horses for their remuda.

A few days later, after pulling the same cow out of the same spot in the river for the third time in a week, Joshua decided that after she had the calf she was carrying, he would sell her to the first cattle buyer to come along. A cow dumb enough to get stuck in the same spot three different times in a week was more trouble than he wanted to deal with and would most likely get herself killed sooner or later anyway. If he could keep the stupid heifer alive until spring he'd sell her. If he couldn't sell her, well, it would be nice to have some beef to eat. Most cattlemen, Joshua included, would rather eat wild game, pork, chickens, even sheep or goats, than to eat their own beef. It just went against the grain to eat what you could sell. But in this case, as he flipped his rope off her horns again, he thought the meat would be particularly tasty.

March brought a break in the weather. Everyone and everything felt young and full of life with the first breath of spring, including Mr. Smith. "Be careful Papa," Sarah told her father as he swung into the saddle on the green broke bronc. Jesse and John had gotten the horse to the point that he could be ridden about half the time by an experienced rider but he was by no means safe. Frank figured as a more experienced horseman than his sons, he might be able to work the kinks out of the horse. "Don't you want to lunge him first to take the edge off him Papa?"

"Honey, I'll be fine," Frank said. "It's been a long time since a horse has been able to put me in the dirt. I've been riding for over 40 years and I doubt this ole hammerhead has any tricks I haven't seen before."

"All the same I wish you'd lunge him first," Sarah said.

"That's fine for you ladies but it ain't the cowboy way," Frank said with a smile as he turned the horse out of the corral and toward the open plain. Frank wasn't even out of sight before the bronc went to bucking and spinning. Frank sat up tall knowing his daughter was watching and rode the hammerhead as easy as if he was sitting in the rocking chair on the porch. Then Frank pulled hard on the reins to bring the horse's head up but the horse went up further than he intended and reared. Frank leaned forward and stayed with him. The third time the horse reared Frank thought he was going over backward. Frank stood in the stirrups and slapped the horse's ears to make him go back down. Instead of going down the horse slung his head from side to side which shook his whole body and threw Frank off balance because he was stretched out over the horse's neck. Feeling himself falling, and knowing he couldn't recover, Frank let go of the handful of mane he was hanging on to so he wouldn't pull the horse over on him.

Frank hit the ground with a thud but his left foot hung in the stirrup just long enough for him to feel his leg snap then the horse went running back to the corral without him. Laying there looking up at the blue Texas sky through multicolored flashing stars of pain, Frank knew his leg was broke and prayed a quick prayer that he wouldn't see bone sticking out when he looked down at it. Blinking the flashing stars from his eyes he looked down and was thankful that the bone wasn't sticking out. "My God that hurts," Frank thought as he tried to stand and fell back down. Sarah saw the whole thing and came running as fast as she could. She helped him back to the house where Juanita and Mary Louise checked out his leg on the porch.

"Below your knee is shore enough broke Mr. Smith," Mary Louise said shaking her head. "We's gonna have to set it and it's gonna hurt but we got to do it anyway. Lay down here on the porch. The sooner we do this the better. Now Mrs. Smith, Miss Sarah, y'all hold his shoulders and I'm gonna set this leg on the count of three. Ready? One, Two," and she yanked hard on the leg.

"Aggh! God Damnit, woman! You said on the count of three!" Frank growled through clinched teeth.

"If I'd waited to three you'd a tensed up and it wouldn't a worked," said Mary Louise matter of factly. "Let's get you in the house and cleaned up so's we can splint this leg. You's done riding for a spell. Miss Sarah, would you go find your brothers and have them make a nice set of straight splints for yo' Papa and set them to work on a pair of crutches? Mrs. Smith, if'n you will help Mr. Smith to bed, I'll get some soap and water and clean towels so he can clean up before we put them splints on him."

"Mr. Smith, are you gonna be alright?" asked Luke with a trembling voice from the end of the porch.

Looking into the young boy's eyes and seeing he was about to cry Frank forced a smile through the pain and said through clinched teeth, "I'll be fine son. It's just gonna take a while to heal. Don't you worry none."

Back in his bedroom as Juanita was helping him undress he said, "I'm sorry Juanita, I guess I really messed up this time. Aren't you gonna scold me or something?"

"No, I'm not gonna scold you. You're a grown man and you already know you messed up. I will say this though, the next time Sarah Lynn asks you to lunge the damned horse, lunge the damned horse." That was the first time in the thirty years they'd been together Frank ever heard that kind of language from his wife.

Luke made himself useful helping out as much as he could with work Mr. Smith used to do. Mr. Smith on the other hand was pleased to have Luke for company. They sat together on the porch and Mr. Smith read to him which encouraged Luke to learn to read for himself. Mrs. Smith had no trouble getting him to do his lessons since he knew Mr. Smith and Joshua both knew how to read and write. He figured if they knew how to read he should too.

Frank also took his crutches and went out behind the house and helped Luke with his target practice. He made him count off the paces to targets and used various other means to make him use the schooling that Mrs. Smith was giving him. He also taught him things like telling time by the sun and direction by the stars. All in all man and boy both had a good time. Mrs. Smith smiled one day when she saw Frank and Luke sitting on the porch. Frank was idly whittling a stick and chewing tobacco. Luke watched him and whittled on his own stick and when Frank spat, Luke spat. Juanita frowned when she realized that Luke was chewing tobacco too.

An hour later, Mary Louise came in the kitchen and told Mrs. Smith that while she was gathering the chicken eggs by the barn she found Luke behind the barn losing his lunch. Mary Louise said she told him "that's what you get chewing that nasty ole tobacco."

Sarah continued to work on gentling down colts while Jesse and John continued to train the horses they planned to sell by riding them as they worked the ranch. Jessica was now pregnant and could hardly do anything for herself what with everyone trying to make sure she didn't over do. Miscarriages were common on the frontier due to over work and no one was going to let that happen to Jessica.

One day Jessica was sitting in a straight-backed chair in the shade of the barn watching Sarah work with a yearling colt. No one would let her help with anything in the house, she'd knitted and sewed everything she could think of for the baby already, and the inactivity was driving her crazy. She had always been amazed at how Sarah handled the horses so she'd come out to watch. "Where did you learn to handle the horses that way?" she asked from her seat in the shade.

"From your cousin Cynthia Ann after the Rangers took her back from the Comanche," Sarah replied. "Do you remember when we went to visit her to try and cheer her up and encourage her to stay with white folk?"

"Yes, I remember. She was so forlorn and miserable. All she wanted to do was go join the Comanche again and take that half-breed daughter with her."

"Yes, that was sad. But can you blame her really? I mean she'd had a family, twice. Then both of those times in her life she'd been ripped away from them. The first time when her parents had been killed and she'd been taken captive, then many years later when she had settled in with the Indians and had made a life for herself as a chief's wife and her village got wiped out. She thought her husband and son had been killed and the only way she could save herself and her baby from being killed had been to start screaming Americano, Americano. Now the whites won't let her rejoin the Comanche and they treat her and her daughter, her own flesh and blood like outcasts. If my life had been wrecked twice like that and that's what I had to look forward to I'd be depressed too."

"I see your point," Jessica said. "But you said she taught you how to handle horses. When did that happen? You were handling horses long before we went to see her."

"Maybe I should say she showed me some new things. One afternoon while we were there I went for a walk with her and we went down by the horse corral. She brightened right up. She handed Prairie Flower to me and went into the corral with the horses. I tried to tell her they were wild but she just looked at me and smiled. She went into the corral anyway. At first the horses ran from her and bunched at the other end of the corral but she started speaking slowly and softly to them in Comanche. She did some things I didn't understand then one of them came out of the group and walked up to her very cautiously. She smiled and continued to talk to them softly and slowly in Comanche. Later I asked her where she learned that and would she tell me how to do it? She told me that in Comanche society the women gentle the horses before the men train them for war and hunting. Her greatest pleasure among the Comanche, other than her family, had been working with the horses. She said once she got her hands on a horse they were hers. Then she explained to me what she did. I only understood about half of it but I've used what I could remember and understand ever since. It works. They don't force the horse into submission. They convince the horse to trust them and give to them on its own. Once the women gentle the horses the men take the gentled horses and train them."

"Well that beats all I ever heard," Jessica said. "Why don't the men take a few lessons from you?"

"Pride," said Sarah as she leaned across the back of the unbridled or tied yearling without putting her full weight on him. "Pure pride. When I offered to show Joshua he informed me that he already knew how to train horses and didn't need any Comanche magic tricks to do it."

"That sounds like something Jesse would say," Jessica giggled.

"They're cut from the same bolt of cloth for sure. If they were any more alike they would be twins but by God neither of them will ever admit it," Sarah said. Then they both laughed. The colt just stood there looking at them completely unafraid.

Chapter Thirty; Fulfilling the Contract

The last week of March Jesse, John, Joshua and his crew gathered all the horses together and drove them to Waco. Luke stayed behind to help out since Frank was still on crutches. Out of a hundred and fifteen horses, the best one hundred were sold to the Army at the contract price of seventy-eight dollars each. Over the next few days, eleven more were sold or traded locally for an average of eighty-five dollars each. The Army bought in quantity but they didn't always pay the premium market price.

The total amount for the sale of the horses came to eight thousand seven hundred thirty five dollars. Of that, one thousand nine hundred fifty dollars was Joshua's. The other six thousand seven hundred eighty-five dollars went to the Smiths.

Of that one thousand nine hundred fifty dollars Joshua owed Fernando one thousand two hundred fifty dollars, which left him seven hundred dollars. That was still more cash money than most folks made in a year. Of those seven hundred dollars, four hundred sixty dollars would go toward a year's wages for the vaqueros and Amanda. That left two hundred forty dollars to buy food, clothing and pay other expenses he would have at the ranch. He was making money but he wasn't getting rich anytime soon. If he could sell some cattle this spring he'd feel better.

The Army was required by law to pay in gold so Joshua and the Smith brothers divided the gold into four packs. They used the four horses they didn't sell for pack horses for the gold, and the other things they had traded for.

They realized that their business with the Army was public knowledge and that every bandit between Waco and Austin would hear about them carrying the money. So they were all armed to the teeth when they rode out of Waco. Joshua and the Smith brothers were wearing two pistols each with their long guns in hand. Jesse took two Spencer carbines, two new Colt pistols, and ammunition on trade for himself and John. The two of them were on the receiving end of repeaters a few times during the war and knew the advantage they could be. Jesse's muzzle loading carbine and John's Sharps were loaded on the pack horses.

For the fifteen dollars the store charged for them with a carbine sling, Joshua couldn't help but get the last one they had in stock for Javier to use. Amanda had the .36 Colt that had been Pablo's and the double-barreled shotgun. Ramon had his Sharps and his Colt. They let everyone see them ride out of town with their long guns in their hands.

On the way to the bank in Austin, they stayed off the trails and out of towns. But even these precautions were not enough. Two days out of Waco, John spotted a rider behind them. "I think we're being followed," he told the others. That night the horses were restless but no one saw anything on their watch.

The next day Joshua rode up beside Jesse, "I'm getting that itchy feeling on the back of my neck like I used to get before a battle during the war. I think we got a fight coming."

"I think you're right. I think we've been followed for about two days now. I think they're waiting until we get into the hill country closer to Austin so they can use the brush for cover and get close without being seen."

"If you're right they'll most likely hit us when we cross Brushy Creek at Round Rock day after tomorrow."

"If it was me, that's where I'd hit us," Jesse agreed. "With all the rain we've had we'll be like sitting ducks when we're in the water."

"What about riding around?" Joshua asked.

"Been raining and the creeks up, there won't be another safe place to cross for miles and I got no idea whether to look upstream or down."

"So I guess you and me take the lead. I think we should give the pack horses to Ramon and Amanda in the middle to get them out of the fight with John and Javier in the rear to cover us going in. If they stay on the north bank they can cover us until we get across."

"Sounds good to me, that's one thing I have to give you Yank, you don't back down from a scrap," Jesse said with a grin. "Ride in with rifles or pistols?"

"I say rifles. The pistols are a little quicker but these Spencers will lay a man down once and for all. With these carbine slings we can use the Spencers till they're empty then just drop them, the slings will catch them, then we pull our pistols.

"We need to make sure everyone puts a round in the chamber and a full seven in the magazine with all six chambers loaded in their pistols and long guns in hand when we hit that creek."

Two days later they rode into the swollen stream of Brushy Creek from the north. The crossing was known as Round Rock because of the unusual large round rock that sat in the middle of the stream. The community of Round Rock was just east of the crossing on the south side.

They pushed their horses into the stream but they were spread out. Joshua and Jesse were in the front and wide apart. Ramon and Amanda were spread out a good ten feet behind them leading the pack horses. John and Javier dismounted on the north bank with Spencers ready to provide cover until the other four were out of the water on the south side before crossing the creek themselves.

Joshua and Jesse's horses reached the center of the stream with water just short of chest deep and the current was fast. The horses were fretful and being careful of their footing when five masked riders emerged from the brush on the south side with pistols drawn.

"Hold it right there," yelled the man in the middle. "We got four more men with rifles trained on you. You're outnumbered and we got the drop on you. Don't make us kill you. Just give us the horses with the gold on them."

For a moment there was no sound but the water in the stream and the birds chirping. Then with a blur of movement, four Spencers, a Sharps and a shotgun roared in unison. Two men were knocked from their saddles and a horse went down. The loudmouth doing the talking took a shotgun blast and a .52 caliber slug in the chest. With a rebel yell Jesse spurred his horse toward the remaining bandits firing the

Spencer as fast as he could work the action. Joshua was right beside him with Ramon, and Amanda closing the gap. John and Javier were firing at muzzle flashes and powder smoke in the trees along the south bank using their horses for cover.

Joshua and Jesse peeled to the right and left respectively as they charged out of the swollen creek and went after the other bandits who were now trying to escape. Ramon and Amanda rode hell-bent for leather south toward Austin. Their job was to get the gold out of the fight. In less time than it took to tell it, it was all over. Seven bandits were dead. Four horses had to be put down including the one John was riding. A pistol ball took Jesse's left earlobe off. Javier had a bullet graze his cheek. A bullet had also grazed Joshua's right rib cage. Now he'd have a scar on the right to match the one on the left.

After a quick discussion Joshua and Jesse agreed to let the two that got away keep going, rather than track them down. Jesse took a small tin of horse salve out of his saddlebags. He put it on his ear and Javier's cheek to stop the bleeding. Javier helped Joshua put salve on his ribs and bandage them. After patching up their wounds as best they could, Jesse caught up one of the bandits' horses and took it across the creek to John who pulled his saddle off his dead horse and put it on the bandit's horse. Leaving the dead where they fell, they rode on to Austin. They caught up with Ramon and Amanda a mile or so down the trail where the two had stopped to reload and wait for them. They agreed that when they got to Austin they'd tell the sheriff what happened and where to find the bodies.

The six rough looking riders pulled up in front of the bank with long guns still in hand later that afternoon. Joshua, Jesse, John, and Javier dismounted, pulled the gold off the pack horses and walked inside. Ramon and Amanda took all the horses to the livery stable.

When the four men walked into the cool semi-darkness of the bank, there were nervous looks from the tellers at the dusty, bloody, heavily armed men, with packs on their shoulders. Mr. Carson came out of his office to see why everything had gotten quiet and he recognized them. "The Smith brothers and Mr. Granger, come in, come in. What can we do for you gentlemen today?" he said as he walked toward them. When he saw the blood and bandages on three out of four men he stopped. "Oh my, it looks like you've had some

194

trouble." Turning to one of his tellers he said, "Run get the doctor quickly. These men have been shot."

"We'd like to deposit our money before anyone else gets a notion about trying to relieve us of it," Jesse said as they stepped further into the room.

"Yes, of course," Mr. Carson said and motioned for his tellers to help the men. "So someone tried to relieve you of the money?"

"Yeah, they jumped us at Round Rock crossing this morning. There was nine of them. Two got away. We decided not to track them down. We'll go tell the sheriff about it when we're done here."

"You can tell the sheriff now," said a voice behind them. Turning they saw the sheriff standing in the doorway. They all four recognized him. He was a Union sympathizer during the war and had a reputation for abusing his authority when it came to ex-Confederates.

The doctor arrived and told the sheriff to wait while he attended the wounded men in Mr. Carson's office. When the doctor was satisfied he'd done all he could for the men, he suggested they come to his office when they finished at the bank. Then they all sat quietly in Mr. Carson's office while Jesse told the tale to the sheriff. "How do I know you Rebs didn't shoot those men and take their money, then make up this story?" the Sheriff asked with a nasty tone.

"Sheriff, everyone here knows I fought for the Union while you were hiding out in the brush like a scared rabbit. I don't take kindly to being called a Reb. As for these men; they are my cousins and honest men you're accusing. Keep it up and I'll forget you're wearing a badge.

"We sold a hundred and eleven horses in Waco. That's where the money came from. You can telegraph Captain Nelson of the U.S. Army in Waco to verify it. He bought a hundred of the horses. Now, unless you've got some legitimate questions for us we're going to conclude our business here and get a room for the night. Tomorrow we'll be heading home. If you'll excuse us," Joshua said as he stood.

That night over supper in a Texican cantina Joshua and the brothers split a couple of bottles of tequila with Ramon, Javier and Amanda to celebrate their success. "You do beat all, Yank," laughed Jesse as the tequila started to sink in and take his mind off the pain of his wounds. "I swear, the way you put the sheriff in his place this afternoon made me proud to know you. I still think you shoulda fought with us rather than agin us in the war but I guess Papa's right and you might work out after all. If I gotta have a Yank for a brother-in-law I reckon I'd sooner have you than some others I could think of. Here's to your health," he slammed back another shot of the tequila and sucked on a lime.

"Ya know," Jesse continued, "I'm glad now that I missed when I tried to take your head off during the war."

Joshua touched the scar on his cheek thoughtfully with a half grin. "You didn't miss by much."

The night drug on and the tequila continued to flow. Javier had a time dancing with the señoritas. He worked the bullet grazed cheek to his advantage playing on their sympathy and impressing them with his bravery in the gun fight. Ramon wandered off with a pleasantly plump and sultry, dark eyed señora that was still twenty years younger than he was. Joshua and Jesse swapped war stories and no one noticed that John and Amanda slipped off together.

The next morning they were all feeling the effects of the tequila with squinty eyes, churning stomachs, and aching heads. The soreness of their wounds was nothing compared to the hangovers. Joshua and Jesse rode slowly along at the head of the group discussing the idea of camping for a night rather than riding into the ranch hung over to face the wrath of Mrs. Smith. John and Amanda didn't say much but they rode side by side and neither of them could stop grinning. Ramon grumbled that he knew better and Javier swore never again every time he had to stop and get off his horse to throw up.

It would have been hard for a stranger to believe that this same bunch shot their way through an ambush just the day before. They spent the night on Brushy Creek west of Round Rock and looked for a westerly crossing the next day. By the time they reached the ranch the following evening it was almost dark. They were all feeling much better and ready for some of Mary Louise's good cooking.

Chapter Thirty One; The Cost of Business

Back in Dallas, the freighting business was growing. Fernando had been making adjustments to compensate for the growth. Dan's store at Fredericksburg could be supplied out of San Antonio easier than Dallas. The Army was closing the post there. They were manning the new posts further west in response to the public outcry for protection. The Comanche and Kiowa continued their raids from the north on their way to Mexico and back to Indian Territory.

Fort McKavett was northwest of Fredericksburg almost due west of Llano. Fort Stockton was west of Fort McKavett. Farther north was Fort Griffin and north of Jacksboro was Fort Richardson. Nathan, Pedro, and Carlos, had been put on the Fort McKavett and Fort Stockton runs. Nathan liked that because Fort Stockton in particular was manned by Colored Troops of the 9th Cavalry and coming back through Austin took him near enough to Mary Louise that he could stop in to see her.

Fernando bought four more wagons and teams. He had two wagons going from Dallas to Trinidad on a regular run with goods to and from the riverboats. Two more covered the stores at the forts in north Texas.

Dan's initial stores were no more than tents set up outside the forts selling goods. The forts themselves were initially just camps.

Nathan, Pedro, and Carlos stayed one night at Fernando's hacienda and one night at the Smith ranch coming back from McKavett. That helped with morale and resting the horses as well as putting a little cash in the hands of Fernando's Segundo to cover the cost of feed and a little profit which in turn made its way into the hands of Fernando's vaqueros. Frank Smith got the same amount of compensation for the use of his corrals, feed, and bunkhouse as a way station of sorts on the next leg of the trip.

Fernando was working in the Dallas office when the office door opened and closed. Fernando looked up from the account ledger he was going over at his desk to see Luella standing there. She was beautiful as always. The royal blue dress with little matching hat set atop her blonde tresses set off the blue in her eyes causing them to sparkle like sapphires surrounded by gold. She smiled and walked over behind him. She kissed his cheek and began to rub his shoulders with an intimate familiarity. "What's wrong darling?" she asked. "You told me your business is going well but you look troubled."

"The grass is green and the Comanche can feed their horses so they're already raiding to the west. The new forts the Army is building to keep them in check are far enough apart that the Comanche can ride east of them undetected almost as easily as they ride west of them. That means we're going to have to hire guards to ride with the wagons. It's more expense and it will cut into profits. Even if we can get into an Army supply train the cavalry escort will be small and we'll still need the guards. The only thing those heathen understand is strength. I'll tell Joshua about it when we go to Georgetown for the wedding. It will be a good time to take him his share of the year's profits and talk about re-doing our arrangement.

"Did I tell you he wired me and asked me to be his best man?" he asked.

"No, I don't think you did. Of course you said yes?" asked Luella still working the stiffness out of Fernando's shoulders.

"Of course," he replied, "and you have exactly two hours to stop what you are doing to me."

She giggled and playfully pinched his shoulder. "Did you tell him you're bringing me with you?" she asked.

"Yes, I did."

"What did he say?"

"He asked if he was supposed to tell my sister," Fernando replied. "I told him that he should tell her I am bringing a very special lady friend and that you would introduce yourself. He seemed fine with that, but I don't think he has ever told Sarah about escorting you and the girls from Little Rock. I wonder if he'll tell her now."

"He'll have to do what he thinks is best and we'll just play along with it however it goes my dear," she said. "I'm looking forward to seeing your hacienda. I've never been on a ranch.

"How do you think your sister will react?" Luella asked. "I have to say I'm a little nervous about that."

"She will be the epitome of politeness and gentility. Beyond that, only time will tell."

The following week while lying in bed, Fernando told Luella that there had been reports of Indian raids and the men were scared even with the guards. So he would be leaving with them on the next run to Fort Stockton which was the fort furthest west. She tried to talk him out of it but he told her he couldn't send his men where he was not willing to go. Therefore, as their leader he must go with them. If he went with them he might be able to arrange a cavalry escort for future trips.

The next morning at breakfast she presented him with her Henry rifle and said she wanted him to have it. He politely declined the offer but she insisted and began to cry. She said it was the most she could do to ensure his return and she damned sure wanted him to come back alive with all of his thick black hair in place. How could she run her fingers through his hair if he got scalped? He accepted the Henry to stop the tears and she calmed down enough to finish her breakfast.

That afternoon he rode out of town and tried out the Henry. He learned the feel of it and was soon hitting everything he aimed at out to about two hundred yards. That distance required what Joshua called Kentucky windage to get a hit. Fourteen rounds was quite a step up from the five he got with his Colt Revolving rifle. Rather than just discard the Colt rifle he decided to give it to Pedro, one of his teamsters to use.

They left the next morning at daylight. They'd travel down to Waco and then west to Fort Concho. Dan had a contract to deliver corn and oats, so they had three wagon loads of corn and oats and seven men armed with revolvers and various rifles. Counting on the number of men and the fact that they already had three repeating rifles; Fernando's Henry, Nathan's Spencer, and the Colt, Fernando spent company funds to provide the other four men with breech loading Sharps rifles. He chose rifles instead of carbines because he preferred to kill Comanche at as great a distance as possible. The average marksman could hit a man-sized target out to three hundred yards with a Sharps rifle. His reasoning for getting the Sharps was that it was better than the muzzle loaders that he and his compadres in the Rangers had used for Indian fighting for years. They were also less expensive and easier to come by than Spencers. Henrys were just plain scarce in addition to costing the equivalent of four months wages for one of his teamsters. The largest majority of people including the Army Infantry still used muzzle loaders and those who had a breach loading rifle or repeater of any sort considered themselves well-armed.

Fernando rode out in front of the wagons acting as scout. It took several days to get to Waco and then more to get to Fort Stockton.

Nathan was always hopeful when going into Fort Stockton. With the 9th Cavalry being a Colored Unit and patrolling up and down the frontier, Nathan kept hoping that one of the men in the unit would come across some word of his brother. His brother's name was Danny. He would be about twenty years old now. His skin color was more brown than black. The family he was sold to was named Carlisle.

This trip produced no more leads than any of the others had, but all the soldiers told him to keep looking, have faith, and they were all on the lookout for him too. Once again Nathan rode away disappointed.

From Fort Stockton they went east to Fort McKavett. That's when they saw the Indian sign. The sign they found was the tracks of twenty-five unshod horses with riders. Fernando kept a watchful eye and saw the Comanche before they saw him thanks to a telescope he carried in his saddlebags. When the Comanche saw the wagon tracks they had a short discussion then followed the tracks. Fernando watched them with the telescope, expecting that very thing. High tailing it back to the wagons Fernando had the men form a triangle with the wagons. They knew they couldn't outrun the Indians so their best bet was to take up a defensive position and fight it out. They quickly unhitched and hobbled the horses putting them inside the triangle. Nineteen horses took up a lot of space and they were packed in tight. The men ran lariats from wagon to wagon forming a make shift corral. They hoped the wagons would shield the horses from some of the coming gunfire. The men took up positions under the wagons and waited for the attack they knew was coming.

They didn't have to wait long. The Comanche came in sight and stopped when they saw the wagons set up for a fight. Staying out of rifle range they looked over the situation. Being accustomed to fighting settlers and soldiers with muzzle loaders they expected to absorb the first volley and then overrun the defenders before they could reload. That tactic had worked well in the past. Seconds after they were in pistol range they would be inside the wagons with their scalping knives.

Screeching and screaming their battle cries and waving their weapons in the air, they charged in two ranks. Fernando told the men with the Sharps rifles to start shooting when the Comanche were three hundred yards out. Everyone else would hold their fire until Fernando fired. At three hundred yards Fernando yelled, "NOW!" and the four Sharps rifles boomed. They brought down two horses and knocked one Comanche from his horse. A fourth horse apparently grazed by a bullet bucked off his rider and headed for a safer place. By the time the riflemen reloaded the Comanche were within two hundred yards. Fernando fired the Henry and all the men fired with him. Between the repeaters, the breach loaders and their pistols the seven men poured a devastating hailstorm of lead into the charging Comanche who in turn fired arrows and bullets into the triangle of wagons. Horses and men screamed with pain, anger, and fear both inside and outside the triangle of wagons. In two intense minutes it was over as what was left of the Comanche raced out of range of the thundering guns that wouldn't stop shooting.

When the wind cleared the powder smoke away the men beneath the wagons saw eleven dead or dying Comanche in front of them and six downed horses. They frantically reloaded fully expecting another attack. Then they counted their losses. Pedro was dead with the shaft of an arrow sticking out of his neck. With him lying prone it was a lucky shot that had caught him in the soft spot between his neck and his collarbone and went feathers deep into his body. His brother Carlos took it hard. One of the guards took a bullet in the forehead. The rest were unscathed.

Fernando took a moment to check the horses. One of the Norman geldings was down with a front leg smashed by a heavy bullet. Fernando put him out of his misery with the Walker, and then his heart jumped to his throat. "Oh God, no," his beloved Chiquita had taken an arrow through her body just behind the stirrup leather. The arrowhead was sticking out the other side and has pulled some of her entrails out through the exit wound. The rest of the arrow was buried inside her. She was bleeding profusely from the entry and exit holes. A bloody froth came from her nose and mouth. She was obviously in a lot of pain. With tears in his eyes he walked up to her and stripped off the saddle. He stroked her neck and said sweet things to her as she nuzzled his chest. Then he cocked the Walker and made the hardest shot of his life.

The bullet hit her in the center of her forehead just above her big brown eyes. Chiquita crumpled from front to back and thrashed for a moment as her nervous system reacted to the violent disruption caused by the bullet smashing her brain then she was still.

Fernando softly choked out "Via Con Dios mi amore." He took the time to reload his pistol and compose himself. Then holstering the Walker he resumed his position under the wagon.

The day drug on and although the Indians didn't leave they didn't attack again. All night the men laid awake waiting, watching, praying, and cursing the darkness. At long last the morning sun lifted the veil of night and the Indians were gone. Somehow they had recovered their dead under the cover of darkness and disappeared.

The morning was spent burying their own dead. Fernando took a Bible from his saddlebags and read the Twenty-Third Psalm over the graves then led the men in prayer. As the others were hooking up the horses with only four Normans in the hitch and one tied off behind, Fernando threw his saddle and bridle in the back of the wagon that Pedro had driven and climbed into the driver's seat. They headed on to Fort McKavett.

Sunday afternoon in early April the wagons rolled into the Smith ranch. Over supper Fernando told them about the Indian attack and losing the men and horses. He told Joshua that he took the smallest mare out of the team and would be leaving her here. He replaced the mare and the gelding they had lost with the two biggest horses he had at his ranch in order to have a same sized pair in the front.

Fernando suggested that the mare be retired to breeding mules. Joshua agreed it was a good plan even though he didn't have a jack to breed her to. A local variety jack would produce a mule but it would be of questionable quality. Joshua said he'd look for a good jack but in the meantime he'd breed her to one of his Kentucky Saddlehorses and hope for big fillies. Fernando agreed that producing quality horses would be better than producing poor quality mules.

Fernando replaced Chiquita with a 15.2 hand black stud with a blaze face. The horse was a six year old with a long flowing mane and tail. He had the dish face and small ears of his Spanish Barb ancestors who were in turn influenced by Arabian blood centuries ago then toughened through the natural selection of life in the wild. His size was an indication that one of Frank Smith's Saddlehorse studs wandered next door to Fernando's range. Such things happened when families had adjoining properties. No one thought anything of it. He was a prancing beauty with the stamina of the mustangs and the size and willing attitude of the Saddlehorse.

Chapter Thirty Two; The Truth and Nothing But the Truth

Joshua spent the night at the Smith ranch again in order to visit with Fernando. That night in the bunkhouse it was just Joshua and Fernando. Luke was inside sleeping on Sarah's trundle bed. The hired hands would start showing up next week for the spring round up. Lying awake and talking, Fernando told Joshua that he and Luella had discussed the possibility of marriage and that she had shared her history with him, including the trip from Little Rock. He asked Joshua if he'd told Sarah about the trip. Joshua said he thought leaving that whole thing alone was a good idea. Fernando suggested it would be better to address it sooner than later. If Sarah got mad she'd have time to get over it. Fernando said he'd stay another day to give Joshua some support in case Sarah didn't take the news well. Joshua agreed that he'd tell Sarah about Luella and the prostitutes as long as Fernando was standing beside him. Joshua was convinced this was not going to go well. Fernando assured him that it would be better to address this now than to let it come out on its own later. Fernando pointed out that the longer Joshua waited to tell her, the more it would look like he had something to hide. If she found out on her own, Joshua might never be able to convince her that he did nothing wrong.

That night Joshua had a nightmare about Sarah's reaction. In his dream she exploded and went into a cursing in Spanish tantrum. This time he understood although he wished he didn't. In between the cursing she told him in English that with three weeks and seven women he could have taken turns every day and given each of them three turns over the trip. Or did he have a favorite? Frenchy smiled at him from the darkness of the dream and disappeared. The dream only got worse from there. Joshua woke in a cold sweat and couldn't go back to sleep. He tossed and turned the rest of the night.

The next morning he looked terrible. He picked at his breakfast instead of showing his usual hearty appetite. Concerned for his health, Sarah asked if he was feeling alright. He told her he hadn't slept well and left it at that. After breakfast he cornered Fernando and said, "Let's get this over with. I'm going out to the barn. You go get her and bring her out there. I'm not doing this in front of her family and don't even try to talk me into it."

A few minutes later Fernando came into the barn with Sarah. Sarah had a look of concern on her face because Fernando explained that Joshua needed to talk to her in private. "What's wrong?" she asked as she stepped into the barn.

"There are some things I left out about the trip from Little Rock to Dallas," Joshua said.

"What kind of things?" she asked looking from Joshua to Fernando and back.

"You know Fernando is bringing Luella Johnson with him to the wedding right?" asked Joshua.

"Yes, is that a problem of some sort?" she asked in return.

"I sure hope not," Joshua replied looking at the ground.

"Joshua, why would that be a problem and what does it have to do with your trip from Little Rock to Dallas?" asked Sarah starting to get annoyed. "Whatever it is you best spill it now because you're starting to upset me and I don't like it."

"I bought the smaller wagons from Luella after she hired me in Little Rock to escort her and her companions to Dallas."

"I don't see anything wrong with that so why are you so upset and secretive? What is it you're not telling me?"

"Her companions were six prostitutes and a piano playing card dealer."

"You spent three weeks on the trail with half a dozen whores and didn't tell me about it? That's nice. What did you do that you don't want to tell me Joshua?" Sarah asked tensely.

"Nothing, I swear to God! May He strike me dead right here if I'm lying," Joshua swore.

"Then I don't see a problem," she replied slowly, then went on a roll, "other than you waited damned near a year to tell me about it! If you didn't do anything wrong why'd it take you so long to tell me?! You said she hired you. Was the pay good?" She paused as Joshua took a long breath and started to reply. "Be very careful how you answer that question Mr. Granger."

Joshua swallowed hard. "She paid me a hundred dollars to get them to Dallas."

"That's good pay for three weeks. What else?" she glared at him.

"Nothing, I swear Sarah. One of the girls offered herself to me but I turned her down every time."

"Every time! How many times did it happen!?" Sarah nearly screeched.

"Twice."

"You turned her down both times?"

"Yes, Ma'am."

"And Luella paid you one hundred dollars to take them with you on a trip you were already going to make?"

"Yes, Ma'am."

"You'd have to have been a fool not to take the job. Why didn't you tell me sooner Joshua? I'm hurt that you didn't."

"I didn't think you'd take it too well that I was on the trail for three weeks with half a dozen whores."

"I guess I can understand that," she said. "I'm not happy about it but I can see why you did it. You've never given me any reason to doubt you so if you say nothing happened then I believe you. I just wish you'd have told me sooner.

"And as for you Tio," her voice rose a little, "are you really thinking of marrying the Madam of a whorehouse? Oh Tio, please tell me something to make my heart stop hurting."

"Sarita, Por Favor, Luella has given up that life. She left it behind in the East. The girls work for her brother. She has opened a dry goods store in Dallas and is doing well with it. Her past is behind her and she has no wish to return to it.

"Sarita, this woman is not like other women."

"I bet not," Sarah chimed in sarcastically.

"That was unbecoming of you, Sarita," Fernando said sternly and she looked down at the ground with a frown. "Sarita, Luella laughs.

She smiles all the time. She enjoys life. She is intelligent. Sarita, she can discuss politics and business in a manner that puts most men to shame. Her intelligence stirs my mind, her beauty stirs my passion, and her charm has won my heart. I have not felt this way since the death of Maria, may God rest her beautiful soul. My whole being is alive again and I am a new man! As Jesus forgave the adulterer, I ask you to give Luella a chance."

"Alright, Tio. How can I refuse when you ask it like that? You know I love you and will do whatever you ask but I suggest we leave Luella's past out of any conversations with my mother."

"Agreed," Joshua and Fernando replied in unison.

Chapter Thirty Three; Family

Sarah and Joshua's wedding was scheduled for June fifteenth. Fernando said he would return to Dallas and be back in Georgetown by the middle of May. They agreed that he would bring Luella to the Smith ranch for introductions and then she would stay at his hacienda.

Joshua and Fernando discussed the freighting business and agreed that on June first they would go fifty-fifty on the partnership. Fernando gave Joshua seven hundred dollars and told him it was half of the profits for the year and he'd bring the rest to him when he came back for the wedding.

When the spring roundup was over Joshua's herd had grown through natural increase and he'd been able to put his brand on a few more mavericks. The cattlemen who had made successful trips north last year came around buying up cattle to drive them north again. Joshua was able to sell fifty head of steers and the cow that kept getting stuck in the mud for ten dollars each. It was three dollars a head more than Mr. Smith had gotten last year and the five hundred ten dollars was welcome. He took the money and his ox cart to Austin to pick up the furniture he'd ordered. He put the rest of the money in the bank.

Luke was asleep on Sarah's trundle bed when his mother came to him again in a dream. It had been a while since she'd visited. "Hi Mommy," said Luke in his sleep. "Where've you been? I miss you so much but I really like Texas."

"I miss you too darling," she told him. "I'm glad you like Texas. You have a new family and I'm happy for you. Everything is going to be alright for you now. One day you will come and live with me again but I want you to be happy here until then. I will always be near you darling. I'll whisper to you through the wind in the trees. I'll kiss you with raindrops. You'll see my smile in the sunbeams.

"Miss Sarah will be a good mother to you and Joshua will be a good father. If you want to call them Mama and Papa, it will be okay sweetheart. I've done the best I can for you and now God tells me I must let you go. I love you darling," and then her image faded away.

"Good bye Mommy, I love you too," Luke said in his sleep and began to cry softly.

"Luke, what's wrong?" asked Sarah as she shook him awake. Sitting up on the trundle bed in Sarah's room he reached for her and she took him in her arms. "What's wrong darling?" she asked again.

Laying his head on her shoulder with his arms around her neck he said through his tears, "My Mommy won't be coming to see me anymore. I'm sad and I'll miss her. Will you be my Mommy?"

"Oh Luke," Sarah said getting choked up herself, Joshua had told her about his visit with Luke's mother and how Luke dreamed about her visiting him. "I'd love to be your Mommy. Is that what you want?"

"Ahuh," he said and held her tight.

"I'm so happy you asked me," Sarah told him as she hugged him tighter.

Raising his head from her shoulder he looked her in the eye. "Really?" he asked with the uncertain beginnings of a smile.

"Yes really," Sarah told him with a smile and she kissed him on the forehead. Looking past Luke, Sarah felt a chill as she saw the vanishing image of a woman in the moonlight through her window. Sarah thought she heard the woman say "Thank you," just before she disappeared. Luke acted like he didn't hear or see anything and returned Sarah's smile hugging her tight again. He didn't let go for a full minute.

After a bit Sarah was able to get him to go back to bed and she made a big deal out of tucking in her son. As she was drifting off to sleep she heard him whisper to himself. "I have a Mommy. I have a family."

207

A week later, Sarah, Jessica, and Mary Louise were working on Sarah's wedding dress. Sarah stepped into the living room wearing the dress. Luke looked up from the book he and Mrs. Smith were going over and said, "Wow, Mommy! You're beautiful!"

"Thank you, Luke," Sarah replied with a smile.

Mrs. Smith gave him a quick strange look. She'd never heard him call Sarah Mommy before. Then she agreed with him. "You look wonderful dear! Such a beautiful southern belle marrying a Yankee," she teased.

"Oh Mother," said Sarah with a smile, "will you ever let that go?"

"Probably not," Mrs. Smith replied. "Now let me check the fit. It should be tight enough to show off what you want, but loose enough to comfortable. Luke, please excuse us while we women take care of womanly things for your Mother."

"Yes, Ma'am," he said and put the book away. He picked up his rifle and pistol from beside the door and went outside.

Mrs. Smith checked the shoulders and surprisingly told them they could drop the shoulders another ½ inch without becoming brazen. If they tightened up the bust at the bottom to give it more lift and take in the waist just a bit it would accentuate Sarah's womanly curves a little more.

"Mother!" said Sarah a bit shocked.

"What?" Mrs. Smith asked. "You only get one shot at this my dear and you want the memory burned into your man's mind for the rest of his life. Your wedding day of all days is the day to accentuate your positives and minimize your negatives."

"I'm just shocked to hear you talk of such things," Sarah said as her face flushed with embarrassment.

"Well, I probably should have said something long ago but I just didn't want to admit that you were a woman and not my little girl anymore. It's just us women here and I've already started so just listen. Joshua is a good man and if you take care of him he'll take care of you. That means more than cooking and cleaning. It means sometimes he'll want you and you won't feel like it but you'll give yourself to him anyway. If you want him happy and not visiting the whorehouses when he goes away with a trail herd or on some other trip you'd better take care of him. If you do he'll be able to withstand the temptations that other women are going to throw at him. If he doesn't feel like you want him he may get his needs satisfied somewhere else."

"Other women would tempt my Joshua even though he's married to me, why would they do that?" asked Sarah. She naively assumed that once they were married, other women, even the brazen one in Dallas would leave her man alone.

"My, my, I don't know whether to be proud or ashamed that your life has been so sheltered that you ask that question," her mother said. "If you think your man is handsome what do you think other women think, sweetheart? Not everyone has the Christian morals you were raised with. Joshua being married won't matter to them and he IS rather handsome even if he is a Yankee. If you ever tell him I said that I will deny this entire conversation ever happened. But as awful as it sounds there are women who don't want to be wives but are quite content to be mistresses to married men. They think of it as getting the benefits without the responsibility. Whores on the other hand are just doing business and only want the money. Joshua being married won't stop them from throwing themselves at him. Even good decent men have been known to succumb to the wiles of a wanton woman."

"Oh," said Sarah as her mother's wisdom began to sink in.

"Even Solomon, who was granted wisdom above all men by God Himself, was led astray by a woman," Juanita continued. "Women have a power over men that few really comprehend my dear. Those who understand it and use it judiciously will never be in want for the love and affection of their men. The women who understand this power and use it as it should be used have husbands who will lay down their lives for them. Those who abuse it or take it lightly will find that power turned against them. These women become the withered, old, hateful, lonely ones.

"In public is the time for you to be prim and proper my dear. But when you are alone with your husband on your wedding night and many nights thereafter," she paused, "then is the proper time let loose the powerful animal within you. Within the sanctity of the marriage bed is the proper place for a woman to give herself over to the wanton savage within. No mistress, no whore, no passing tramp can compete with the passionate wife who freely gives her all to her husband. Your Spanish blood runs hot darling, use it to your advantage."

"Mother!" Sarah exclaimed.

Juanita gave her daughter a smile as she realized her own cheeks were flushed, not from embarrassment but from memories that she kept to herself. "My but it's hot in here today. I must get some air," and she strolled out the front door leaving the three younger women staring slack jawed at each other. They had just glimpsed a side of Mrs. Juanita Smith that none of them would have even guessed existed. And that was as it should be, she thought to herself as she closed the door behind her.

That evening after supper, Sarah and her mother were walking alone in the moonlight when Sarah said hesitantly, "Mother, I've been thinking about what you said in the parlor today."

"Yes?" Juanita encouraged her to continue.

"Are you saying that I should give myself to Joshua anytime and every time he wants me?"

"You must follow your heart on that my dear," her mother answered. "Sometimes he will want you when it really isn't healthy for you, like right after having a baby, for instance. I can tell you this from my experience. Your father is a wonderful man. He has never denied any reasonable request I've made of him. Nor have I ever denied him any reasonable request he has made of me.

"But you must understand that your body is only one instrument, although a very important one, through which you wield the power I was talking about today. The power itself comes from your heart. When you listen to that little voice inside, you will usually know what to do in any situation. When the little voice isn't talking, you must pray and remember what the scriptures tell you about being a wife. When in doubt read Proverbs 31. Stay in God's will, pray for your husband, support your husband in all ways, and you will have a long and loving marriage. That is the wisdom that my grandmother gave to my mother and my mother gave to me. Now I pass it on to you and fully expect you to pass this wisdom on to your own daughters when it is time."

"Yes, Ma'am," said Sarah respectfully. She took her mother's hand. Juanita smiled at her giving her hand a squeeze. They continued their walk hand in hand each woman lost in her own thoughts of the past, the present, and the future.

Chapter Thirty Four; Luella Meets the Family

Late on May tenth Fernando pulled into the yard of the J-G ranch in a buggy. Luella was with him. Joshua was plowing a field for another corn crop and the vaqueros were out working the ranch. It was almost sundown and Amanda expected the men in for supper any time. Fernando made the introductions between Luella and Amanda then put away the buggy horse and the pack horse he had tied behind the buggy. The visit was totally unexpected and Amanda was nervous. Being in her customary men's clothes didn't help her feelings of insecurity around well-dressed Luella. Luella did her best to put Amanda at ease by helping her in the kitchen. In the meantime Fernando got one of the tents out of the bunkhouse and set it up for him and Luella.

When the men came in Fernando was outside smoking his pipe enjoying the relative cool of the evening. "Hola," he said as he stood to greet them.

"Hola," Joshua returned as he slid off the mule. He led it into the corral to strip off the plow harness and rub it down. "I'm guessing you brought company," Joshua said.

"Si, Luella wanted to see your ranch that you've worked so hard for. It only made sense to bring her here first. Tomorrow we go to my sister's and then the day after that on to my hacienda."

"Where is she?" Joshua asked looking around.

"She is inside helping Amanda. Amanda was uncomfortable at first but I've heard them laughing since then. When you are finished we will join them. I believe we are having venison stew with cornbread tonight. It smells wonderful."

Supper was indeed venison stew over rice with cornbread and it was very tasty. Amanda apologized for the plain and simple fare but Luella was complementary and had a second helping which made Amanda smile. Ramon was quite the conversationalist asking Luella questions about places and things, weather and land, the kind of things that would interest a vaquero about other places and didn't get personal with his questions. They all got a laugh when Luella told the story of Nathan cleaning the turtle and Frenchy screaming and running in the other direction. Javier was quiet and shy.

After supper the vaqueros retired to the bunkhouse, Luella insisted on helping Amanda with the cleanup. Fernando took Joshua out to the tent and gave him another seven hundred dollars.

"That is the second half of your portion of the profits for the last year. All accounts are paid. We have no debt. I held one thousand dollars for operating capital to start out our next year. I brought the tally book with me so you can look it over," Fernando told him.

"I trust you Tio. I don't need to look at the book."

"You may not need to, but you should look it over anyway. It is only a good business practice. Let's go over it together," and he showed Joshua the tally book laying on a box he was using for a table.

The next morning Joshua showed Luella some of his ranch and explained about his plans for the future. Between the cattle, horses, the freighting, and doing as much as he could for himself he was slowly getting ahead. He wasn't broke but he was a long way from where he wanted to be. Luella complimented him on his progress. Joshua pointed out that if it wasn't for help from his family he wouldn't be anywhere near the position he was in today.

After lunch Fernando and Luella went to the Smith ranch. They arrived at the Smith ranch about an hour before sunset. When Luke saw who was in the buggy he yelled "Ms. Johnson!" and started to run off the porch toward the buggy but Frank grabbed him and said calmly, "Easy, son. You'll spook the horses that way."

"Yes, sir," Luke said. Frank let go and the boy walked out to the buggy to meet their guests.

Luella stepped out of the buggy and gave Luke a big hug. "My how you've grown," she said. "Why you're almost a full grown man."

Luke just smiled quietly and she took his hand. Frank made it out to the buggy on his cane. "Welcome," he said as he took her extended hand and got a firm handshake instead of the dead fish grip and curtsy he expected. "You must be Luella Johnson. I'm Frank Smith, Fernando's brother-in-law. If I'm not mistaken my lovely wife Juanita should be coming through the door right about now," he said with a smile and turn of his head. "Right on time," he continued when he saw that Juanita was coming down the steps of the porch.

"Ms. Johnson, I'd like to introduce you to my lovely wife Juanita Smith. Juanita, Ms. Johnson."

"Welcome to our home," Juanita smiled genuinely and politely as she shook Luella's hand. "Has Fernando made sure you had a comfortable trip?"

"Oh yes, it's been very pleasant. We considered taking the stage but decided that the carriage would be much more comfortable. I think we made the right choice."

"Well, Mary Louise will have supper ready shortly. Why don't we get you set up in Sarah's room and you can freshen up before supper," Juanita suggested. "Luke can bring your bag in while Fernando puts the horses away. Sarah is out with the boys on one of her colts this evening but they should be back in time for supper. Our daughter-in-law Jessica is taking a nap at the moment. You'll meet her at supper too." Luella followed Juanita into the house and Fernando handed Luke her carpetbag. Luke took it into the house. A few minutes later Luke came out of the house packing his bedroll to the bunkhouse with a frown on his face.

That night at the supper table the conversation was light and friendly. Luella told them she was from New York City by way of Cincinnati and had dry good stores in both places. Her store in Dallas was doing well. She was excited about being on the frontier and getting to see the ranches. She would love to learn to ride a horse. "I've never had the opportunity before," she told them. "Living in the city we always rode the trolley or took a hack. Only the wealthiest women rode horses there and it was more for sport and show rather than necessity."

"Well, if you want to stay here a few days, I'm sure that we can find a horse for you and we have sidesaddles. I'd be happy to show you how to ride. Around here it's more of a necessary thing," Sarah volunteered.

"That sounds wonderful. Fernando would you mind if we stayed a few days and Sarah showed me how to ride?" asked Luella.

"If you wish it, we will make it so," he said.

"Thank you," Luella said with a smile. "I'd love to take you up on your offer. Can we start tomorrow?" she asked Sarah.

"We'll start right after breakfast. I've got just the horse in mind for you," Sarah answered.

The next morning Mary Louise put on a good breakfast for their guests. She did manage to spill a little bit of hot coffee that barely missed Fernando's lap. When Fernando jumped back she feigned shock, "Oh, Mista Nava, I'm so sorry. I don't know whatever is the matter with me this mornin'. I'm sorry for being so clumsy. Can I get you a cool rag to cool it off with?"

"No, no, I'm fine. You just barely missed me," Fernando said coolly.

"I'm truly sorry," Mary Louise replied.

After breakfast John was sent out to bring in Sarah's string of riding horses so she could pick a good one for Luella. In the meantime, Sarah and Jessica assisted Luella in picking out a suitable skirt and blouse to ride in.

"I know back East women that ride horses wear the latest fashion in riding habits but out here on the frontier we don't worry about those things. Out here riding has a purpose and we ride in what's comfortable. Forget about petticoats but you will want some bloomers to protect your legs. This skirt looks like it will work just fine with this blouse," Sarah told her as she handed Luella a skirt and loose blouse that were similar to what Sarah was wearing. "By the time you get dressed and out to the corral John should be bringing in my horses."

Out in the corral with her horses, Sarah had just dropped a loop over the head of a small, older palomino gelding when Luella walked up and leaned on the fence. "I'm excited about learning to ride from you," Luella said. "Joshua told me what a good rider you are and about the time when you were young and you rode a bucking horse to a standstill. He said it was a palomino. I don't know what that means and I didn't want to interrupt the story by asking. I don't think I could ever ride one that mean. Is it true that sometimes cowboys will put a new rider on a horse they know will throw them just to get a laugh?"

"Joshua's been known to exaggerate, but yes that's true," Sarah said with her back to Luella and facing the horse. With a perturbed look that no one saw she took the rope off Diablo and patted him on the neck. "Go on old man. Looks like we won't be using you today after all," she told the horse.

"Is there something wrong with that one?" asked Luella.

214

"He's old and seems a little stiff this morning so I'll get you another one," Sarah said. Diablo snorted and bucked his way to the other side of the corral. Luella smiled but didn't say a word. Sarah dropped her loop on a pretty, but lazy looking steel gray horse with black mane and tail. The horse had never bucked in his life and would only run if you spurred him hard or gave him a whack with a riding crop. Well, Sarah thought to herself, this won't be as much fun as I thought but at least Fernando won't be mad at me.

"What is a palomino?" asked Luella.

"A yellow horse with light colored mane and tail," said Sarah without thinking.

"You mean like the old stiff one?" Luella asked innocently.

"Yeah," Sarah said blushing, "like the old stiff one."

From that point on Sarah had a grudging respect for Luella and treated her accordingly. After turning out the horses she wasn't going to use she let the rope fall and the gray stood perfectly still, ground tied. She traded the lasso for a halter and lunge line. Sarah showed Luella the different parts of the saddle and what they were called. She also pointed out that her saddle had what was called a leaping head. Sarah explained that she first saw a sidesaddle with a leaping head while she was in school in New Orleans before the war. The prim and proper ladies riding instructors called it a novelty item that was sure to be a passing fad but since it was the latest thing from France, they wanted the girls to be aware of it. Sarah said she immediately saw how the leaping head would make riding sidesaddle more secure in rough country or on rough horses and had one added to her saddle. Texas had both rough country and rough horses.

"The sidesaddle," Sarah went on to explain, "only has a stirrup on the on (mounting) side of the saddle. The lady puts her right thigh between the two horns on the pommel (front) of the saddle. The knee wraps around the left side horn with the right calf resting on the horse's left shoulder. The lady is not to sit sideways but is to sit square facing forward with her left leg hanging more or less straight down with her left foot in the stirrup.

"This is where the leaping head comes into play," Sarah continued. "As you can see the leaping head is on the left side of the saddle, lower and a little behind the pommel. It is also curved. This allows a lady with a properly adjusted stirrup to push her left leg upward into the leaping head while tightening the grip of her knee around the pommel horn thus giving her some purchase on the saddle to stabilize herself should the ride get rough for any reason. Without the leaping head you would have very little to help hold you in the saddle if you were to need it."

"That makes perfect sense to me," said Luella. "So basically you can grip the saddle with your legs to help you stay on?"

"That's it exactly," Sarah said with a smile. "However, there is a drawback to the leaping head."

"What is it?" asked Luella.

"Well," Sarah said, "If you have a really mean bronc or your horse falls with you, there is no way for you to jump off."

"That's good to know. I'm glad you have calm horse for me," said Luella. Sarah's stomach turned a little when she thought about how it could have gone with Diablo. "Now how do you get in the saddle?" asked Luella with a puzzled look.

"Well, the proper way is to have some strong, gallant, handsome man lift you into the saddle," Sarah said. "Personally, I lead the horse over to the porch and step into the saddle from the porch. The only problem is you don't want to dismount until you're done or you have a strong gallant man handy, or something like the porch to help you get back on."

"It is rather elegant. I think I'm ready to give this a try. Is there a handsome gallant man around or should we use the porch?"

"Let's just use the porch," said Sarah. "It's easier than hunting up a man. Now I'm not going to bridle this horse just yet. I'm going to lead him. I want you to concentrate on sitting square in the saddle and getting your balance. Once you can sit the saddle properly we'll work on using the reins. Here's a riding crop for you to use with your right hand. It's not for beating the horse. You use it to give the horse signals on that side since you don't have a leg on that side to signal with."

By lunch Luella was doing well with sitting properly in the sidesaddle at a walk and trot. Sarah explained that they should stop for the day because Luella had used muscles that she hadn't used before and she was going to be sore. Tomorrow they would work on sitting the canter and once she had that down they'd start with the bridle and getting the horse to go where she wanted it to.

On the fourth day at breakfast, Sarah announced that Luella had progressed rapidly and they were going to go for a ride in the open country today. Juanita offered Sarah the use of her own sidesaddle since Luella would be using Sarah's. Sarah started to decline in favor of using her Mexican stock saddle but the stern look from her father made her accept her mother's offer.

In her room after breakfast Sarah pulled her pistol out of her dresser drawer, loaded it, and strapped it around her waist with the belt and holster she had for it. Seeing this Luella pulled her pistol out of her carpet bag and dropped it in the pocket of her skirt. Sarah suggested that they find her a belt and holster so she wouldn't lose the pistol during their ride. Sarah asked her father and he came up with a holster and belt for Luella.

Out on the open range east of the house Sarah and Luella rode along talking and Sarah got up the nerve to ask her about the trip from Little Rock to Dallas. "Joshua told me about the trip from Little Rock to Dallas and how one of the girls threw herself at him. Woman to woman, I need to know what happened," she said.

"Well, Joshua was a perfect gentleman the whole trip. Frenchy took to him right away and let him know it. Joshua was embarrassed and turned her down. You have nothing to worry about Sarah. If Joshua was any straighter you could saw him up for lumber. What did he tell you?"

"He said the same thing," Sarah replied uneasily.

"You need to trust your man, honey," Luella told her. "He told me all about you. Why when I met you I expected you to have wings and a halo."

"Really?"

"You and a ranch of his own was all he talked about."

"Hum," said Sarah smiling smugly as they rode on in silence for a while.

Chapter Thirty Five; The Baby

That evening, after supper, the ladies went for a walk in the gathering twilight. "The baby has dropped," Juanita commented to Jessica pleasantly. "It won't be long now."

"I'm a little scared but I'll be so happy to have this baby," Jessica said. "I can't get comfortable to save my life. I feel like I've swelled up as big as a buffalo. It's the strangest thing too, sometimes I want to just hold Jesse's hand and then a minute later I want to slap him when he hasn't done anything or said a word in the minute since I wanted to hold his hand."

"It's the pregnancy, dear," Juanita told her with a smile. "Your emotions will start to even out again after you've had the baby. It's perfectly natural to feel that way although I know it drives men crazy. I'll send Jesse to town tomorrow to bring your mother out like we agreed."

"Thank you, Mrs. Smith. I'm such a Mama's girl even at my age. It will be comforting to have her here with me."

Three days later Jessica went into labor. Jesse was out on the range working as usual and Luke was sent to bring him home. When Jesse heard that Jessica was in labor he let out a happy Rebel yell and rode hell bent for leather back to the house. His father was waiting for him on the porch when Jesse slid his exhausted horse to a stop and leaped from the saddle.

"Just wait out here son," Frank told him. "It's women's business in there right now. Your mother, her mother, Mary Louise, Sarah, and Ms. Johnson are in there with her. You'll just be in the way."

Jesse paced back and forth on the porch for three hours flinching every time he heard Jessica cry out. His father had to hold him back at one point to keep him from running into the house when he heard Jessica yell something very un-lady-like. Then they heard a baby cry.

A few minutes later Sarah opened the door and let Jesse in. Jesse ran through the house to his and Jessica's room with his spurs jingling and his hat still on. He ran right past his mother and mother-in-law to the bed where Jessica was sitting up, "Are you alright?" he asked breathlessly.

"I'm fine," she said smiling weakly. "I'm just tired."

"Thank God," he said. "I was afraid you were dying in here."

"She's fine," his mother told him. "Would you like to hold your son?" She handed him the red and wrinkled baby wrapped in clean white cotton cloth. Jesse took the baby like he was taking a bottle of nitroglycerin and had butter on his fingers. "Relax," his mother told him. "You're not going to break him."

Jesse held the baby for a minute then handed him to Jessica. "What are you going to name him?" asked Mrs. Smith.

Jesse looked at Jessica and she nodded, "I thought we'd name him Robert Lee Smith," he said.

"That's a fine name. A name he can be proud of," Mrs. Parker commented.

That night by candlelight, Mrs. Smith recorded the birth of Robert Lee Smith in her family Bible. The date was May 21, 1867.

Meanwhile in Sarah's bedroom two women laid awake lost in their own thoughts about motherhood. One was excited at her prospects and the other was thinking that if she wanted children she had better get with it before she got too old.

Two days later Fernando and Luella left for his hacienda with the pack horse and the steel gray gelding tied off behind. Sarah gave Luella the very pretty but lazy gray gelding as a gift and Fernando promised her a sidesaddle.

Chapter Thirty Six; Domestic Realities

May 23, 1867 found Joshua walking beside his ox cart. He thought to himself that this was not what he'd had in mind when he dreamed of having his own ranch. This month he had spent more time on the ground than in the saddle and he didn't like it. Yet he had to admit that they needed the garden and they needed the corn crop for feed for the saddle stock. So while he didn't like following a plow it needed to be done and he was the only one who knew how to do it and do it right. Thankfully Amanda helped with the planting after he got the plowing finished or he'd still be planting.

Vaqueros weren't farmers and didn't want to be. It was often more trouble than it was worth to get them to do that kind of work. They'd put in endless hours in the saddle in all kinds of weather, fight

Indians and rustlers without complaint, but had been known to look for greener pastures when required to do "farm work."

Joshua walked along beside the ox cart with makeshift cages of seventeen squawking chickens and two mean roosters along with the boards and poles that had been the chicken coop. He would reassemble it when he got home. Tied behind the ox cart was an English purebred Devon cow for milking, followed by her purebred heifer calf. The cow had been bred back to the farmer's Devon bull. Also tied to the cart was a yearling Devon bull. In a year of two he would be able to breed the bull to the cow and later the calf. The idea was to have a few milk cows and be able to sell some.

Joshua felt more like just another dirt farmer than a successful businessman and rancher. But he wanted to make the nicest home he could for Sarah. That's why he'd bought the chickens, cow, heifer calf, and yearling bull from a local family who was selling out and going to California. Joshua knew that having milk cows would be a good thing and Sarah would be pleased. She and Amanda could take turns milking the danged things. He was not real excited about farm chores himself. The chickens would be nice though for eggs and occasionally cooking one of them.

When he'd heard that the family was selling out he had saddled up and went to visit them. They wanted to go to California and like most folks they didn't have much cash money. Joshua offered to buy their chickens and milk cows. They had agreed to sell the chickens and one of their two milk cows with her calf but Joshua wasn't able to talk them out of their Devon bull. He was finally able to talk the farmer out of a yearling Devon bull calf out of the farmer's other Devon cow.

The farmer knew he could make money off that bull even with just one cow and he wouldn't sell him. The yearling bull calf would be a nuisance on the trail. Longhorn cattle were notorious for being poor milk producers but if Joshua could cross them with a Devon bull, the calves would be better milk producers than their mothers and he could possibly sell them as milk cows for more than he could as beef. Beef cattle in Texas in 1867 were plentiful and cheap. Dairy cattle on the other hand were few and far between. That's why Joshua grudgingly gave thirty dollars for the Devon cow and her calf and another forty dollars for the bull calf. As he was counting out the money he kept telling himself that this was an investment and at the very least it would improve his herd.

After Joshua had made the deal he went home and got the ox cart agreeing to be back in two days. Meanwhile the farmer was to catch and cage the chickens and dismantle the chicken coop so Joshua could take it with him and put it back together at his ranch.

What Joshua didn't expect was for one of the farmer's children to give him a puppy. What the heck was he going to do with a puppy? But how did you tell a five year old little blue eyed girl that you won't take her puppy when she walked up and said, "Mr. would you take my puppy? Everybody needs a good dog. I just know she'll be good for you. Papa says her mama is a good cow dog but my puppy is too young to make the trip to California. She's the runt of the litter and the last one I have. She needs a good home."

So he gave the little girl two bits and took the dog. The female puppy was about a month and a half old and it was a little early to wean her, but life was hard that way sometimes and she'd just have to learn to eat. The dog was a purebred brown and white mutt. She'd been howling and barking ever since he'd put her in the ox cart. She missed her mother. Just from looking Joshua figured there was some kind of hound in her bloodline and the farmer did confirm for his daughter that the puppy's mama was good at bringing in the cows for milking. The barking and howling was really getting on Joshua's nerves but he couldn't just abandon the puppy after he'd promised the little blue eyed girl he'd give it a home.

When Joshua stopped for lunch he built a fire to make coffee and pulled out some jerked buffalo meat that Amanda had sent with him. He gave the now quiet but sad looking puppy a piece of the jerky and she gobbled it right up. Joshua untied the leather thong he'd used to keep her in the cart and picked her up. Holding her up in front of him almost face to face he asked, "What am I gonna do with you? I don't even like dogs." Then the puppy licked his face. "Now why'd you have to go and do that?" he asked her. The puppy just looked at him and wagged her tail. "I reckon Luke will take to you. Every boy should have a dog."

Joshua sat her down on the grass then stretched out on the ground for a nap with his hands behind his head. The puppy snuggled up next to him and was soon snoring right along with him.

Back at the ranch it was Amanda who took to the dog first. Luke was still staying with the Smiths. She named the dog Missy and Missy stayed by her side constantly, sleeping on the floor at the foot of Amanda's bed.

Meanwhile in Dallas, Nathan received a telegram from Fort Stockton. He had some difficulty reading it but was able to make it out.

For Nathan Wagoner, teamster, stop. New Recruits in from New Orleans, stop. One private Dan Carlisle, stop. From Platoon Sergeant Manning, 9th U.S. Cavalry Fort Stockton Texas, stop.

Chapter Thirty Seven; Finally Home

June 15th was the big day and it had finally arrived. The weather was typical of June in Texas, hot and sunny. The bride and groom arrived in town on the 14th. Joshua took a room in the hotel and the Smiths stayed with the Parkers. Fernando and Luella also arrived a day early. On the fifteenth there was the typical hustle and bustle of last minute emergencies and preparations that go along with any wedding. Sarah's dress required a last minute fix from Mary Louise. Mrs. Smith scolded the Smith brothers who were supervising Ramon and Javier. They were barbequing the beef in the lot behind the church where the reception would be held. The four men had tapped one of the kegs of beer brought in from Austin and had a mug or two with the priest who came up from San Antone. They blamed it on the heat and promised not to drink any more until the reception.

Joshua was nervous and had to be reminded not to wear his gun to the church. Fernando looked dashing as always in his black suit and tie. Joshua checked the best room in the hotel again and again to make sure everything was perfect for his new bride.

The wedding was held at 6:00 p.m. to avoid some of the Texas heat. After checking Sarah over one last time at the door of the church, Mary Louise fluffed out the train of the wedding dress for her baby doll and boldly took the liberty of kissing her on the cheek as tears of joy streamed down her own cheeks. There were gasps of astonishment from some of the wedding party at her boldness and

222

forgetting her place but neither Sarah nor Mary Louise noticed nor would have cared if they had. Frank led Sarah through the door and down the aisle while Mary Louise took a position at the window to watch the service; she was not allowed in the white folk's church. Nathan arrived from Dallas just in time to watch at the window with her.

Sarah was a lovely bride in her off the shoulder dress that revealed her strong soft shoulders and Joshua cleaned up quiet nice to make a handsome groom. Sarah's image as she walked down the aisle on her father's arm was definitely burned into Joshua's mind just as Mrs. Smith said it should be. The Presbyterian preacher offered an opening prayer then the priest administered the vows and blessed the couple in the Catholic style, which included a full Mass.

Not exactly an orthodox wedding for the Catholics or the Presbyterians but then Texans have always made their own rules so folks took it all in stride. Some of the old timers remembered when the Old Three Hundred families had to adopt Catholicism in order to be allowed to settle in what was then Mexican owned Texas. They respected Mrs. Smith's wish that the Catholic Church recognize her daughter's marriage. As far as blue-blooded Texans went her blood was even bluer than theirs. She was to Texas what a duchess would be to England. Her family had been in Texas before the Old Three Hundred. Her Grandfather had come from Spain with land grants and had fought the Kiowa and Comanche to hold them. Her father, a first generation native Texan, had welcomed the Old Three Hundred. Her Uncle had died with the heroes of the Alamo and her father had fought Santa Anna right alongside the Anglos, one of whom was now her husband. Her brother had fought in the Mexican War and had served with the Texas Rangers. Her sons had fought for the Confederacy. All her life, she had supported the men of four generations of Texans. She'd kept the home fires burning for them while they shed their blood and risked their lives for Texas. Yes, she was more Texan than any of them and she could see her daughter married in any style she wanted.

While only family and friends were invited to the wedding, the whole town was invited to the reception. It was an event that would be remembered and talked about for years. There was plenty of food, music, and dancing. A discreet bottle of good Kentucky Bourbon was passed around among selected wedding party members and guests. There were two kegs of fresh beer brought in from the Germans in Austin. In true Texas style, the celebration lasted way past sundown, but the bride and groom said their goodbyes early and headed for the best room in the hotel where they spent their first night as man and wife.

The following day Joshua and Sarah headed for the ranch. The J-G crew would make their way back to the ranch the next day or the day after depending on how much celebrating they did. The newlyweds arrived at the ranch late in the day and Joshua unsaddled their horses while Sarah went in and surveyed her new home. She felt proud of it all as she stood just inside the doorway and looked around at her home, not her mother's home, her home. It felt right. It felt comfortable and in her mind's eye she saw children running across the room and heard their laughter as they chased each other around.

She set the picnic basket that Mary Louise prepared for them on the table and walked into the bedroom. She'd seen it before on visits but now it looked different somehow. It was adequately furnished and she smiled knowing that Joshua wouldn't have spent the money for the dresser with mirror, wardrobe, washstand with another mirror, and the small room size stove for himself. He'd bought them for her. She looked at the sturdy bed and felt her cheeks get hot as she imagined being in her husband's arms in that bed very soon.

She went back to the door of the cabin and looked around. They had a fine start in life and she was pleased. They had a herd of cattle and good horses. In addition to the cattle and horses Joshua already had and the horses that Sarah owned, her father had surprised them by giving them fifty cow and calf pairs and ten head of brood mares along with the land he had promised for her dowry. They still had money thanks to Joshua being thrifty, the five hundred dollars Sarah saved from her half of selling the first ten horses to the Army, and the profit from the freighting company they were half owners of. The milk cows and the chickens were luxuries that most young couples didn't have starting out. The acre garden was doing well and the five acres of corn was looking good too. She bowed her head and said a quick prayer of thanks to God for all the blessings He had given them.

224

All was right with the world and she couldn't imagine being any happier than she was at this moment.

From the lean-to shed in the corral Joshua glanced over at the cabin as the sun set behind it. He froze the image of his bride, his best friend, the only woman in the world for him, in his mind so he could look at the memory later. She was standing in the doorway of the sturdy little cabin looking over the little ranch smiling like a queen overlooking her castle. He saw the details in the glowing red and orange sunset; Sarah's long hair flowing half way down her back as she looked at him and smiled pulling out the hair pins. She fluffed it in a way that made his blood run hot. She smiled as she turned away into the house. "Don't be long Husband. I need you in here," she said over her shoulder.

That night Joshua and Sarah dined alone on the contents of the picnic basket that Mary Louise had prepared for them. They sipped the French wine Fernando gave them from tin cups at the table in the main room of the cabin. They both got quiet as the time drew near for their second night together. Each of them was nervous but eager as well as a little bit scared.

When the last of the wine was gone they looked into each other's eyes. Joshua gently took Sarah's hand and stood. Silently, slowly, almost reverently, they walked hand in hand into their bedroom and closed the door. Joshua wrapped his arms around Sarah from behind and she leaned back into him. "Welcome home," he whispered in her ear.

"It's good to be home," she said turning in his arms and kissing him as she wrapped her arms around his neck.

THE END

Dear Reader,

I hope you enjoyed Texas Yankee: Homecoming. Thank you for sharing in the story. If you enjoyed it please feel free to tell your friends and leave a review on Amazon.com. Texas Yankee: Honeymoon, the second book in the Texas Yankee Series is now available on Amazon. You can find behind the scenes information on Texas Yankee the Series Facebook page. If you would like to send me a note, my email is jerry.p.orange@gmail.com I promise to respond. Happy trails and may God bless you. I look forward to spending more time with you in the future.

Sincerely,
Jerry P. Orange

Made in the USA
Columbia, SC
19 September 2020